The Discovery Center

The Center Duet, Book 1

Liz Hambleton

For the women of this world.
You're stronger than you think.

Contents

Chapter 1

Deceit

ALAINA

That asshole.

Deafening silence filled the room. The words before me appeared foreign. My shaking hands held a tablet filled with lies. The only semblance of truth was my husband's picture and his signature.

I ran my finger over his image and shifted my hips on the metal chair. Thoughts of that morning felt like a knife to the gut. Tears pricked my eyes from the memory of my husband thrusting inside me only hours before. He whispered promises with every stroke. "Everything will be fine," he had said. "I love you."

I believed him.

I trusted him.

I bit the inside of my cheek until it drew blood. The tang of metal filled my mouth. Deceit tasted bitter.

"This isn't right." My voice shook despite my best efforts. "Please check again. You've made a mistake." I shoved the tablet back across the table. Its scratch echoed in the empty room.

I clawed the desk until my fingernails bent. A large hand covered mine. "No, ma'am," a deep voice said.

"We don't make errors in this process. Three individuals verified his response. We completed and recorded Charlie's psychological evaluation. You may view it if you choose."

"No," I shot back with force. The words before me had done enough damage. Watching him reject me would have killed me. My heart felt heavy in my chest, and tears fell despite my efforts to keep them hidden.

How could he do this to me?

"Would you like a moment on your own?"

I shook my head and continued to fidget. The room was too bright. I squinted and pinched the bridge of my nose, releasing the stranger's hand.

"Shall we move forward with the next steps?"

Another nod from me. A tissue appeared on the table, and I took it, wiping my eyes.

"Your things are being loaded into storage. The City will house you in the Center for up to one year. Apartments come fully furnished. In three months, a full review of the joint property will take place. If by that time you have chosen a new partner, they will take part in the division."

My head shot up with a sharp intake of breath. The man spoke with such certainty and coldness. He dressed in white, mirroring the room. He wore his blonde hair slicked back in a firm part. Bright blue eyes looked back at me with indifference. Noticing my sudden shock, they softened.

He moved closer to me, offering his hand once more. I saw mine tremble when I reached back. "If I may be so bold." He paused, and I concentrated on his eyes. The pools of blue grew kinder with his touch. "I've been through this personally. It feels like you can't imagine finding another, but this shock will wear off faster than you expect. Wonderful people inhabit the Center, and one of them will be your partner."

"For ten years, maybe," I snipped. "Until I'm cast aside again in hopes of someone better."

"Not better. Different. Our lives ebb and flow, and one cannot do that with the same person. It's the way of things." For a moment, I saw the flicker of sadness cross the man's face.

Someone had hurt him once.

I pulled my hand back. "It wasn't our way. It wasn't what we agreed to."

"I completely understand how you feel, but it doesn't change what is."

Another tear fell down my cheek. "Can I see him?"

"No. Not until you both have new partners, and even then, it's not recommended unless children are involved."

"So, this morning, when he made love to me and told me everything would be fine, that's the last time I'll ever see him? A lie while he's inside me is the last thing my husband of ten years gifts me with before he abandons me?"

His throat moved with a hard swallow. I tested his well-mannered resolve. Everyone that works for the City seemed so calm - so polite. Except for the officials, who made their living with aggression and force. "It wasn't a lie. Everything will be fine. I will help you through this process. You'll see."

I looked to the wall, away from his gaze. My head spun with incessant thoughts. Charlie's words played on repeat in my memory. Then, I realized what I'd missed that morning. *He never promised to stay.*

I banged my hand on the table in my rage. I felt so stupid. The man didn't jolt back, and he reached his hand out again, showing me empathy. A pang of guilt hit me for being so rude to him.

My words fumbled out, barely a whisper. "How can you do this job? Break a woman's heart a hundred times a week. It must be awful for you."

"It's rare that... someone thinks...," he trailed off.

I nodded in understanding. No one stayed with a partner for longer than ten years. I'm the only fool left in the City that wanted someone forever. "I was in your position years ago, though," he repeated. "It's not always the women that are heartbroken. I found someone else, and I realized I could help those that... need a nudge toward this lifestyle. I'll help you."

I slowly exhaled. I wanted to lash out, but kindness begets kindness. "What year are you in with your current partner?"

"Year nine."

"And are you afraid that she'll choose to separate?"

"No, because we've decided to separate."

"So, you're unhappy." I let out a huff. "You aren't selling this well."

"We're blissfully happy. The happiest I've ever been. Her happiness with another will increase my joy because I love her. In three months, we'll sign the separation agreement and move to child-free centers like yourself. We will find a partner and continue the next decade apart."

He recited the words as if he had memorized them. But there was something about the way they left his lips, the monotone and lack of feeling, his stiff back, and empty eyes. It all made me wonder if he believed them. *Maybe he had to.*

Tears fell on my thighs. I wrapped my arms around my stomach to still myself. Who could be happy in his situation? The man waved his hand over the tablet and opened a document. "You only need to do a thumbprint today. I'll visit you in a few days and we'll complete the rest."

He stood up, lifting the tablet. I raised my thumb to the screen and the words, *Separation Fulfilled*, flashed. A choked sob left my throat. His arm wrapped around my shoulders, and the sobbing intensified. Minutes passed like that, being held in the arms of a stranger, feeling numb.

"I know, Alaina. It feels awful now, but this will pass."

"What's your name?" I asked once my crying subsided. "I know you told me. I just can't... can't remember."

"Liam. I'll walk you to your new home. There's already food and drinks and some of your items stocked, so you can lie low for a time."

He took my elbow to lift me, and I followed on lifeless legs. Ten years and nothing but a broken heart remained. Our next decade would mean children. That's what he said.

He lied, Alaina. He's already starting the singles' activities without you at another Center.

I tried to cry in silence down the hallway. White doors appeared every few steps, and I wondered what news the people inside received. Did they, too, get the shock of their life?

No, because no one in the City thinks like you.

My mother would call me a fool. She flipped husbands every ten years with no apologies. Her partners knew upfront there would be no lifetime love story. She never cried a single tear over any of them. I would shed enough for both of us.

My parents visited the boarding schools to see me during and after the separation. Maybe I shouldn't complain. Three men had taken the role of father figure without question, and I cared for them all. Her current partner had dinner with us most Sundays. I tried to recall how many years until she'd find her next husband, but everything blurred together.

I didn't want that life. I wanted one person, forever. I wanted Charlie.

He doesn't want me anymore.

The temptation must have been too great, or I became too boring. I did everything I could to keep him interested in our marriage. I never said no. The apartment was clean, we never fought, and we had sex five times a week.

Liam linked our arms, stepping out into the sunlight. The transport buzzed outside the doorway, and I could see my dog Jupiter in the backseat.

He doesn't even want the fucking dog.

"This way, Alaina." Liam steadied me inside. He shifted into the seat across from me and tapped away at his tablet after we sped off. We faced each other in the vehicle, but I hung my head, not wanting to look in his direction.

"I imagine I won't be in the same location as him," I muttered.

"No. That would be..."

"Against the rules," I interrupted.

"I was going to say cruel."

"Don't you find this entire process cruel? I'm being punished for loving someone because he couldn't fight temptation."

Liam set the tablet down and leaned forward, his elbows rested on his knees. "And why, Alaina, are you? Why are you fighting the temptation to find someone new? You know, the first few months at the Center are very exciting. You're beautiful and smart. You could have any man. And men are three to one these days."

I scoffed at his compliment. I never saw a great beauty looking back at me in the mirror, and my reflection would show a crumpled mess right now. Men outnumbered women and had for a hundred years, but all I thought about was my broken heart and bruised pride. I'd fallen for Charlie's lies.

"Seems odd you're so happy for your soon-to-be ex-wife when you'll have so much competition finding a new woman. Why does any man want to leave a sure thing? Idiots." I snapped at him.

Liam's face hardened, and I knew I had struck a nerve. He licked his bottom lip and narrowed his eyes at me.

"I... I'm sorry. I'm just upset..."

He gripped my chin between his thumb and fingers, lifting my eyes to meet his. "Maybe in a few months, I'll see how I fare in the competition for you."

My breath hitched, and I slapped his hand away. "Don't be cruel."

His jaw ticked, and he sat back. "We aren't so different, you know?"

"You don't know me," I whimpered. I searched his eyes, which were no longer filled with kindness but lust. They bore into mine, and something inside me trembled.

"Don't flatter me to stop my tears, Liam."

His lips drew up on one side. "I'm being honest. Sometimes with people, you just know." He sat back and released my face. "I'm also risking my livelihood telling you that in your... current state."

Lost in my thoughts, his risk meant little to me. Charlie had changed my world forever. I had a year to find a new partner to cohabitate with, or they would partner me against my will. Charlie had left me alone, but I couldn't choose to stay that way.

"Has anyone ever... changed their mind? If Charlie... if he gave this more thought?"

"No," Liam barked, and his back stiffened. "It's never happened."

Another nerve hit.

"Never?"

"I didn't stutter."

"Please don't be mean," I whimpered. "Your kindness is the only thing holding me together right now."

Liam's ice-blue eyes softened once more. He laid his palm upright on his knee and gestured for me to take it. "My frustration isn't with you, it's with your ex-husband. He should've been straightforward with you. A woman such as yourself should have been given the respect of honesty. To hear he made love to you this morning with no regard to his plans... It angers me."

"He loved me. He wouldn't hurt me."

"But he did just that in the worst way possible. He's a coward. It's lucky you decided against children with that match."

The transport came to a halt, and I lost my balance in my seat, falling forward. Liam gripped the sides of my arms to steady me.

"Are we here already? Is this The Discovery Center?"

He nodded, his grip on me still firm. My fingers dug into his muscular arms. Letting him go meant taking the next steps. I wasn't ready.

"What do I do now?"

"We settle you into your apartment. You meet new people." He looked down at me and tilted his head. "You could wait for me."

Jupiter barked and broke my trance. I blushed and loosened my grip. Taking a tissue, I cleaned myself up in the mirror. I nodded to Liam once I felt ready to enter the battlefield. That's how it felt, like a yearlong battle to find another partner.

Sunshine hit my skin once more, and we entered the complex. All eyes laid upon the fresh meat, making my skin prickle. My heart thudded in my chest while men stared unabashedly as we walked.

Liam pulled me closer to his side. Heat radiated off his firm body. "They won't be shy about their advances. Prepare yourself for that. You hold the power of no, and they must listen. There is no tolerance for breaking the laws of coupling."

I never reviewed the laws of coupling before. Charlie and I met in the boarding school and always knew our first decade would be together. I thought that would turn into forever. *He lied to you.*

"I need a copy of the laws. I'm... unfamiliar."

"There is a new tablet in your apartment, loaded with the document. Here we are."

We stood in front of a pale blue tower. Several curved balconies lined the building's front, with vines and flowers covering the cement. A few women stepped out and waved, holding books and watering cans.

"This complex is female only. There is security as well. You won't need it. It's safe here."

I followed to a gray door that read, *0628.* "That's my birthday," I said.

Liam gave a smile and pushed open the door. "What a coincidence. Does that make you feel more at ease?"

I shrugged. A soft white sofa stood in the center of the apartment, facing a wall of artwork. Liam pointed out the picture in its center, which divided into a screen for entertainment and connected to my tablet for work. I made my way to the open kitchen, already stocked with some items, and set my bag down.

"This is a one-bedroom, but your room is spacious and opens to the balcony. The City delivered your favorite flowers and various plants this morning."

"How does the City know my favorite flowers are Madonna Lillies?"

Liam looked downward with a tight smile.

"Oh, Charlie. How thoughtful of him." The sarcasm dripped from my lips with a bite. I moved through the stages of grief without missing a beat. From denial to pain to anger.

"I'll leave you now, but I'll check on you in a few days. When you feel up to it, open the welcome packet on the tablet."

An awkward silence stretched between Liam and me. "Do we hug or something? I don't know what protocol is here."

"Protocol was that I put you on the transport and send you on your way. Alone."

"Oh," I murmured, and goosebumps covered my skin. "Thank you for... doing more... for me. I appreciate it."

Liam stepped forward and pulled me into a hug. His warm skin against mine almost pushed me into another round of tears. I inhaled his scent of spice and vanilla.

He released me and moved toward the front door. His hand touched the handle, and he paused. "I know you feel alone right now," he said, his body still facing away from me. "But you aren't alone. I understand how you feel. I'll return in a few days." He left with the soft click of it closing behind him.

Determined to find the bed and sleep until my nightmare went away, I stripped off my clothes and let them fall in a trail behind me. My new oversized bed held a neat pile of items in its center, which I chucked onto the floor.

The sight of something in the stack stopped me in my tracks - a small envelope with my name written in tight lines on its front. I recognized the handwriting. Calculated letters in deep black ink that I'd witnessed a thousand times before.

A note from Charlie.

Chapter 2

The Start

JULIE

I had spent most of my life in blissful ignorance, and fuck, I missed those days. I had never struggled with myself or my place in this world - not like Alaina. I supposed artists' suffering is a real affliction, and I should have been kinder to her in the beginning. My life was stacked so full of all the should haves that it made me sick. I had every intention of making it up to her.

I'll make it right.

Youth made us all inherently selfish. It made us believe the world revolved around us and had to bend to our will. I felt that way once when the world seemed much smaller - when the world ended at the borders of the City - when I didn't know any better.

Her incessant questions annoyed me in school, but never enough to leave her side. She questioned everything about life, and at the selfish age of sixteen, I simply didn't care. Despite her senseless chatter, I loved Alaina like a sister from the moment I met her. Our bond would never break, even after all this, even if I never see her after.

I never understood how she came from her mother, the woman bred to win at this life. Her mother would take over a room, a company, and definitely a man. Visits to our school were a chore to her, but she did them dutifully. She always dressed in a flawless outfit with a perfect smile. Her heels clicked down the hall of our boarding school, her stride oozing confidence. Every head would turn in her direction, but Alaina's stayed down to the floor. Secretly, I envied the confidence and style Alaina's mother possessed. Her flippancy towards her daughter, I hated, but her presence, I admired.

To say my parents were boring would be an understatement. My biological father voluntarily skipped on a second partner and was housed with a cousin. They frequented the pleasure houses, went to work, and lived a quiet life. My mother chose a second husband, almost identical to her first. She knew what she liked, I supposed, but I remembered thinking I would much prefer to mix up my partners.

They never spoke to me about the future. Being female meant I wouldn't have trouble finding a partner. While other tables had parents scolding the boys about their grades or body so they could match with someone decent, or match with a woman at all, mine sat awkwardly across from me. They pushed food around their plates and asked about my classes. My eyes would drift to Alaina, and she would grant me a small smile, both of us thinking, *"When will this be over?"*

And then there was dutiful Charlie. He was traditionally handsome, smart enough too, but not interesting. No one would enjoy fucking that. A woman could tell when a man had the fortitude to make a woman come undone. Certain men couldn't rest until the woman beneath them felt exhaustion from her release and desperation to go again once her strength returned. It took patience and servitude. Charlie had neither.

What he had were stability and safety. Two things Alaina was desperate for. Two things Killian never possessed.

Alaina showed no interest in Charlie or any man when Killian roamed our halls. She thought she hid her obsession with Killian, the resident outsider, but I knew. I saw how they looked at each other. They snuck off together, and I covered her tracks more than once. I let them have their fun, and I thought it would pass on its own.

It didn't.

When Alaina announced she and Killian would couple. I laughed. She appeared genuinely confused at my reaction. I told her I was happy for her and I loved her, all the things a best friend should say when that kind of decision is made. But it was the wrong decision. The City would eat them alive. They would only feed on each other's ideals and get into trouble.

That's what I thought before I knew the truth about this City. I followed Killian for a few days, looking for something to use against him. When I saw him sneaking into the archives of our school, stealing things, I threatened him. He didn't care, but when I threatened Alaina... when I told him I would report to the council she had disobeyed with him, that I would find Abigor, the council leader himself, and tell him, he agreed to leave. I never thought Killian would vanish. Maybe he would show indifference toward her and pick another woman, but he left us all. That wasn't what I wanted.

For years, I stood by my actions. His choice to leave was his own. I had merely told him to stay away from her. It wasn't until it was too late, and Killian was gone for half a decade, that I realized I had sentenced my friend to misery. It could have been different for her, and I took that away.

I thought about that moment then, when the call came. At that moment, I worried much more than she did about the finality of her suffering for years. She didn't yet know she suffered. She had numbed herself with a half-life. For the past few years, something in her had died and had taken a piece of her joy with it. My heart had turned to ash years ago. It carried a small beat for my boys and her, but without them, soon, nothing would remain.

I sat at my desk, nervously rocking from side to side, waiting for the call. I had already paced my office a thousand times, just waiting. My boss knew I would leave early today, and the hours ticked onward. I had made the arrangements, but nothing was certain.

Last week, I called Liam to catch up. I'd asked about Rachel and work and flirted like an animal. We had always cared for each other, and once he seemed comfortable, I had planted the seed.

"Oh, my friend Alaina will visit the Separation Center enter soon. You know, I'm so worried about her. We've been close since grade school, and she has this wild idea. Oh, Liam, you wouldn't believe it. She thinks her husband will renew their marriage."

He sighed. "That hasn't happened since my time here. Years, you know. He won't."

"You're right. It's such a shame. She's beautiful, flawless really, and she may just fall apart with devastation."

A damsel in distress. A damsel who believed that coupling forever was a possibility. That's all Liam needed. Hook, line, and sinker. I heard tapping in the background and knew he had started a search for her file. I almost felt bad about exploiting his weakness. A man like Liam hated the way of things. He didn't want ten years at a time. Anyone with eyes saw that in him, but he didn't want to believe it himself. Alaina, or her ideals, would be irresistible to him.

"First match with a man named Charlie?" His voice rose in a question.

"Yes, that's the one. Is her picture there? Isn't she something?"

"Yes. Yes, she is. Give me a second, Jules." I waited, muting my phone so he wouldn't hear my heavy breaths. More tapping and I prayed he took the bait. I had never prayed much before, not until last year, not until I learned how.

"Okay, so I hope this isn't too forward..." *No, he didn't. He hoped he could rescue her from another heartache.* "But I've assigned myself to her case. I'll take good care of her and assign her to my Discovery Center. You may not know this, but I had a similar situation before. It's embarrassing really." His voice faltered for a moment, catching in his throat.

Everyone knew Liam's rage the day his wife separated from him, but I didn't want to hurt him. I ignored the statement and carried on. "Liam, that's so gracious of you. What a prize you will be for your next match. I'm so lucky to know you. Alaina will be too."

The words made me sick to my stomach because I knew Alaina wouldn't be staying in the City. I could almost feel the pride radiating off him through the phone, and it made my stomach twist into knots. Liam had his faults, many as they were, but what happened to him I wouldn't wish on my worst enemy.

"It's no issue at all. I'm honored to meet your friend."

"Please call me if you need anything. And if it isn't too much trouble, let me know how it all goes. I won't say anything. I'm just so concerned about her. She's a fragile thing."

"Absolutely. Speak to you soon, Julie."

"Oh, and one more thing. Don't tell her we know each other, okay? I don't want her thinking I sent in reinforcements or something."

"You know I can be discreet."

I had hung up while my body vibrated with nerves.

The phone rang and ripped me from my memories. Liam's face lit up on the screen. I took a deep breath and turned on my chipper voice.

"Hi, Liam. It's so good to hear from you."

"You too, Jules. I wish I was calling under better circumstances. I've met with your friend, Alaina. It went how you imagined. I've only stepped out for a moment to apprise you. I'll escort her to Discovery Center 7, and I'll send you a message when she's settled. You should come down."

"Oh, my. That was today, wasn't it?" *Damn, I was getting good at lying.* "I'm so grateful you called. You are so kind."

"Anything for you, Julie." He disconnected the call, and I gathered my things. I had maybe an hour or two. I messaged my husband, not that he cared. It was almost the weekend, which meant he was probably throwing credits at the pleasure house to keep someone's mouth shut or around his dick. *Maybe both.*

When I called Alaina an hour later, she didn't pick up on the first try. I paced in frustration. She had no way of knowing what I was about to do for her. I pulled every string for her to be in this group. She had to get out. If she didn't answer, I would just head down there, but she rang right back.

"Alaina!" I spoke with panic in my voice. The cup of coffee I held splashed over the side and ran down my arm. "I just spoke to a man named Liam. He told me what happened. What the fuck? I'm coming down there. Just let me tell my piece of shit boss I have my period or something."

She gave a weak chuckle. "He's not a total idiot. He knows you have two boys."

"It will still make him uncomfortable enough to let me go. I'm packing up now."

"I'm fine, really."

"No, you're not," I almost yelled at her. "Why do you do that? Act like everything is just great when it's a disaster. I'll be there in thirty minutes with copious amounts of liquor."

I killed the call before saying goodbye. Adrenaline coursed through my veins in a rush. Already at my home office, I had called Alaina in front of a blank wall, so she didn't know I had left work already. Not that she would notice. The woman looked horrid.

I feared Alaina may falter that day, but she would come around. She would remember who she was. She belonged outside these walls, and I could get her there. I needed to get her there, after what I did.

I gave myself a long look in the mirror. This was where it began. Once I walked into the Discovery Center with my attachment band, things went into motion. The first domino would fall, and nothing would stop each piece from following behind it.

I hesitated, scanning my reflection. A few wrinkles met the corners of my eyes and my smile lines creased my cheeks. A few lighter strands ran throughout my dark hair. Older and wiser rung true in my case. Wisdom brought its demons, and I had plenty.

I looked the part of a City Ambassador. Perfect hair and makeup with an impressive body. I presented myself as the ideal City woman. Alaina's mother would be proud. She inspired this reflection. She inspired my mistakes, too.

I spoke the part, spitting lies about *the way of things*. I pushed their agenda to everyone in my path. Sometimes I made myself sick. *Fuck, I made myself sick all the time.*

What I didn't see in the mirror, what no one noticed, was my broken heart. Sometimes I wondered if it would die in my chest from the memories. The pain reached such an intense level that I swore it would bleed through my skin.

But perception was a reality for others. The woman they walked by, poised and perfect, wore a crisp white blouse with no sign of blood, no sign of devastation that boiled under the surface. The pain remained within me, and I would carry it in silence. *It dies with me.*

I could do this. I could be anyone to anybody to save Alaina the pain I had suffered. The attachment band gleamed against my wrist, bright orange. There was no question, no decision to make. I decided on this fate long before today. I couldn't save my angel, but I would rescue Alaina.

Chapter 3

Tequila

ALAINA

The sides of the letter creased in my tight hold. I wanted to crumple it into a ball in my fist, but I couldn't bring myself to destroy it yet. I hated my desperation to open it. I hated how he tricked me. I wished I was the type of woman that could burn it to ashes without a care in the world. I wished I hated him.

Why the fuck do I care what that liar has to say?

I cared because I loved him. The tablet on the floor vibrated and sang a harsh tune, startling me out of my fury. I dropped the letter on the bed and punched my finger on the screen to silence it. I noticed the words, *Julie -incoming call*, only after I'd ended the transmission.

"Shit," I mumbled to myself and rang her back.

"Alaina!" Her panicked voice matched her face. The cup of coffee in her hands splashed over the sides when I picked it up. "I just spoke to a man named Liam. He told me what happened. What the fuck? I'm coming down there. Just let me tell my piece of shit boss I have my period or something."

I chuckled at Julie's sentiment. "He's not a total idiot. He knows you have two boys." My heart sank at my words. I always wanted children, and I thought Charlie did as well.

Not with me.

Once matched, couples had to have children within the first three years or forgo the option until their next coupling. The medics for the City promised two healthy children. Then the city sterilized you unless you produced girls. Julie never had to deal with a period again. She bragged about it often.

The sex of the children was difficult to manage. More boys continued to thrive while the females struggled. Julie's boys, ages eight and nine, would leave for the boarding schools in a month.

Julie rolled her eyes. "It will still make him uncomfortable enough to let me go. I'm packing up now."

"I'm fine, really."

"No, you're not!" she yelled through the screen. "Why do you do that? Act like everything is just great when it's a disaster?"

My jaw fell open, and she flung a bag over her shoulder. "I'll be there in thirty minutes with copious amounts of liquor." She killed the call, and I moved my attention back to the letter.

It begged me to read it. I'm an emotional cutter. If the wound hurts, dig deeper, and pour salt inside.

Julie would be here to pick up the pieces. My best friend of over a decade was on her way with tequila. I smoothed the envelope and ripped it open.

Alaina,

I know you're angry, and you have every right to be.

This morning, I wasn't sure we were doing the right thing. Fuck - the past year, I wasn't sure. I love you more than I have loved anyone or anything else. But I'm wondering if we want the same things. Are we just scared? You always seemed so sure that we should match forever. I never argued with you, but I never felt the same way.

When we left to go to the Separation Center, I just had this feeling that we were missing our chance at life. I hate myself for letting it get this far. I should have told you how I felt sooner.

I can't imagine loving anyone the way I do you, but what if we never try? Don't we owe that to ourselves?

If in ten years, we are still missing each other, we can come back together.

This may not be the end of our story.

I understand if you hate me, but I don't think you will forever. You may find that I'm right and there is someone out there that brings out another part of you, someone who fulfills you in ways I can't, and we both need that right now.

I'm so sorry for hurting you.

I love you.

Charlie.

I read the letter several times. I turned it over and checked the envelope. *That was it?*

Liam was right. Charlie was a coward.

I sat on the edge of the bed until the chime of the door rang through the hallway. It was in my hand when I let Julie inside, and she snatched it away, reading its contents while she mixed margaritas.

"Say it," I spit out from my reclined position on the pristine white couch. The apartment was too clean. Nothing felt like home except the Madonna Lillies on the porch. I considered throwing them over the railing.

"What do you want me to say? What I'm thinking, the truth, or what will make you feel better?" Julie sat a large glass on the side table and sat at my feet.

I picked up my drink, shaking the ice inside. "It's not even noon. I probably shouldn't." Then I swallowed half the contents. I barely noticed the sweetness, but the tequila warmed my belly.

"Atta girl," Julie chuckled and followed suit.

"Say it all," I let out. I smelled the alcohol on my breath.

"Charlie was a good first match, but that's all he was. I love Charlie, but I also love Jupiter." The pup raised her head from the floor, and her tail gave a slight thump. "Forever matches don't happen anymore, anyway. It's not natural. We were all kids when you met Charlie, and I think you took the path of least resistance."

"You were the one who pushed me onto the path!" I yelled at her. "Or, have you forgotten? I think you said I needed to forget my fantasies and be reasonable. You sounded like my mother."

Julie exhaled and took another sip. "I regret that now if you want to know the truth. But you wanted more than ten years. I thought you would let that idea die."

"I'm not like you," I whimpered. "Or like my mother. I just thought-"

Julie patted my leg. "The idea of having to marry repeatedly was too scary for you, so you set your mind that it was Charlie forever to solve the problem. I knew he wasn't right for you, but in my defense, I thought, what do ten years matter?"

"Do you hear yourself?"

Julie rubbed her free hand on my thigh, and I pulled myself into a tight ball, rejecting her comfort. "But in your heart, you know being with Charlie forever would be another task for you. A chore or checklist item you had to complete," Julie continued. "There's someone else, and in another ten years, there will be another someone else. That's harder for some people than others. I understand."

"Why does everyone today keep telling me they understand? None of you understand. I love Charlie," I sniffled. "You act like I'm supposed to have seen this coming."

Julie bit her lip and tilted her head. I tapped the side of the couch to call Jupiter. She rested on the floor next to me, and I stroked her soft fur in silence, sipping the remaining cocktail.

Julie brought the pitcher from the kitchen and set it on the table. I sat up and refilled my glass. "I should have seen it coming," I huffed. "I'm a fool."

Julie's normally carefree demeanor shifted. She clenched her jaw and groaned.

"Aren't we all, sometimes? We all do things we could take back. We wish we could start over, unwind the mistakes."

"I can't see you making a mistake like this."

She flipped her expression and shot me a smile. "You are beautiful and smart and kind. Don't put yourself down. Now drink."

Julie thought I was a fool.

We spent the rest of the afternoon unpacking. The City delivered several things to the storage unit in the complex's basement, and boxes filled each closet. The apartment represented a home more and more with each passing hour. The artwork I'd handpicked replaced generic pieces. Jupiter's toys, bowls, and bed found a corner by the patio door.

My skin tingled from our drinks. Still somewhat sober, but feeling pleasantly numb, we returned to the couch. This would be the first night in ten years I wouldn't sleep in my bed, next to my husband.

"Will you separate from Drew?" I asked.

Julie ran her delicate fingers through her magenta hair. She had a wicked smile that answered the question before she spoke. "Oh, yes. I love him," she choked out. The words almost caught in her throat. "He's the father of my children, so I have to love him, but we are driving each other nuts. The next two months are a countdown. We're both ready."

"Seems like no love lost to me. I guess that was a dumb question."

Julie slapped her hands on her thighs. "Number one, stop putting yourself down. Number two, I have so many contacts that work here, I'll be able to live here. Now that's something to drink to. Back together again like the good ole days."

My heart lifted with that information. Julie worked directly with all the Discovery Centers, and everyone loved her. I had a fleeting thought that she could check on Charlie, but I shoved it away. She wouldn't do it, and I shouldn't want her to. Knowing he met someone else would hurt, not help.

I envisioned him spending his first night at a singles' event. It was Friday, and I scoffed, rereading his letter in my mind. *When we left to go to the Center, I just had this feeling that we were missing our chance at life. I hate myself for letting it get this far.*

Bullshit. He knew all along. He'd been so different... so distant this past year. And in truth, I didn't care. So, I ignored it, but I can't anymore. *What does that say about me... about us?*

"So, Drew won't care if you go out with me a few times? Since you both know you are separating."

Julie's eyes went wide. "I already have the wrist bands. So does he. We just haven't brought it up, because you know, the boys and stuff."

"Wristbands?" I crinkled my nose.

"You know, your attachment band. They left you one on the stack you threw on the floor." Julie rushed to my bedroom and returned with a few rose gold bracelets. I shot her a confused look, and she gave a dramatic exhale and returned with my tablet.

"The coupling rulebook is on here, and I'm guessing by your face you've never even glanced at it."

"Not since school really, and even then, not much."

"Ugh, woman. Okay, so at the Discovery Centers, everyone wears attachment bands. Singles don't leave the center much, so you may have never noticed. The City connects them to your chip."

Julie put my bracelet on her wrist, and it turned black. "See. It won't work for me." She put it on my wrist and a glow of light purple beamed around the circumference.

"Purple is single. Orange means married, but single in the coming half year. That's what mine will glow."

"How many colors are there?"

She flung the tablet into my lap. I fumbled it in my arms. "A lot. Start reading the laws."

I scrolled through the document on the screen. Forty-seven pages of laws. Nightmares of boarding school study sessions resurfaced. The screen flashed, and another tune poured out. I frowned and rolled my eyes. "It's my mom."

"Hm..." Julie tapped her finger on her bottom lip. "Reading for an hour about our city's coupling laws or speaking to your mother. Tough choice." I hit the decline button. Within seconds, it rang again.

I groaned and reluctantly answered. Julie giggled and left for my bedroom.

"Oh, God, Alaina. Look how puffy you are. Please tell me you aren't crying over this. You should be elated. Your next match will provide me some grandchildren."

"How are you, mom? Good to see you. Oh, me, I'm fine. Thank you for asking." She pursed her lips through the screen at my passive-aggressive response.

"I'm wonderful because my daughter can forget this silly notion that she'll be with the same man forever. That's simply not how things are done. I'm grateful Charlie gave you the gift of freedom."

Tears threatened to escape once more. I tightened my grip on the tablet and fought the feeling.

"You didn't even love him, Alaina. You settled."

I turned my head away to hide my expression. The ache in my chest continued, but I feared she was right. I was more scared than sad.

"You should let loose with all the singles' activities," she continued. "I'm jealous, honestly."

"Really, mom. I can't even think…"

"She is," Julie bellowed from the bedroom. She walked out holding two dresses, new to my eyes. They certainly didn't come out of my demure closet.

My mom clapped through the screen, and I shot my head back and forth between the women. A bracelet glowed orange on Julie's wrist.

Julie threw the dresses on the back of the couch and snatched the tablet. "I'll catch you up later, Mrs. M. Bye."

"Bye dear-" She disappeared mid-sentence with a tap of Julie's finger.

"Try those on," Julie ordered. I sat on the couch, mouth agape.

"I can't even think about this right now."

"Then don't. Put on a dress, and let's get dinner. It's just food. You need to eat."

I ran the fabric through my fingers. Julie must have brought these over with her bag of tequila. My body felt the hum of alcohol. I exhaled a heavy breath and rose with the dresses.

"There you go. Oh, and I invited that Liam guy."

That stopped me in my tracks. I turned to Julie. Her sly smile looked almost evil, and she popped her weight out on one hip. "He seemed awfully concerned about your well-being. Had a few questions about you, and I wouldn't classify them as professional. Based on your scarlet complexion, I guessed right."

My mind raced, but no words came out. "Put on the green one. It makes your tits look good."

"Fuck," I muttered under my breath. I closed my eyes and tried to picture Liam again. *How would he look out of that white uniform? How would he look with no clothes?*

I rolled my eyes at myself and put on the fucking dress.

Chapter 4

Belonging

ALAINA

"I hate Mexican food."

Julie rolled her eyes. "You love Mexican food." She pulled out a chair and motioned for me to sit.

"I love tequila. There's a difference."

"It's fucking tapas, Alaina. Everyone loves tapas. And look around. This isn't like your normal margarita bar back home. This is special."

I plopped my ass in the seat and felt my breasts shake in the revealing dress. Eyes were already scanning my body from the second we entered the restaurant. I felt self-conscious about every movement.

Julie made a valid point. This place was gorgeous but not too upscale. Black walls with gold and silver hand-painted skulls surrounded us. Bright red roses cascaded down every window ledge. Live music carried through the rooms, and people danced a beautiful salsa on an open floor towards the front.

Julie caught me scanning the restaurant. "See, it's special. It's set up for mingling and fun and..."

"Coupling," I cut her off.

She pursed her lips as a server came over, dressed in head-to-toe black with slick dark hair and perfect skin. His bracelet beamed purple under the cuff of his sleeve.

Julie made a circular motion between us. "Dos Patron Silver Mojitos, por favor. And there will be two more, so no need to ask."

"Dama absolutamente hermosa," he purred. His eyes shot to my bracelet then met mine. My breath caught, and I moved my gaze back to the dancers. "Every employee of La Rosa prides themselves in the salsa and rumba. All dances that may please a woman. You need only ask and we will guide you, preciosa."

I blushed and nodded.

"Gracias, Rafael," Julie intervened. He turned on his heel and left.

"Do you work with La Rosa?" I asked. "You act like you know him." My mouth suddenly dry, I grabbed the glass of water on the table and gulped it down.

"Yes, but his name's on his shirt. You should be more observant."

"Oh, I'm seeing everything. Like the avalanche of men staring at us right now."

It took ninja focus not to turn my head to the tables surrounding us, but I could feel their eyes on me. My green dress felt small under their intense glare. It hugged my body, hitting just at the top of my knees, but the chest dipped low, exposing the curve of my breasts. Julie believed in showing one part of your body to the fullest and flaunting assets. All my outfits typically came up around my neck with full sleeves and pants. *Maybe that's why Charlie left me.*

"The world is seventy percent male, eighty percent at the Centers. What do you expect?"

Her accuracy didn't change the point. "I expect to have a few days to process everything."

"You can process while you drink tequila looking hot as hell. I don't see an issue."

"Do you work with Liam?"

A sip of Julie's drink caught in her throat. "What?" she coughed.

"Why would you invite him here? I've been separated for less than a day. Are you worried I won't find someone? You had to find my last match," I whined.

Julie creased her brow and shook her head. "No one should force a match. I made a mistake pushing you and Charlie."

I couldn't respond. There were no words to say. Julie had been a driving force in my marriage with Charlie. Men weren't lining up for their ten years with me, but I had another choice.

"Why are there more men at the Centers? More than... out in the City?" I asked, changing the subject.

Julie wiggled her wrist. "More orange dick," she smirked. "Most women wait until it's officially official."

I huffed and sat back in my chair, feeling my chest bounce once more. I closed my eyes in frustration and felt a warm hand cup my right shoulder. My body stiffened, and I opened my eyes to see Julie's wicked grin pointed at someone behind me.

"Liam, how wonderful you could join us!" She licked her lips and scanned his body. I took a deep breath, and my posture relaxed. Liam gave a squeeze on my shoulder and released me. I heard the chair next to me scratch across the floor for him to take a seat.

A pale five o'clock shadow covered his chin, and his blonde hair lay tousled instead of firmly parted. His piercing blue eyes appeared almost neon, even with the dim lighting. He had ditched the white uniform for black pants and a fitted shirt. His firm chest peeked through the V of the neckline.

He turned his body toward me, leaning in slightly. "You look beautiful. I'm glad you had dinner out tonight. I hated the thought of you caged up inside that apartment. You're too special for that."

"Oh, hell yes," Julie beamed. "Welcome, Liam."

I sputtered a laugh, unable to stop myself. "Glad you could make it out. What about your um, I mean..." The words behind my throat felt stupid, but they made it halfway out before I could stop them. I wanted to ask where his wife was. Did she know he came out to flirt with me?

He placed both hands on the table, and an orange bracelet glowed. Of course, she knew. She probably had the same agenda on her own somewhere else. I fiddled with the purple circle that encased my wrist. Warmed by my skin, it felt like equal parts handcuff and beacon, calling every male in sight to lock me away.

Rafael dropped the mojitos at the table and Julie pushed hers toward Liam. "Rafael, spin me around the floor once or twice." He beamed and extended his hand. I opened my mouth to protest but decided against it. Julie should have a fun night. She came across as so sure of her path for separation, but part of her must feel pain. Two sons had come from that union. *Wasn't she sad?*

"Do you work in the city?" Liam grazed a fingertip up the side of my arm, and I shivered. He brought it down to Julie's mojito, gave it a sideways glance, and took a sip.

"I'm insulted you haven't memorized my file. You seem so..." I waved my hand in a circular motion.

"Enamored with you," Liam asserted. "I am, and maybe I did a bit."

"A bit?" I arched an eyebrow up at him and sipped my drink. "How many people leave the centers as alcoholics?"

Liam chuckled. His laugh was deep and vibrated his firm chest. "I wouldn't worry about a few extra drinks on your first night out. It's allowed."

"Anything goes, right? All bets are off."

"Not anything," he whispered. His eyes were full of longing as he moved his hand to my thigh. "Like I can't take you to my bed tonight. That's not allowed until I'm separated. But I can tell you I want to. I can tell you all the things I'll do to you until you scream my name and come undone."

I gulped my mojito, eyes wide. The stories were true. The men here would make their intentions known. And a part of me didn't hate his affection. I looked at other men while married to Charlie, resigned that I could only enjoy them from afar. Everything changed this morning, and my mind couldn't keep up.

I was married eight hours ago.

"Liam," it came out choked, barely audible. I cleared my throat and tried again. "Liam, you are very forward."

"I am very interested in you."

"Why?"

Liam tilted his head, and I saw him glance toward Julie. My eyes shot to her and back in his direction. I crossed my legs, tightly winding them around each other and turning away from Liam. His fingertips remained on my thigh.

"I think we have a lot in common," he answered.

"You don't know me."

"I'd like to get to know you. Do you work for the City?"

"Doesn't everyone in one way or another?"

Liam leaned back, removing his touch. "Do you like your job?"

I thought about that for a moment before answering. My job had security, which was the most attractive factor. Now my life flailed in the wind, and the need for a stable environment seemed less imperative.

"I don't know anymore. I work with analytics and data for several clients. Most are owned by the City, and it's just sharing information. I wouldn't say it's a calling like you find yours. I'm good at it, so that's something."

"You would be good at anything you wanted. You're smart and self-driven. What do you want to do?"

You.

The thought hit my mind, making my eyes bulge. Damn mojitos. Damn tequila. Damn my desire to punish Charlie.

He won't care.

"Um, I never really thought about it. Now that I have some time off, I guess I should. I wanted to make decent money and be home for kids every night while I had them in my house."

"Did you try to have kids?"

"That's a bold question."

"It is."

I spun the empty mojito glass on the table. Another server came by and replaced it, and I muttered thanks.

"No, Charlie wanted to wait until the next decade to try. But I guess he wanted to wait until the next woman."

"I've told you he's a coward and a fool."

"You also told me that separating every ten years is the way of things. Why does it matter who you have kids with? Do you have kids?"

"I meant that it's the way for most people to make you feel less..."

"Rejected," I finished his sentence.

"No kids," Liam continued. His voice strained when he said it, and guilt washed over me. "We decided not to, but Charlie is a fool. A chance to have a piece of you in the world — that's something a real man wouldn't pass up."

Julie crashed her body back into her seat across from us. A mist of sweat covered her arms and chest. My mouth hung agape at Liam's words.

"Alaina, get out there. It's exhilarating. You don't have to know how to dance. They do it all for you." She ran her hand through her hair and reached for the rest of the Mojito.

Liam took my hand and stood. I followed, still stunned by his words — by this day — by my body's reaction to him.

I was married eight hours ago.

I stuttered something about not knowing how to dance, and Liam pushed a finger to my lips and pulled me against him. We moved in unison without effort. The band played so loud it thudded in my chest, drowning out any attempts to speak.

Song after song, we moved together in the most sensual experience one can have in public. It felt dirty, but everyone around us engaged in the same manner. Bodies joined, mimicking what they would undoubtedly engage in later.

But not us.

This would end here.

Now.

I moved my palms to Liam's chest and pushed away. He held me firm at first, then allowed me to move backward from him. I almost stumbled into another couple. "Sorry," I murmured, shoving past them. My feet carried me away while my head floated above the clouds. Dizzy and flustered, I held onto the wall, making my way to the bathroom.

The entire day caught up to me in an instant. I woke up a different woman this morning. I walked into the Separation Center, sure of my future. My mind flashed with images of Charlie, the dinner I planned to make him tonight, the way he looked on top of me when we made love.

He doesn't love you.

Did I ever love him?

Images of Liam's arms holding me intertwined with the thoughts. The way goosebumps covered my body under his grip made me question everything. My head spun in circles. Is there a place I belong to or was this all a terrible dream?

Shit, was this a nightmare?

No. I knew the reality of my situation. The burn of rejection and the excitement of desire pushed adrenaline and fear through my veins. My heart pumped so loud it thudded in my ears.

And now what? Now in a sexy dress downing strong drinks, I stumbled to the bathroom to cry or vomit or scream. Maybe all three. Maybe none.

My hand shook on the door, pushing it open. An arm wrapped around my waist, pulling me back against a man's chest. I whimpered and spun around. "I just need a minute," I explained. But it wasn't Liam who had yanked me away.

This man contrasted Liam in every way, dark to Liam's light. Chestnut hair that hit his shoulders in waves and brown eyes that held mine. I moved away from him, startled, slamming my back against the wall.

"You... you can't just... just grab me. I know the rules," I objected. But I didn't know shit. The forty-seven pages got only a cursory glance from me, and he smirked at my bluff.

"I expected a different outcome for tonight. This makes things... complicated."

I shook my head and scoffed. "What?"

"I didn't expect this from you... this bar... that dress." He raised one eyebrow in disapproval.

I examined his unfamiliar face and brooding stance. Nothing came to mind. "You have me mistaken for someone else. Excuse me."

My attempt to dart away failed. His hand and body moved forward in one quick motion, pushing me back against the wall. Fingers wrapped around my bicep. The cool metal of his gold bracelet hit my skin, and I looked down at it. Red glowed.

His lips grazed my ear. "I'll be watching you tonight. We can talk another time." His grip tightened. "Not everyone is as they seem, Alaina. Go home. You don't belong here."

Before I could object, he disappeared into a crowd of people. My chest heaved and his words replayed in my mind.

He said my name.

He knows my name.

What the fuck was that?

Chapter 5

Sugar Skull

ALAINA

Julie fumbled down the corridor while I stood, stunned. Too drunk to notice the shock upon my face, she babbled about being the next salsa queen. "Did shoo pee?" she slurred.

"No, not yet."

"Well, why the fuck are you standing out here? Let's go." She scurried into the restroom and lifted her dress before the stall door shut behind her.

"Did you see that man that I was talking to? Dark hair, kind of messy."

"Getting back on that wagon. I like it!" She hiccuped in the stall and continued with the longest pee I had ever heard. I'd never seen Julie like this. She kept herself polished and put together, but both our worlds were changing.

"No... no. He thinks I'm someone else. You didn't see him?"

"Nope." She popped the p in nope, driving home the point.

I went into the stall next to her. My brain still felt fuzzy from the day of tequila. I placed my face in my hands and exhaled. *He knew my name.*

Julie opened the door with my panties still down. "Dammit, Julie!" She shrugged and leaned against the stall door. I lifted myself and brushed by her, washing my hands and dragging her out.

"I think it's time to call it a night," she admitted. "I'm not feeling too great."

"Agreed," I said, arm in arm with her. I found Liam leaning against the wall by our booth, waiting for us. He somehow looked even better. Beads of sweat misted his open chest from all the dancing. Tequila improved everyone's appearance, but he exuded sex. *Maybe good sex for a change.*

He looked over at Julie. "You should probably get her home. I'll get you a shuttle."

We fumbled outside, and Liam tapped on the door of our ride. It opened, and he assisted Julie to her seat. "Are you coming?" I asked him.

Liam shook his head. "I can't trust myself around you. I should get home to my wife."

His admission, although honest, felt like a slap to the face. Liam had a wife for another few months. I had a husband for ten years until this morning. This was the way people operated. It was *the way of things?*

The door slid closed without my response. I simply gave a tight smile and settled back for the ride, hoping Julie kept the contents of her stomach to herself. I waved to Liam, who shoved his hands in his pockets and stepped back so the shuttle could leave.

Behind him, I saw the stranger, arms crossed and jaw tight. He stared through the shuttle window directly at me. Our ride inched forward as each transport took its time entering the street. He followed along with us, bobbing in and out of people, never breaking our gaze.

I nudged Julie. "Hey, do you see that guy? Do you know him?" She grunted, half asleep, and whipped her hand at my side. "Goodnight," she slurred.

We continued a slow crawl towards the main road. Citizens left restaurants and bars, walking in our path, tipsy and giggling. I heard it all, but I didn't break my focus from the man who kept his stride along with us.

I raised a hand to the window and brought my face closer to the glass, getting as close as I could to examine him. He knew me. A spark of memory flared somewhere inside my mind.

Perhaps I recognized something familiar in his walk, in the way he held himself, but I didn't trust my thoughts. I wanted to know him because he said my name. I needed something about today to make sense.

Our vehicle stopped at the signal before we would speed off toward home. He moved to the window in three long strides and brought his hand flush to the other side of the glass.

My breath caught, but I kept my hand up. "Who are you?" I mouthed.

"A friend," he said back, and we sped off into the dark.

Julie slept in my bed after a short video chat with her husband. He laughed at her antics. The entire conversation felt completely off to me. Her husband cared little about the other men she met and how she danced the night away without him. He insisted she stay with me, and I agreed. She was drunk, and she offered a needed distraction on my first night alone.

The next morning, she groaned and left the tangled sheets, promising carbohydrates for us both. I smelled pancakes and coffee moments later, which lulled me out of the warm bed. Day two of this shitshow had to be better. Pancakes promised a good start. Some routine would be nice. No more surprises would be better.

"I own things to cook with?" I yawned. Charlie was the better chef, and none of the pots and pans in our house belonged to me. I made my way to a barstool, resting my elbows on the large counter that overlooked an impressive stovetop. I considered the gorgeous kitchen a plus for being ditched at the proverbial altar. I made a mental note to find positives each day.

"You own all the necessities and enough food to get by for a few days, but you need to head to the market. And I'll warn you now... it's a market for many things."

Julie passed over a cup of coffee made the way I loved. She was sometimes a wild drunk, but forever an excellent barista. I inhaled its caffeinated goodness, the second positive of the day.

"I guess you mean a market for men and coupling." I made air quotes when I said coupling. I hated the word. It sounded so mechanical.

"You bet. It seems like all the infractions come from the markets nowadays, no matter how many guards we put there. Something about men and meat. Fuck, I don't know."

"Keeps you busy, though. Job security," I mumbled over the hot cup.

Julie nodded. She worked for the City, managing security teams and overall safety at several Centers. The stories she told had me terrified or laughing so hard I peed my pants. I never thought I would have to experience the places myself.

A tall stack of pancakes hit the counter, and Julie smiled. "Never get groceries on an empty stomach."

"Good idea," I chuckled back. The warm food filled my queasy belly. We took our second cup of coffee on my patio. The sun hit it just right, warming my legs but not blazing down to burn them. Another item to add to my thankful list.

"You seem different today," Julie admitted. "More resigned to things. Did Liam's presence help?"

"He's nice to look at. Fun to dance with."

"What more do you need, right?"

I frowned. "You didn't see that other guy... at the bathroom. You passed out in the shuttle, but there was this mysterious guy."

Julie smiled into her coffee, averting her eyes. "Your time here will be fun, but also filled with weird guys. Sorry, but they are out there. Part of the package."

Too tired to go over the strange encounter, I sat back in my chair to finish my cup. It crossed my mind that Julie may report the incident as a threat to safety, and that made me nervous. The man knew me, and I wanted to know how before someone else intervened. Maybe my curiosity would get me into trouble, but my life wasn't exactly at a high point. *A little trouble wouldn't hurt.*

To avoid a nervous breakdown, I needed to have something other than Charlie's betrayal occupying my mind. Julie didn't need to know more about the stranger until necessary. The tequila haze allowed me a dreamless sleep last night, but Charlie would creep back in, eventually.

"Are you coming to the market with me?" I asked.

"Oh, that goes without saying. You want me there."

I sat up with wide eyes. "It's that damn bad?"

"It'll just be a culture shock for you." Julie raised her arms above her head like a professor. "Since the dawn of time, men shop for women while they shop for apples and broccoli. You check out fruit, they check out your ass." She plopped her arms back down, and I giggled. "And you, my dear friend, have a lovely ass."

The market was indoor and outdoor shopping with lines of independent booths that sold everything from produce to artwork. I had never been there, but I would make the best of it. I had Julie by my side to fend off any unwanted advances.

Julie undersold the enormity of the shopping experience. Hundreds of people walked the streets, and every ten feet offered something new to explore. Officials stood at every corner, and for once, I felt relief with their presence. If I said no to someone, they would make sure they obeyed.

I strode in and out of shops, wanting to purchase something for my home. I needed an item just for myself, for this new life, that brought me joy. We popped from booth to booth, examining quilts, artwork, jewelry, candlesticks, and everything else imaginable. A colorful space caught my eye. I walked into the open tent to find beautiful sugar skull artwork covering its walls.

The skulls mirrored the ones lining the restaurant walls the night before. Yesterday, I dealt with the worst moment of my life, but the evening proved to me how strong I was. Julie would always be there for me, and this unexpected adventure was here to stay. Despite the oddness of Liam's insertion into my world and my weird encounter with a mysterious stranger, it had been fun. I'd danced and had far too much tequila.

Also, I loved sugar skulls. Their culture and beauty had drawn me in ever since I was young. They represented departed souls, and I had always felt a little lost, out of place. Their meaning was a dangerous fact to know because the City outlawed symbolism. I knew lots of things I shouldn't. I didn't think like the others in the City, a fact proved again yesterday.

I ran my fingers along the edges of woven fabric and porcelain wall hangings. An older woman stepped from behind a bench and greeted me. "I make everything by hand. If you like, there are a few things in the back I keep special, away from sticky hands or accidental bumps."

I grinned from ear to ear. "I would love to see them."

In my youth, I painted. Truthfully, that was an understatement. I had lived and breathed a brush and canvas. I ate up every opportunity to get into a studio. While others in school dreaded the mandatory expression classes — art and theater — I would countdown the minutes until their arrival. That part of me had lain idle for so many years, but it crawled back into my mind and heart in the tent that morning.

She motioned for me to follow her, and I saw a red glowing bracelet bounce on her wrist. She pulled a few large containers from the back wall filled with canvases. I flipped through with excitement. Julie moved to my side, scrunching her nose. She never understood art or appreciated expression in that way.

A piece stopped my fingers in their tracks. A tan canvas had the typical skull, but she had painted it in a garden setting. Feathers surrounded the head and pink opened flowers filled the eye sockets. Vines curved along the jawline, bringing the entire piece together. A single ladybug sat in the center of one eye. It's bright red contrasted with the rest of the paint. In cursive, around the skull read, "*They whispered, you cannot withstand the storm. She whispered back, I am the storm.*"

"This one," I said, and lifted the item from its container. The quote had once felt kitsch to me, but now I understood. Women needed the reminder sometimes. We often felt incapable, but great power was within us.

I can be powerful. I can change.

"It's beautiful," Julie agreed as we left the small shop. "Where will you put it?"

"I think I'll start redecorating the bedroom. It feels more personal."

"And hopefully you will spend a lot of personal time in there."

I rolled my eyes. So far, the trip had been uneventful. I noticed all the eyes on us. They would flick down my body and then to my wrist. A smirk would follow with an attempt at eye contact or an invitation to come over and speak.

I tried every camouflage tactic available. I wore a hat, sunglasses, and long sleeves to cover my wristband. The damn thing glowed through every shirt I owned, and Julie had told me to give it up and get a move on. I resigned myself that the cuff may have been unavoidable, but no one could force me to act upon my singleness. Not yet.

"What does the red glow on the bracelets symbolize again?" I asked as we left.

"That someone chose a partner to marry or they are already married. Once married, you leave the Center."

My heart sank a little. Some gorgeous woman partnered with the unknown man at La Rosa, no doubt. *Why do you care, Alaina?*

"Most of the booth owners are going to have red bracelets because they come in to sell," Julie continued. "But red doesn't always mean married, you know. If they are still bouncing around town and acting unattached, they could just be making sure there isn't something better."

"That's awful and mean."

"Is it?" Julie cocked her head to the side in question. "I know this concept is new to how you have been thinking, but not to the rest of society. Everyone is looking for the best potential match at this point in their lives. If you love someone, you want what's best for them. If it's not you, let them go."

"Even if you are in love with them, and you could be what they needed?" I huffed out a breath and marched onward. Julie hooked her arm in mine and remained silent. Thoughts of Charlie, still fresh in my mind, made my eyes prick with tears.

A scuffle broke out up ahead, and people crowded in a circle. "And here we go," Julie groaned. "Every damn Saturday."

Curiosity got the better of me, and I headed toward the commotion.

Four black vehicles lined the street. Two men and one woman were on their knees in front of them. A guard spoke to another woman with an aggressive stance. She returned the conversation with her chin up and hands on her hips. He pointed a finger at her while he spoke, and she occasionally waved her hands around in frustration. She wasn't in danger, but that many officials frightened me. Women were untouchable. The City kept females safe, but our numbers dwindled each day.

The three citizens in front of the shuttles kept their heads low, hair hanging down to conceal their identity. After a few tense minutes, the woman yelled loud enough for all to hear, "Fine, you take them, and I'll pick them up at the border. You won't see us back here again. Agreed?"

The man gave a nod to the other officials, and they lifted the three individuals from their knees and loaded them into the shuttles. Red bracelets glowed from their wrists banded behind them.

"I wonder what's going on?" I asked myself aloud.

"Probably got out of line in this meat market. Ninety percent of the infractions are people coming on too strong, touching others when it's not wanted. Stuff like that."

I frowned in confusion. "But their bracelets are all red. I don't understand."

"Like I said. Red doesn't mean wed. Let's go." She tugged at my elbow, and I stumbled after her. The shuttles moved away towards the outskirts of the center. The other woman scurried out of sight before I saw where she went.

"What are the other ten percent?"

"Ugh," Julie groaned. She released me, and I walked behind her toward the food area. The smell of freshly baked bread filled my senses. "Don't worry about it. I should have said ninety-nine percent because that's all that goes on here."

The crowd grew, and people wedged between me and Julie. She sped off ahead, and I lost her in the sea of people. Someone stopped directly in front of me, and I almost slammed into them. Aggravated, I moved around their wide stance, only to be held back by an arm wrapped around my waist. My heart jumped, and I turned around, ready to argue.

"You," I gulped. The man from last night held me against him, chest to chest. My cheeks flushed at our closeness. He pulled his loose hair back today, and I noticed he had shaved recently. The smell of woods overtook me, and I inhaled against him, unable to pull away.

"She may not tell you what that was about, but I will. Coffee tomorrow at La Rosa. Ten o'clock."

I froze. A million questions tangled in my brain, but none escaped my mouth. All I could do was nod. He pulled me tighter for only an instant, and I held my breath. What may have been a minute felt like an eternity in his arms.

"Ten," he repeated, then disappeared into the crowd.

Chapter 6

Forever

ALAINA

I could hardly catch my breath and force my legs to move. I saw Julie in the distance, leagues ahead of me. The encounter once again had been shielded from her eyes. I tried to catch up to her before I lost her completely.

Another stranger with an orange bracelet found his way to her first. Their shoulders touched, both of them enthralled by a hushed conversation. I grabbed a basket and slid in next to them.

"Hey," I gasped. What I had meant to come out as nonchalant and easy was breathy and panicked.

"You get lost?" Julie shot me a look. "This place can be overwhelming. Sorry, I thought you were right behind me."

"Oh, no no no no. I'm fine." I sounded like a crazed person instead of relaxed. *Get your shit together, Alaina.*

The man pulled Julie toward him and shot me an aggravated glare. She pushed him off, clucking her tongue. "Enough, Aiden. I'll see you around. Nice talking with you." Julie gave me a wink, and we headed further into the store. He sneered at us, but Julie cut him off with nothing more to add to their conversation. I gave a weak wave and smiled, my legs shuffling after her.

"How about we do a pasta night?" she asked. "We can continue our carb coma, and it's easy to make a big batch so you have a few nights of dinners ready."

I gave an eager nod without response, and she gave me a strange look. "What's wrong with you? Your chest is all red and splotchy, and you're breathing weird."

"Nothing." My high-pitched voice gave me away. My shoulders slumped, and I sputtered a defeated breath. "Um, I just saw this cute guy. That's all."

Julie gave an excited clap through the handles of her basket. "Now that's the spirit, love!"

To my relief, that ended her inquiry. We hit a few aisles with no wasted time chatting or responding to the unending stares of other patrons. Men walked around with mostly empty baskets, their purple bracelets on display, impossible to ignore. Only a few women floated around the store, and all had male escorts. Three men trailed behind one woman. She held her head high and darted her finger around a cheese aisle, directing them on things to drop into her cart. *Was this how I should be?*

Julie had a basket full of food and an interesting bottle of wine. I avoided any eye contact and grabbed some breakfast bars, oatmeal, and sandwich items. Every flick of my wrist beamed purple despite my best efforts.

We walked home in peace without interruption, and the time relaxed my busy mind. I had almost forgotten about the next day's meet-up when we entered the apartments.

Given the time to observe my new home, I saw its beauty in the sunlight. Not only did every patio have a gorgeous terrace as high as I could see, but the front walkway was a flower garden. They'd scattered benches with colorful pillows throughout a variety of plant life. Stone walkways weaved all around the building lined with trees. The Blue Forest that surrounded the city provided the perfect backdrop. A black iron gate encased the entire place, but I didn't understand why. Security walked around the outside bars, but no lock was present. The gate creaked behind us as I brought it to a close, and that's when I saw him again.

My stranger sat across the street with another man, both similar in height, build, and dress. It looked like the man Julie had spoken to at the market. She'd called him Aiden. They stared at me from a small sandwich shop. They had barely touched the plates in front of them. His friend said something to him while keeping his eyes locked in my direction, and my stranger nodded.

Julie came up behind me, and I jumped. "Enjoying the view?" she joked and gave the men a wave and a smile.

"It is beautiful," I said. I moved my gaze to our surroundings for a moment, hoping she didn't catch me gawking. I caught Julie's fallen face instead. She wrapped her fingers around one of the steel bars and tilted her chin upward. I moved my gaze from her to the men.

"Julie, is that Aiden from the market? Is something wrong?"

Julie flashed a quick smile. "Absolutely nothing. Admiring the view as you were."

"Yes, the forest looks so peaceful at dusk."

Julie unclenched her grip from the bars. Her movements were stiff and robotic. I could tell their presence unnerved her.

"Oh, please. Don't act like you were looking at that awful forest that suffocates this place. You like the hotties. I would let that man on the right do unspeakable things to me." My skin burned with an emotion I couldn't pinpoint. *Was it nerves or maybe even jealousy?*

His eyes remained locked with mine. I flipped the latch on the gate and forced a smile. "Right, I know. Let's get dinner started. I'm starved."

Julie turned, unaware of the thoughts I hid from her. A security guard passed in front of the gate, knocking me out of my trance, and I left the garden to follow Julie. I could feel my stranger's gaze on me with every step, and for some unexplained reason, I liked it.

Julie and I cooked and laughed and relaxed in a wine haze on my new couch. Before she left, I hung my new picture in the bedroom, replacing a useless floral piece. It fit despite its obvious differences from the minimalist decor. Soon, the apartment would resemble a home, one item at a time.

Julie grabbed a shuttle home, and I scanned the area while walking her to the ride. I searched but saw no sign of the mystery man or Aiden. I caught Julie looking too, but I said nothing.

I finished the last glass of wine on my patio, staring out into the darkness. I heard a few women on the floors around me chatting about their weekend. My mind was filled with worries about the next morning. While the neighbors pondered what dress to wear to the market tomorrow or which brunch cafe to meet and greet at, I tied myself in knots over my plans.

Sleep didn't come until well after midnight, and when I dreamed, Charlie didn't enter a single scene. Each nonsensical flash had a man with dark eyes and wavy hair. He stood by a line of blue trees, watching me. I awoke more than once with him in my memory, and when the alarm went off at eight, I groaned, finally having fallen into a decent sleep only two hours before.

What does one wear to a liaison with a possibly crazy but definitely sexy man? Something I could run away in, perhaps. Something that made my ass look good while I sprinted for my life. I laughed at my internal dialogue. *What the fuck am I doing?*

I almost vibrated with nerves walking up to La Rosa. I wore a sleeveless high neck top and jeans. I had given up all hope of hiding my glowing bracelet.

The restaurant hopped with energy. Chalkboards out front written in colorful patterns listed all the specials focusing on drinks. My liver wouldn't survive the year at that rate.

Reaching for the door, I halted. What did I say? I'm meeting a friend whose name is, what? I didn't see him at the tables out front, but I hated the idea of walking around the restaurant like a lost puppy.

An arm slipped around my waist, and I stiffened. I knew who held me, but I felt conflicted about how to react. I sensed a familiarity with him but an uneasiness as well. I inhaled the woodsy scent, shuddered a breath, and separated my body from his. He looked me over, still touching my waist with his fingertips.

"H-hi," I stuttered. He reached his other hand around to open the door and guide me inside. We walked past the entryway and slid into a back table. Rafael brought menus, and I smiled, recognizing him. The men spoke something in Spanish, and he left.

"I ordered you a coffee. I thought you might want a break on the alcohol for a meal."

I smirked and opened my menu, pretending as if it captivated me more than the dark-haired stranger.

"What do you know about it?" I chided.

"I know everything."

A shiver ran down my spine. The instinct to run lay oddly dormant. That comment alone would make a sane person grab an official and beg for their safety, but I sat there, scanning eight ways to eat eggs.

"Well, you know a great deal more than I do. Like your name. I don't know that. You never gave it."

"You never asked." When I rolled my eyes at him, his smile became infectious and reached my lips. "You do always seem a bit... breathless when around me, though," he continued. "So I'll put you out of your misery. Most people call me Kit."

"Do I qualify as most people?"

"No, you're special, Alaina. But you can call me Kit."

Rafael brought a French press of coffee, and I inhaled the sweet aroma. Coffee made all things possible. He pushed the lever, saying something else in Spanish to Kit, and poured me a large cup. When he left, he took menus from the surrounding tables. Kit must have asked for privacy.

"Are there some things you want to tell me?" I asked between sips.

"Are there things you wish to ask?"

Yes, why is your bracelet red? My heart thumped with the thought. A million questions swam in my head, and all I cared about was his relationship status. Stupid. Without realizing it, my gaze shifted to his wrist. I tried to hide the question behind my eyes, but it pushed through.

"It's not real." He grabbed the spare coffee cup and poured himself a cup — black. "The bracelet is because I'm mandated to have one. Security sends you home otherwise. Red keeps people at a distance."

Maybe Kit knew everything because he sensed everything. He read people and situations. A gift I had never possessed.

I flushed at his admission and shrugged my shoulders. "Okay," I said, avoiding his stare. My pathetic attempt to act like that fact didn't excite me failed miserably.

He reached a hand across the table, stroking the back of mine with his thumb. "I'm not trying to keep you away." Goosebumps ran down my arm.

"How can you fake something like that? Our chips sync with the band. And they feel like shackles," I whined. I rubbed my arm where I knew a chip lay implanted underneath the skin. "Everything I do centers on this glowing light. Before, everyone saw me for my work or my friendship. Even strangers would recognize me for my artwork sometimes. Now everyone just sees this." I shook my wrist and frowned.

"It's newer technology. Our chips are not, but one can manipulate the coding for the bracelets. It's complicated, but not impossible."

He was right. My mother never wore a bracelet, and curiosity struck me on how they determined your partnership status before. Maybe they all wore signs then, and if the City allowed it, she would likely display a blinking banner over her head.

"What if I wanted mine red? What if I wanted some peace?"

"It's not that simple. They inspected and updated your chip at the Separation Center. Mine has been the same since birth, and easier to... alter." Kit explained.

"What about the others at the market, the ones handcuffed? Are their bracelets fake?"

"Clever girl." Kit sipped his coffee. His grin told me I guessed right.

"Why? Why mess with it?"

"To remember who they are, as you said. To be something more than your ability to match. To help others be more than what the City wants. I see you." Kit had a grip on my wrist now. Our eyes locked while I sat, frozen. "I see your thoughts and ideas. And I love your paintings. They are... hauntingly beautiful."

"I haven't painted anything in five years," I murmured. A realization hit me and I pulled my hand back, attempting to break his hold on my wrist. It remained, and I struggled, not wanting to make a scene.

"I don't know you, Kit. What do you mean you see me and you have seen my paintings? Who... are... you?"

The look he gave could have burned the restaurant down. His intensity made my core clench, and it stilled me in the seat and halted my speaking.

"I'm a friend to you. Someone who feels like you and thinks like you."

Silence fell between us. Two plates hit the table with a swift clatter, and Rafael exited, noting the tension that hung in the air.

"I don't know you or why I'm here. I don't know what I think anymore," I admitted. "I thought I was happy with my husband. I thought we would be happy forever."

"No, you didn't," he shot back. "You thought you were safe. And this world is dangerous despite the illusion of order."

I stared down at my eggs, and ordered sunny side up, the way I liked them. Was that a coincidence, or did he indeed know everything?

"I loved Charlie. I loved our life together."

"And would you love the next decade with him?"

"Yes," I assured. "I don't want to be here, ogled by strangers. I'm set out like an auction item. Those men don't want to be partnered with a friend, another man, for ten years. Forced to visit the pleasure center sites to get off. I see the desperation sometimes, you know. I'm not that blind."

"You're observant, I know that. You're resourceful. You'll need to be."

His comments fell flat while I pondered the truth of my marriage. That Charlie risked being partnered with a roommate, a friend, rather than the security of staying with me, hit me like a brick. No one leaves the Discovery Centers alone. No one lived alone anymore. Those left, which are always men because of the gender gap, must find release in each other or the pleasure centers. Adultery meant life in prison.

Charlie felt so sure we should separate that he rolled the dice on being alone. He risked sleeping alone in his bed for ten years with only a digital woman to fulfill his needs. That's how much he wanted to get away from me.

My cheeks heated, and tears filled my eyes. I lifted my hand to my heart and rubbed my chest. "He didn't love me either," I admitted.

"Either?" Kit raised an eyebrow. I nodded. The tears dropped on the table, and I wiped them with my napkin.

"When you have children..." Kit paused and waited for me to look at him. I brought my eyes to his and bit the inside of my cheek to stop the crying. "When you have children, and you will, do you want to send them to boarding school?"

I scrunched my brows in confusion. "There isn't a choice in the schools. They go before your next decade - when they are between the ages of seven and nine. For a man that knows everything, you don't know that?"

"I asked if you want to send them away, not if you must. Would you want to stay with them?"

"That's not the way of things." I made air quotes with my hands, already exasperated by the phrase.

"It's just a question. Maybe one you never asked yourself, but think about it now."

I pictured myself with children before and now. I always saw two girls in my future, even though it would be damn near impossible. In my imagination, we painted together and played outside. I read to them at night and braided their hair. The part of leaving them on the steps of their school and only seeing them on occasional nights and weekends never entered my thoughts. Letting myself picture it with Kit, the vision hurt. No, I didn't want to send my kids away.

"I can't imagine leaving them." I frowned. "Maybe it would be different when it's time."

"Maybe it wouldn't. Maybe I think like you." Kit poked around at his food, taking occasional bites. My stomach growled, and I ate in silent thought.

What are you doing? Why are you talking about this with him?

When our plates were clean, there were more questions than answers. This morning wasn't going as planned.

"I still don't know what you want or why you are here," I admitted. "I'm more confused than when we started."

Kit finished chewing his last bite, his eyes never leaving mine. He sipped his coffee and leaned forward. The waft of woods encircled me, and I moved closer, waiting for his reply. Something familiar washed over me. A part of me recognized his voice, the dark eyes, and strong jaw. *Why can't I put it together?*

Our faces stopped only inches apart. I flushed again but refused to sit back. "I'm here for you. I'm here to take you with me."

I waited for more, but he leaned back in his seat.

"You want... to have the next ten years with me. Is that what you are saying?"

"No, Alaina."

Embarrassed, I bit my lip and shoved my back against the seat with a thud. Without an escape from the tiny booth and my idiotic question, I stared out the window, feeling awkward.

I felt the table move as he left his seat, then the presence of his heat as he sat next to me on the same side. I kept my eyes on the street.

"Fuck the ten years bullshit and this place," he hissed into my ear. One arm wrapped around my shoulders, and one laid on top of my thigh, drawing me closer. "I don't want the next decade with you. I want forever."

I turned my head toward him. "What—," I started, but his lips met mine before I finished the thought. I allowed myself to get lost in the embrace. It felt right and eerily familiar. I couldn't place his touch, but I knew it from somewhere. Everything in my body hummed when he parted my lips with his tongue and brought us impossibly closer.

He released me with a growl, and I scanned his face again.

"Forever," he repeated, brushing his thumb against my bottom lip. I shuddered but didn't respond. Somewhere in the back of my mind, I knew Kit. I knew his touch, his kiss. I knew he meant it when he said, forever.

Chapter 7

Faithful

ALAINA

I should run. I should, somehow, un-wedge myself from the irresistible man that has me pinned me to the booth and find an escape.

His hold on my body lingered after he hissed the last word into my ear.

Forever.

I remained still except for my eyes, which darted back and forth, searching for answers. A shaky breath left my body, and I moved my hand to his that clutched onto my thigh. He pulled me closer, and I felt his breath against my skin, quick and shallow in anticipation.

"Shhh," he whispered into my neck. "Not now. We aren't going anywhere now, bug."

Bug.

No one had called me Bug since boarding school. My second father, Thomas, gave me the nickname Laney Bug, and it drove my mother insane. I had never grown tired of the affectionate title. The schools were strict. You could only call others by their full names. Any moniker died out quickly, but Bug stayed with me.

I loved Thomas with my whole heart. I had felt lost after my biological dad had moved on and they had shipped me away. Thomas visited me often, while my biological father rarely came to the boarding school. He brought me a ladybug necklace I keep stored in a crystal jewelry box. I wore that necklace every day during my last year of school, carefully hidden under my shirt collar. After he died, I became fearful of losing it and the precious memories tied to the metal. Only a few people knew of its existence and fewer understood the significance.

A warm feeling passed through me, unlike the nervous quivers I felt before. I longed for the past and the happy memories. I missed the people that cared for me instead of caring about what I could do for them. As a teenager, you don't see them as clearly. I took that unconditional love for granted.

At the end of school, my entire life was consumed with coupling. The thought of being alone terrified me. It scared almost everyone except... except just one man. Except the one holding me.

"Killian?" My voice trembled, barely a whisper. I looked him over, arching backward. He pulled me back against him, our bodies flush against each other. I had the sudden urge to shift my leg in between his, wrap my arms around his middle, and nuzzle my face into his neck. Charlie became a far gone glimpse in the back of my memory. "Is it you?"

He brought his forehead to mine, our faces inches apart. "Took you long enough," he scolded.

"You look so different. You are so different. You're... bigger. And your face."

"Fifty pounds of muscle changes that. Also, repeated broken noses, a broken eye socket, and other messes I got into. I don't recognize myself either, so I understand. Maybe I secretly hoped I would need to touch you again to spark some memory."

Memories flooded back, and tears threatened to follow. Julie's voice sounded in my mind. *"He'll get you into trouble. Charlie will keep you safe and happy."* And here I was, undoubtedly in trouble, but I couldn't pull away.

"Where did you go? You just left," I said. My hands gripped his shirt, pulling him closer to me.

Killian made a motion with his hand, encouraging me to lower my voice. It had become louder and frantic with my excitement. Killian and I were... *entwined* before I met Charlie. I only spent time with Charlie after Killian disappeared.

At school, we would eat lunch at the same table every day. He helped me in classes. Everyone mocked me for my ideas about a forever partner, but not Killian. He silently nodded in agreement when the topic arose.

He had a habit of disappearing often. In my heart, I thought he would come back. Years passed, and that dream died.

No one came for Killian on visitors' days. He had spoken of how his family disagreed with him in all things, and I never pried further. I looked for him when my dads would come by, noticing his loneliness. They would welcome anyone to spend time with us, but Killian faded into some corner of the school I never found.

Then one day, a group of us laid out some blankets on the lawn to study. I remembered how the sun felt on my skin, and I basked in it rather than reading the history of our civilization. The lesson that semester was incessant on how mass shootings and suicides plagued the nation before the city mandated coupling. It droned on and on about the importance of having an accountability partner to watch out for one's mental health and wellbeing. It was no wonder my panic about coupling reached an all-time high shortly thereafter. The lessons depressed me, and I couldn't find Killian to share my misery.

I napped while others read and caught him staring when I opened my eyes. I knew he wanted me, although we were forbidden to seek partners yet. I wanted him more than anything.

Killian had an air about him that wasn't exactly that of a bad boy, but he wasn't a good guy either. His mannerisms drew you in, but his ideas put you off. Not me, though, because I secretly agreed when he argued that coupling may be a crutch used to soften the blow of our council's regulations and harsh penalties.

Free speech against leaders existed once. Conspiracy theorists had entire archives about oppression. Anything like that in present times was punishable by death. Things were in order because of coupling. *Or were they?* If you asked Killian, things were in order with weapons and an iron fist.

Walking back to the school that day, the last day I saw Killian, he said he had forgotten something and broke away from the group. I tried to go after him, and he said the oddest thing to me.

"Julie knows what's best for you. Stay by her side, okay?" Then he walked straight for the tree line, far from where we had set up our blankets. I never thought he could go far. There's nothing past the border but death.

The wall around the City means protection, and no one ventured too far into the trees.

That's what I told the police when they questioned his disappearance. I doubted they believed me. No one went near the forest.

They investigated the school for a few days. When they pressed me more about Killian, I knew surprisingly little. I could only convey how he made me feel. Special, loved, and cherished came to mind. The way he looked at me then made me ache for his touch. The way it felt to have someone understand me for once, to have someone uninterested in changing me. He thought I was perfect, but then he left, and I fell into Charlie's arms.

But that's not something you could explain to investigators. That wouldn't help them find Killian. I kept those feelings buried deep, not admitting them to Julie or myself. She never knew about the few times he found me in an empty hallway. Something in his eyes signaled for me to follow. When I did, he rewarded me with my first, and if I'm being honest, my favorite, kiss. There were other firsts too, moments I kept to myself. Moments I thought about when I was by myself, and sometimes... with Charlie.

When Charlie courted me, I tried to force all the memories of Killian away. But the occasional dream brought him back. Sometimes they felt like nightmares, having the same vision again and again of him leaving. The memory of him walking to that forest, away from me forever, that's what played on repeat in my mind. His departure took something from me. It took the piece of me that hoped for something better.

Killian's hands moved to my face, and he brought his lips back to mine. I drew my head back.

"You just left," I sputtered. "How could you leave me like that? I thought you... I thought maybe we..."

"So did I," he interrupted. "I came back for you, but you looked so happy with Charlie. It wasn't time, anyway. Things weren't ready. Waiting ten years was the worst hell you could ever imagine. I should never have left. I was young, and I listened to the wrong people."

Rafael coughed at the edge of the table. Unaware of his presence, I jumped in my seat, and Killian's jaw tightened. "Ellos estan aqui," Rafael muttered as he grabbed the empty plates.

My Spanish was just good enough to be dangerous. "Who's here?"

"I have to go." Killian kissed me again, and I tried to object. "I'll come by soon. Your birthday, right?"

I shot my hands up in frustration. "What?"

"Your apartment is your birthday. June twenty-eighth. They always are."

I nodded.

Rafael gave a curt nod, and Kit returned the gesture. "Soon," he said, striding off before I knew what hit me.

"Algo mas?" Rafael asked.

I squinted back at him. "No, nothing else. Do I just leave now? This is crazy."

"Diez minutos." Rafael raised both hands, displaying ten fingers to drive home the point. I turned back to my booth and refilled the coffee. The bitter liquid mirrored my feelings. I gulped it down in frustration, thinking about the men in my life and how they always disappeared.

I relished the alone time on my unaccompanied walk home. I had been with someone every minute since I got to the Center. When I gave it some thought, I realized I had been with someone every minute since I left the womb.

How many minutes since I had last been with Killian?

It felt like I stepped back in time when I saw him again. All the feelings rushed back and swarmed my thoughts. Over a decade ago, I shared the most secret and intimate moments with him. Every step brought back another flash of memory.

Killian's hurried movements – rushing us into a spare closet, shoving things off a storage table. He lay me down, and my inexperience betrayed me with every shiver and tremble of my limbs.

Even then, when he was so young, hard lines covered Killian's body. Rough hands swept up my bare skin, but his fingers – they were always gentle, finding their way inside me for the first time. He listened for every catch of my breath and moan to escape my lips, making each movement count.

By the time I made it home, my face flamed red letting the thoughts circle my mind obsessively. Killian had been more than a lust-filled youth. I gave him a part of myself and he was back for more.

Shaken by my thoughts and my new reality, I made the goal to spend the afternoon by myself and maybe find myself a little. With Jupiter, of course, my one true loyal companion.

I had a better lay of the land after chasing Julie around town for a few days. The entire City was a circular design, and The Discovery Center was a smaller circle inside. The Center was mapped out like a pinwheel with apartments wrapped around its entire circumference and a singular exit. Mine was on the Northeast side, but it only took a twenty-minute shuttle to circle the entire place.

The next ring inside the circle held the market, gymnasiums, salons, and any other business you could imagine. Parks and gardens filled the Center. As we strode through the market the other day, my head kept turning to the stone pathways and colorful flowers at my side. Today I would grab Jupiter and take a jog to explore some nature.

Charlie never cared for dogs, and the gift from my father, Thomas, annoyed him. It thrilled me, and although I acted inconvenienced when I opened the box a few birthdays ago for Charlie's benefit, I secretly cried tears of joy holding the Husky puppy in our bathroom. I thought Charlie would come around, but Jupiter loved me more. I needed something to love me the most and without question. *Charlie only cared about himself.*

I put on a matching workout set that hugged my curves. It was comfortable, and I felt good wearing it. Men would look anyway. Why not lean into it? Before heading out the door, I grabbed my hat. It helped me avoid eye contact in a pinch. Thankful I had the massive pup for some extra protection, I strode toward the green space, confident about the afternoon ahead.

What would I fill my time with during the next few weeks off of work? I might as well firm up my ass, as everyone seemed keen to stare at it constantly.

About twenty minutes in, almost dead from exhaustion, I made a promise to myself to run every day. It would be good for Jupiter, who impatiently dragged me up a hill. Out of breath, I found a bench in between patches of tulips and flopped my sweaty self down, heaving some much-needed breaths into my burning lungs.

"Fuck, I'm out of shape," I muttered to myself.

"You look great," a man running past yelled in my direction. I gave a small smile and looked away. He slowed, and noticing my avoidance, continued on his path.

"You do," Liam's voice purred from behind the bench.

"Fuck!" I yelped. I stood up in shock and Jupiter barked. I calmed her with a pat on the head.

"Were you hiding in the damn bushes? Where did you come from?"

"Quite the mouth on you today." Liam chuckled. "I saw you a mile back. I followed your path. Surely you can't blame me for taking another opportunity to see you."

A sheen of sweat covered his forehead and muscular arms. Dressed in all black, his shirt clung to every muscle, which flexed with his deep breathing. Guilt immediately followed my thoughts. I wasn't betrothed to Killian, but I felt loyal to him. I averted my gaze before I looked lower at Liam's joggers. That might send me over the edge.

Fight the attraction, Alaina.

"Sorry," I mumbled. "Charlie hated how much I cussed. He called it unladylike. I guess the habit is rearing its ugly head now that he left. An act of defiance even though he'll never know it." I lifted an eyebrow, still averting my eyes from Liam.

"I like the thought of you becoming more... you. Even with all the cursing, which in this case may be my fault. I startled you. Have you eaten lunch yet?"

I nodded and turned back to him, confident I could keep my gaze on his upper half. "Well, I had a large brunch, and I'm still full."

"Ah, the ladies love the weekend brunches. Men also partake in the mimosa specials if they are brave enough."

"The men partake in anything that will get them closer to the ladies."

"Like stalking someone jogging?"

"So you admit it." I pointed a playful finger at his chest, and he gripped my wrist, bringing us closer.

"I admit, I'm always on the lookout for you, Alaina."

A rush of heat washed over me as I looked into his ice-blue eyes. They crinkled with his smile, and I hated to admit, he had me under his spell. I thought of kissing him and then remembered kissing Killian. The feelings jumbled inside my busy mind, and I couldn't form words. After a long silence stretched, Liam released his grip.

"Where did you brunch?" he asked.

A surge of nerves came over me. The desire to keep that information private, to keep any interaction with Killian private, overtook me. I pulled my lips back into a tight smile. "You know, after that run, I think I am hungry. Is there a dog-friendly place around here?"

Liam puffed out his chest and brought my palm up
to his lips. He planted a gentle kiss in the center, and
although the gesture felt kind, the orange glow in my
line of vision overtook my thoughts. *Liam goes home to
a wife.*

His playful expression fell. "What's the face? Too
much swoon for you?"

I still had a million questions about Liam, Killian, this
place, and the new "way of things". If I wore an orange
bracelet a few months ago, would this all be easier?
Would it hurt less?

"Do you still fuck your wife?" The shock of my
statement hit me hard, and Liam stiffened in response.
He inhaled sharply and clasped my hand. "Oh my, I'm so
sorry. I just... that just came out. I don't know why I said
it out loud. Oh, shit."

Liam released his breath and brought his other thumb
to my lips. He stroked the bottom lip, pulling it down.
I remained silent, terrified of what he, or I, might say
next. My words and thoughts fumbled from my mouth
without thinking.

"Not for a long time. It's difficult to explain..." He
trailed off. "I'm not like Charlie. I don't think like that."

"No," I gulped. "You are nothing like Charlie."

"What I mean is..." Liam pinched the bridge of his
nose and looked down to his feet. "Some men don't want
to have sex with a woman that wants to leave you."

"But you said... it's the way of—"

"I know what I said at the Separation Center," Liam
bit back. His chest rose and fell with quick breaths. I
saw the redness on his face, but I didn't know if it was
embarrassment or anger.

"I wouldn't like it either," I muttered. "I wouldn't want to be with someone who could let me go."

Liam smiled, and his shoulders relaxed. He looked over at Jupiter. "I don't know of a place where Jupiter could go with us to eat. Let's drop him off at your apartment and then go get a bite."

Liam turned and pulled me after him, holding my hand in his. I followed, still shocked by my earlier question and our conversation.

"Is that a good idea, going to my apartment together? Is that allowed?"

He chuckled to himself, wrapping his fingers around my palm.

"Let's find out."

Chapter 8

Choices

ALAINA

It never gets easier taking a man to your apartment, even the second time around. Liam had been there before, but now it felt like my home. He entered a space I considered my own. It was funny how quickly I'd adapted to this new life. A life I didn't want, but I couldn't escape.

What do I want?

I had reunited with Killian, whatever that meant, and now I ached for him. A literal pain entered my core, and even the sight of a broad-chested and handsome Liam couldn't take the longing away. These two men had left me adrift.

Many times already, Liam had met my needs and showed kindness. Yes, he wanted something from me, but he didn't have to be so friendly at the Separation Center. The mess I was in last week, how could he have known I would heal up the way I did? Not that I'm all the way patched up from the shock of everything. Far from it.

Given the chance to stop at home, I changed into something not covered in sweat. Jupiter heeled at Liam's feet, her head cocked up to him while he stood and waited. The pup was cautiously optimistic about this large stranger that loomed in our living space.

"You can take a seat," I bellowed from the bedroom. "I'll just be a few minutes." Obsessed with Killian or not, I still wanted to look good. I swept my hair into a ponytail and changed into fresh jeans and a tank top.

I emerged from my bathroom to find Liam standing in the doorway of my room. "Interesting piece," he said, nudging his chin toward the sugar skull.

"I meant to wait in the living room," I deadpanned, yanking my top over my bare stomach.

"I knew what you meant." His smile stretched across his face while his eyes flicked over my body. "Where should we eat? I'm suddenly ravenous."

My heart thudded in my chest. Even with Killian's return, I couldn't deny my attraction to Liam. *Is this what it's like to want a man?* I hadn't wanted Charlie this way. He and I had an arrangement more than a desire. That was clear now that we were apart. How many years had I been blind to what it felt like to want someone, not need them? "Your choice. Remember, I've been here less than a week. Do with me what you want."

His eyes flicked to the bed, and I regretted my stupid mouth once more. *Why can't you keep your thoughts to yourself?*

I rushed to my doorway to exit, but his hands made their way to my hips and stopped me. "Now, now," I whispered, my breathy tone giving me away. The rush of his touch so close to my bed affected my ability to function. Heart pounding in my ears, I forced myself to calm down. "There are rules... you well know. Flirtation is one thing. Don't push it."

He released his grip and backed up. "I have an idea. Not La Rosa again. You must have grown tired of that place by now." He winked and left the hallway, patting Jupiter on the head before walking past.

I froze at his comment. The mention of La Rosa gnawed at me for a moment. For all Liam knew, I visited the restaurant once. Why did he say, *again*? I pushed the worries away, hiding my curiosity.

"Okay, well, I trust you. Whatever you think." I rushed out the door after him and locked it behind me. I turned and noticed the other door numbers for the first time.

0921, 0704, 1223: There was no order for the assignments. Killian was right. They must be birthdays.

"You should trust me, but be careful who else you give that trust to."

Liam's choice of words, once again, caught my attention. "Of course," I agreed, but I knew at that moment I trusted no one but myself.

Liam brought us to a cafe on the northwest side of the Center. I hadn't been this far with Lori yet, and Liam acted as my tour guide, helping me navigate through the area while giving me a history of the Center. I enjoyed discussing less carnal things. Liam had a one-track mind, and although I found him alluring, my libido needed a break.

"That tower is where I live. It houses employees of the City, Discovery Center, and the Separation Center." He pointed to a large, oppressive building. It stood dull and grey, the least ornate thing I'd seen thus far, but it made sense. Why draw attention to those who were here by employment and not by choice? "I moved here about a month ago, and I live alone," he continued. "When my wife and I decided to separate, and the space came open, it seemed like the best option."

His need to update me about his living situation did not go unnoticed, but he was still very much married.

"This side feels so... different. I can't place my finger on it. Something is less... touristy if that makes sense."

Liam sipped espresso and a charcuterie board of snacks hit the table. My stomach growled at the sight of food. Liam gestured for me to eat, and I popped a date in my mouth, moaning at the sweetness.

"This area houses most operational facilities for the Center. You are seeing more government buildings. And the Blue Forest is on this side. That thing is oppressive."

"Oh, I find it beautiful, you don't?"

"I find it dangerous. There is a reason thirty-foot fencing and a frequency wall line the border. It's certain death outside the City."

"You don't feel a little... caged in?"

Abigor, the head of the Council, ordered an increase in size and strength at the City's border when I was a girl. I remembered how everyone was afraid of not being protected, but I felt suffocated, trapped even more from the supposed dangers. *What was out there?*

Liam didn't answer. "Still, there is something magical about it," I sighed. "All the stories can't be true."

Liam swallowed hard. The sandwich he ordered arrived, and he cut off a piece and handed it to me. "Some stories are most definitely true. You should talk to your friend Julie if you ever feel the need to have a visit. She would set you straight."

"You know Julie well?" I asked.

He shrugged, chewing and looking at the forest. "She works with security for the City, right? She'll agree with me."

Locals named the acres of trees that lined our lives *The Blue Forest*, but the official name came from some soldier or politician. The government re-titled everything honoring one of their own after the shadow times. The new laws and social standards they implemented saved humanity. At least that's what the history books taught. So, every park and landmark got a fresh coat of paint and rebranding.

Killian had told me once what they named the forest before our grandparents' time. The fact felt dangerous to know, and I had forgotten it. If only I'd realized the importance of things like that in my youth. There were truths taught and then the truths you learn yourself. The latter was more important to me, now more than ever.

Everyone called it blue because of the Jacaranda trees that lined the edges and sprinkled throughout the foliage. Their purple and blue tints drew your eye, but the area itself remained off-limits to anything but a look.

Criminals lurked in the forest, although some called them refugees. The last time I heard any news about the people captured in the forest was at my boarding school. The memory returned as I sat with Liam, and so did memories of Killian. He sat clearly on the side of the refugees, while the entire school grew panicked at the thought of criminals so close to our property.

Frequency walls lined the forest, cutting off any ties to all life outside the City. It was not visible to the naked eye, but we all knew that twenty feet in meant certain pain and possible death.

Nothing went in and nothing came out.

Despite all that, Liam saw danger in the purple leaves each spring, but I saw beauty. Something about the expanse of bright colors that almost touched the sun and the waves of trees that stretched on forever called to me. If criminals filled those woods, they picked the perfect spot. They were free in a sea of beauty.

Free.

"This entire place is breathtaking, oppressive forest or not. I may not have chosen this life, but I'm grateful for the view."

I took a bite of a sandwich, a pesto grilled cheese, another favorite of mine.

"What you really should lay your eyes on is the building over there. The one with the red awning. You're an artist. I saw that in your file."

I turned to see the art gallery on our left. The first story had floor-to-ceiling windows where supplies lined rows of its warehouse. The floor above looked like classrooms. They had placed chairs in circles among various rooms. One room bustled with activity. People focused on a central object, a woman perhaps. Their brushes flicked across canvases as their heads bobbed from side to side, inspecting their subject. A woman walked the circumference of the space, hands behind her back, nodding at the pieces before her.

My eyes grew wide. "Do they teach? I would love to take a lesson."

"You don't need lessons. I've seen your pieces. You are masterfully skilled."

I blushed at the compliment. "To your eyes, maybe. No artist thinks their work is ever perfect or ever done. Or ever good, if I'm being honest."

Liam finished his sandwich and wiped his hands clean. A dangerous smirk crossed his lips. I glimpsed at his outstretched hand, but my attention remained on the class, watching the rhythmic strokes of their brushes. He wiggled his fingers, motioning for me to take hold. I slipped my hand in his and rotated back in his direction, my eyes the last to leave.

"The classes are constantly full," he admitted. My heart sank. "They don't need more students. They need another teacher."

"I'm not a teacher. I don't have the credentials for that."

"Life experience is the world's best educator. Carrie, the woman you see walking around the students, she asked me not too long ago if I knew of anyone that could help. Talented artists are few and far between. So, while you are on a break from your current employment, she has four or five classes she wants you to co-teach. If you do well, perhaps you could start a new career with this new life of yours."

"I... I don't know what to say," my voice sputtered. "That's so very thoughtful, Liam. I'm taken aback."

"Sometimes, things work out the way they should. When I saw your file, I knew you would be perfect for the job."

"It's so nice of you to think of me."

Liam's fingers tightened around my hand, and he pulled me closer. "A real man will take care of you. Look out for your wants and needs. He should satisfy you in every way."

My cheeks flushed. His intentions to coerce me into this life, and maybe a life with him, hit home. He saw me. He saw my wants and desires. Something that Charlie never grasped. Never wanted to.

We finished eating, mostly in silence. Liam kept his grin. He thought this was a big score for him, and for all he knew, no other man held my attention. I had no words, still in shock at how things were working out. His thoughtfulness made him more attractive, and it was obvious he felt the same way.

Sure, he wanted a partner. All the men at the Center carried that burden, but Liam could have his pick. No children and on his third match made him a prime target already. Every woman in her thirties and ready for match two planned for children. Men without kids in their early forties were rare and sought after. They had security, savings, and patience. And who wouldn't want to make a baby with the chiseled man that sat across from me? Hundreds of males passed me each day, and none held my attention quite like Liam.

Except maybe Killian.

Liam's interest in me was surprising. Although men didn't have enough women to go around, I didn't see myself as a prize. I knew the current standards of beauty, and I held most of the general characteristics. My curves were in the right spots. Blessed with unblemished skin and decent looks, I kept myself up as best I could.

Nothing about me drew a lot of attention. I didn't possess a perfectly symmetrical face or large, perky breasts. I was simply slightly above average. Thinking Charlie and I would be together forever, I never wanted to enhance or change anything.

Once our table cleared and our stomachs were full, Liam took me by the hand to the studio. Its name, aptly *The Discovery Center Art House*, curved over the entrance awning. The stained glass doors opened, and I glimpsed over the government order that flashed to our left as we entered. It read the same as any in the City. They must review all art to ensure it abides by the laws. Artistic expression held no freedom.

A memory surfaced from boarding school. A young woman had painted a man with a bleeding heart that he held in his hands. He wore a clean-cut suit and had a stiff haircut, but red paint stretched across the canvas in thick pools, making it appear covered in his blood. The piece was meant to convey that behind the most powerful men lies sadness. The problem was, that the man looked eerily close to a high-ranking official who happened to be the girl's father. The teacher submitted the artwork and after examination, chaos ensued, along with hours of lessons about acceptable expression. The girl wanted to reach her father on an emotional level, not to cause him harm. He never came on visitor days, and she missed him.

Only Killian knew I cried when they told us they burned it.

"Carrie," Liam's voice bellowed. Already entranced at the rows of supplies, he tugged me along after him. I grazed my fingers on brushes and canvases along the way. Liam and Carrie kissed on the cheek. A bit of overkill, but still adorable. Her bracelet glowed red under her gauzy sleeve. Her bright red hair flowed down her back, and I resisted the urge to run my fingers through the soft ends. She oozed everything artist, and I wanted to be near her. As if her closeness might rub off on me somehow and make me more worldly and special.

"And this must be Alaina," she cooed. "It's so wonderful to meet you. Please, let me show you upstairs. We are setting up for our next class. Would it be too forward to ask you to assist, already?"

"Oh, I would love to," I said. "Unless... Liam... I didn't know if you had other plans for us."

"I planned to see that bright smile on both your faces."

Carrie gave him a wink. "Didn't take you long to get me someone. I owe you, Liam."

Liam waved his hand at her. "Not at all." He turned to me and brushed a thumb over my cheek. Heat trailed to my center. "I'll find you later." He kissed my forehead and left.

Carrie wiggled her eyebrows and ushered me to follow. I grabbed a smock from the hooks along the stairway towards the studios. It smelled of paint and cleaner, and an immediate sense of relief filled my bones. The years of avoiding the one thing that made me happy pained my heart with regret. *Why did I give up so much for Charlie?*

"We have about three or four classes a day," Carrie echoed ahead of me. "There are seniors' classes, children's classes, beginner art... you name it, we do it. But I have strict rules for my students." She stopped at the top of the stairwell and looked back at me. "This isn't a club or bar. I'm not in the business of matchmaking. I'm in the business of creation and soul searching."

I smiled and nodded with vigor. Her words were so unlike everyone else. "I completely agree and understand. What classes are going on now?"

"The human form," she continued. Her shoes clicked on the floor while she tied her apron behind her back and gave a few sharp claps to the room as we entered. "Everyone, I want to introduce you to Alaina." Several faces peered around their pieces to greet me. I offered an enthusiastic wave back, my heart leaping from my chest. "She'll be teaching with me today, and perhaps from now on. Right now, she's observing. Be sure to ask for her thoughts and opinions. I've seen her work. It's fascinating."

The compliment sent my heart bursting into a million pieces. Securing the smock, I clasped my hands behind my back, mirroring her stance, and took a slow walk around the artists. A young woman draped in purple fabric sat in the center of the room. She had one leg straight out and the other tucked underneath her. A sad expression crossed her face, and I wondered if it was genuine or coached. Her bracelet beamed orange.

Floor-to-ceiling windows cast light over one side of the room. A few splatters of paint trickled over the glass. The other walls had no space between hundreds of paintings. They were all tucked together, edges touching, covering every available inch. I wondered if every room had wall-to-wall art like this and if Carrie considered covering the ceiling next. The room encased me in art and sunshine.

The students showed wonderful technique, and I assumed this was an advanced class. Walking around the circle, one woman asked about my thoughts, and I gave her a few tips about shadowing. Reaching the windows, I peered outside to the Blue Forest in the distance. That's what I would paint next. Its beauty called to be captured.

The streets below held citizens strolling in and out of buildings, enjoying the beautiful day. Crowded sidewalks had friends hugging and couples holding hands. The rays of the sun hit their bracelets and caused beams of sharp light to blind my eyes every so often.

There was a stillness in the crowd from a few men on the sidewalk below. They spoke closely, hands placed on one another's shoulders. The talker looked like Aiden, the man Julie met at the market.

The listener ran his fingers through his wavy dark hair, and I felt his presence, even though I couldn't see his face.

Killian turned and looked directly up at me through the windows. The other men walked away, and Killian's face cast an emotion I couldn't pinpoint. He crossed his arms over his chest and sat on a bench facing the studio. I waved my hand, gesturing for him to come up. He shook his head no and brought his ankle up over his knee, slouching on the bench.

Is he just going to sit there and stalk me?

The thought made my skin tingle, but panic overtook my excitement when a dark shuttle reached the corner and several officials leaped out in unison.

Killian remained calm when they grabbed him and tied his hands behind his back. His body fell limp as they shoved him around and slammed him to his knees on the sidewalk. Unsure of what to do, I stepped closer to the window, bringing my open palms to the glass.

After a small crowd surrounded him, they hoisted him inside the transport. It drove off, and my eyes filled with hot tears threatening to escape. Through the blur, I scanned the crowd. The other men with him a moment ago were nowhere to be found.

The one person I recognized kept his eyes on the transport until it rounded the corner and fell out of sight.

Liam stood tall, hands on his hips. He crossed the street, cocky and sure of himself. He looked as if he had won a bet with his long, confident strides carrying him away. A sick feeling fell over me, and a few tears escaped down my cheeks.

Killian had disappeared again.

This time, it wasn't by choice.

This time, I would do something about it.

Chapter 9

Offender

ALAINA

I twisted my bracelet around my wrist so much a red ring appeared on my skin from the motion. The repetitive action would have to hold me together for the few remaining hours of the class.

After seeing Killian taken by security into that dark vehicle, I let silent tears fall, facing the window for a few tense minutes. No one noticed, enthralled with their work. When Carrie's heels clicked my way, I continued my circle around the students and observed the walls of art that encased the room. They were beautiful, but devoid of anything real. Just like everyone else in this fucking City. They left me empty.

Avoiding anyone's attention until I put myself back together again, I gritted my teeth and pushed through the day. I wanted this job. I needed this opportunity. Whatever trouble Killian got himself into couldn't take this away. Maybe he was a man destined to disappear, but I refused to let him slip away this time without me doing something about it - without at least asking questions.

Carrie thanked me for staying so long on brief notice and asked when I could return. We decided I would take the next two weeks working in the beginners' classes three days a week. "The children's group takes the most work and the most patience. I won't scare you with that right away," she joked. "But at some point, everyone here has to suffer through some fingerpainting."

"Oh, I don't mind," I insisted. "I want to have children soon, and it would be a wonderful experience." The words fell out without thought, true as they were. I brought my fingers to my lips at the admission, but there was no putting them back now.

"Yes, that's what Liam said," Carrie snickered.

"Oh," I choked. We picked up the classroom, moving canvases to dry on pieces of lumber in the spacious hallways. My voice echoed from the emptied room. "What else did he say?" Instant regret filled me once the words were out. She worked with Liam, and, no doubt, she would report back any exchange between us.

"He's definitely smitten with you. Obsessed a bit, I would say. That's odd for him because he finds most women... how has he put it... predictable - a bunch of followers?"

I tilted my head and scrunched my face at her words. *I follow the rules, don't I?*

"Anyway, it's nice to know you may share that affection." Carrie entered the room and pulled at the fabric covering the floor, folding it into a sloppy roll. She waited for a response and I gave none, so she continued. "Rachel is pleased, you know. She's been worried about him since the first separation."

Lifting the other end of the fabric, I gave Carrie a blank stare. Her words might as well be in another language. I shrugged my shoulders, answering, "I'm not sure I catch your meaning. Liam and I just met."

"Oh, really? Well, time flies when you are having fun."

Piecing together a few bits, I asked, "Is Rachel his... wife?"

"Yes, but they have decided to separate. They are great friends and it's cordial, unlike his first."

"Because his first wife..." I trailed off.

"They planned on being together forever, or at least Liam did. He got the shock of his life, I'm afraid. The entire experience changed his outlook on everything. His life plan, his job, you name it. I think..." she trailed off. She scratched the back of her neck, taking a moment before she continued. "I think he still wants that. To be with someone forever." She turned to face me. Her eyes pierced into mine. "That's crazy, right?"

I offered a slow nod but said nothing. Carrie and Liam must have been friends for a long time. She knew him better than just a colleague. I caught my breath and broke our eye contact. "Have you known him for long?" I asked.

"We share many acquaintances. Anyway, Rachel gushes about how great their time was together, so you are a lucky lady."

I carted the fabric out of the room and into the laundry area. I returned to Carrie, confused as ever by our exchange. I still found this way of life odd and offputting. Desperate to change the subject, I flipped the conversation back to the task at hand. "Do you need more help to clean up? I'm happy to do my part of cleaning along with teaching."

"I'm a bit of a neat freak if you couldn't tell by all the drop cloths. A big contrast to the artist's line of work I know, but I feel it helps to have a fresh space, so the art is all you notice. No one wants dirty floorboards drawing their attention. There's a non-stop list on the outside of my office each week of things to do. If you get to something, just mark it off."

"Great," I said, eager to make my exit. "I don't have a class tomorrow, but I'll run by and help you out. I'm someone who needs to keep my hands busy."

Carrie wrapped an arm around my shoulders and escorted me to the door. She grabbed a set of keys from a rack and handed me the bundle. "Use these any time." I gave her a quizzical look. Keys were an antiquated technology, and I vaguely remembered seeing them in my mother's office as a girl. "I know, keys right. So old school. But they make me feel nostalgic for my grandfather's art studio, and well, we all find joy where we can."

I placed the keys in my pocket. There had to be six or seven on the set, and I wondered how many doors they opened. The studio wasn't that big. I assured Carrie I would see her tomorrow and skipped out the door. I made it a few steps before I slammed right into Liam's firm body and almost fell on my ass. He caught me before I hit the floor, and a rush of fury swept over me. Hours before, he had a part in taking Killian. *Well, he either knew about the event or orchestrated it.*

"Funny seeing you here," I grumbled.

He cocked his head and gave me a one-sided smile. "You aren't taking any supplies with you? A perk of the job."

My sarcasm apparently lost on Liam, I narrowed my eyes. "What do you mean?"

Liam barged past me, his mission clear in his mind. He gave the door a few harsh knocks and greeted Carrie once more. They talked for a moment while I paced the sidewalk, unsure of what to say or do. The angry part of me wanted to walk off and leave him there.

But that wouldn't help Killian. I needed Liam to trust me and help me understand what those damn officials did with him.

Hands full of paint and a few canvases, he marched back, beaming with pride.

"Let me help you," I said, and grabbed a few things from his overflowing hands. My need to be polite was a fraction stronger than my need to kick him in the balls. Liam had information about Killian. I knew it, and I had to play the part to get it out of him.

We walked in silence for a few minutes back to my apartment. A rush of panic hit me that Liam would want to come in to set the things down. He may be easier to resist, but that didn't change that twice in one day this hulk of a man would be in my space. Halfway through our journey, I started talking.

"There was some, um, chaos on the street today outside the studio. I could hear the commotion from the class. I thought I saw you. What was that about?" My babbling could go on forever and give my intention away. I scolded myself for rambling already. *Stop talking, Alaina.*

Liam gave a slow smile and never broke his stride. "Potential nonresidents. We keep finding them more and more. Why not just register? I don't get it."

"Potential?" I asked and then clamped my mouth shut with force.

"Well, there is a chance someone just had a defective band. It happens. The technology is newer. But some people interfere with the bracelets themselves."

"Why would anyone do that?" Kit's words rang in my head so loud I feared Liam might hear them. *The bracelets are not real. I'm here to take you with me.*

"Oh, you're a smart woman. Think about it. Some women and men want to appear to be something they're not. It's typically a problem with vendors. They come in with their red attachment band and want to try their luck with someone in their interim year. Maybe they're bored. Maybe they're a coward."

Liam loved that word — coward.

"That's a big risk for a possibility. I saw a vehicle with security rush someone away. Where do they take them?"

"Depends on how many offenses."

"People do it multiple times?"

"Oh, yes. One group of men we caught altering their bracelets twice in one month."

With only a few blocks from my apartment, I slowed my stride. I needed more information, and I wasn't up for a lengthy conversation inside, where my bed was, just the two of us. Liam stopped, noticing I trailed behind him.

"Let me carry some of that for you."

"Maybe we could take a quick rest on this bench. You were saying?"

"Okay, sure. What was I saying?"

"Where do they take them?"

Liam set the things down and joined me on the bench. He reached his large arm around my shoulders and drew me toward him. I let him. Proximity would only help my cause.

"First offense, City officials take them to the Separation Center. The offenders take part in a week of mental evaluation and psychological assessments to rehabilitate. People who do things like that don't understand the delicate balance of our society. They've forgotten how things used to be. We shield that from most people, but if you offend, they show you firsthand the terror society suffered through. They give them the knowledge of why it's so important to trust the council and the City."

I knew very little outside my history classes about the shadow times. Mental illness ran rampant, and hurt people always hurt people. There were mass suicides, cults, and shootings, and families retreated to their homes. That didn't help the mental strain. Things only became worse. Humans are social animals, and every week our school lessons reiterated how much you need a partner to stabilize you. More than once I'd had the thought the partner was there to watch you, to tell on you, or to report your wrongdoings to the City.

Eventually, everyone becomes indoctrinated with the mantra. It was tattooed on my brain with such force, my obsession with coupling had overtaken all reason. It had overtaken my need to find out what happened to Killian. I wouldn't make that mistake again.

I remembered every evaluation I went through with Charlie. We all had to do it once a year when we partnered. I endured hours of interrogation about my spouse in that tiny, dark room. My sweaty palms ran down my pants while I answered each question the official asked of me, no matter how personal. I could almost feel the heavy monitor on my chest that pulsed along with my heartbeat.

How often do you have sex?

Do you orgasm?

Do you self-stimulate? Alone? Together?

Does he perform cunnilingus on you?

What did those questions matter to the City? But I answered them, squirming in my seat, my face aflame with embarrassment.

I ensured Charlie passed the assessment each time. But of course, he would. He fit the mold. He was normal.

"Three offenses is a different story," Liam continued. "If you carry on like that, there is no hope for you in our world."

I turned to Liam, still deep in my thoughts about our City's history and Killian. "So then what?" I asked.

Liam curved his head around me and pointed in the distance. The blue trees swayed in the winds. I closed my eyes in understanding.

"Exactly," Liam affirmed. "It's criminal at that point. Officials open the field and shove them in. I would say best of luck to them, but I don't mean it. At that point, good riddance. People like that won't ever comply with the way of things."

I shuddered at the phrase, and Liam pulled me closer. My head craned to the side, facing the Blue Forest. "I wish I could kiss you right now," he breathed into my neck, but I didn't respond. His fingers grazed my arm with a light touch. I remained still and calm. My thoughts were with the woods and all those presumed criminals.

Julie burst through the door full of smiles a week later. "Alaina, my girl. I'm back and I've gone shopping." She halted a few steps into the living room. "What... Wow, Alaina. Oh, my."

I had converted the living space into a makeshift studio. I pushed that damn white couch haphazardly to the furthest wall possible and draped it with drop cloths. The floor stuck to Julie's shoes, lined with thin plastic. Three easels stood in the center of the room. Three separate canvases flowed together for my piece, so I kept them all up at once. Carrie allowed me to take anything with me to paint at home, grateful I helped clean even when I didn't have a class. I never left without an armful of supplies.

"Making this place your own, aren't you?" Julie's eyes were wide, scanning the room. "How do you get to the entertainment dock?" I had covered the wall outfitted with a large screen and tablets with plastic.

"I don't," I replied. I inhaled the hot coffee in my hands and sipped. "I thought you said you were coming over tonight. Not that I mind the extra attention," I lied. I minded. The entire week, I came up empty in my search for Killian. Liam came by every day, and we jogged together. It's difficult to host an inquiry while jogging, especially when I'm out of shape. I felt his eyes on me the entire time, observing every inch of my body. I hated how much I liked it, and I hated how it distracted me from my goal.

I learned only a few tidbits. No one had perpetrated three offenses in over five years. They hadn't chucked Killian into the woods just yet. That offered a small bit of comfort. I also felt confident about where he was and when he would get out. Assuming they believed he tampered with his band for selfish reasons, he'd leave the Separation Center that day.

I determined Liam had nothing to do with Killian's capture. The timing was bad, but officials constantly scanned residents to ensure their bands are properly registered. Killian was in the wrong place at the wrong time, but something was still off about it. He was standing with other men, Aiden included. They abandoned him and he sat there... waiting.

I could barely sleep last night. If he didn't find me, I would have to get to the Center somehow and locate him.

And here was Julie, and her timing unnerved me. I heard the clang of alcohol bottles in her bag. I needed my wits about me and an excuse to avoid drinking.

"Well, this is impressive," Julie went on. "I'm so proud of you for painting again. You are so good. And it's wonderful Liam set you up like that."

I pursed my lips. "Did I tell you Liam arranged the job at the studio?"

"No, he did."

Undecided if this annoyed me, I changed the subject. "Where are we headed tonight? And what shall we do with our day?"

"Confession time before you make a plan." Julie set her bags on my cloth-covered couch and lifted a finger. "I'm using your space to drop off, clean up, and dress up. I have a lunch date today. I'll be back this afternoon. Do you mind?"

I didn't and shook my head no, with perhaps too much enthusiasm.

"No lecture about dating before my separation? Wow, you have come around," Julie chided.

"No lecture, but I'm surprised. Getting ahead of the game there. What if you meet someone you want to match with before your year even starts? Seems like you would miss all the fun."

"Oh shit, that won't happen. Not with this guy, especially. He's just nice to drink with and nicer to look at. I'm getting my sea legs. Maybe you should try a proper date instead of the incessant jogging with Liam. Something more relaxing would be nice."

Liam and Julie apparently talked quite a bit.

"Our jogs aren't dates." But as soon as I said it, I questioned the statement. *Are we dating?*

"Whatever you say," Julie responded in a singsong voice. "Just... be kind to him. He's a good guy." I nodded in response, curious about her defense of Liam. She rushed off before I could ask any questions.

Julie borrowed my bathroom for the better part of an hour and emerged, looking confident and elegant. She didn't know what overdressed meant and would wear a ballgown to a bagel shop if she felt like it, but she pulled it all off with grace. Any man would be lucky to have her arm today with her tight black dress and red lips.

"You look amazing," I said. I had almost finished my coffee and frowned in the cup. Running low meant rationing.

"Thanks. Do you want me to bring you back anything? Will you be here in a few hours?"

"You know what? That would be great. I could use a good meal. Thank you." I'd avoided the market all week, hence the lack of coffee. Liam offered for us to go together, but it would have been an opportunity for him to touch me and pull me close to him through the crowds. I wanted to keep him at a distance until I knew more.

I hugged Julie goodbye. She practically skipped out of my apartment with glee. A long bath was the only thing on my agenda. It would kill some time and might calm my nerves. My muscles ached from my week of runs and stressful sleep.

When the tub filled, I killed the lights and slipped in. The scalding water pinched my skin. I took baths entirely too hot, but the momentary sting was worth the relaxation. I sunk deep into the tub with only my nose and lips above the water. The hum of my apartment vibrated in my submerged ears, and I stretched my back, feeling my bones pop.

I bobbed there for a while, eyes closed. When I relaxed for the first time all week, a sudden light shone through followed by a large palm covering my lips. My eyes flew open, and a cold bracelet hit my cheek, glowing purple. Nose to nose with the intruder, I heard nothing but my breath push out against his hand.

"Don't do that now. All the effort it took to sneak in here, and I'll just get kicked out if you scream." Killian's eyes bore into mine, and I froze. Uncaring about my nakedness in the bright bathroom, I placed my hands on his cheeks.

He came back to me this time.

My heart swelled at the sight of him. He wore simple black cotton pants and a shirt. His face looked slightly drawn but still strong and defiant. And at the sight of me, his eyes filled with lust.

Once he realized I wouldn't yell out or set off an alarm, he ripped me out of the tub. One arm wrapped under my knees and one behind my back. Water slapped around us on the floor, soaking his shirt when he held me against him. His hands full, he opened the door with his foot, heading straight toward my bedroom.

Chapter 10

Free

ALAINA

Killian, being the only one dressed, made quick work of removing his clothes. He placed me on my unkempt bed and removed his shirt with one hand, yanking it from behind his head. My limbs vibrated with excitement watching him.

Every inch of him was lean with muscle. Pale white lines covered his chest and arms. On his ribs were two raised circles of pink scar tissue. His body had been through something... something awful.

I could feel his length on my leg when he freed himself from his pants, and my desperation grew to see and feel every part of him. I reached my hand between us and wrapped my fingers around his cock, feeling it pulse against my fingertips. He moaned, and I laid my head back with a shuddered exhale. He trailed his hand up the side of my body, thumbing each rib, and studied my naked chest with hungry eyes.

Any modesty left in me subsided. He wanted me. He had always wanted me, and this was our time to be together after all these years. All I could think at that moment was how he would feel inside me and how I could make him feel; how his face would look when he came. All those years ago, we never got this close. He would touch me with skilled fingers, and I took him in my mouth only once. Long-forgotten memories flooded back, making my body flame with desire for him.

His skin burned hot against mine, but my teeth chattered involuntarily. I shivered after being ripped from the blazing hot tub. He brought a thick blanket around his back, encasing us in its heat mixed with the heat of our bodies, and settled between my legs. Already impossibly hard, he became rock solid when his tongue entered my mouth. I released my hand from his cock, and he groaned again.

We kissed in a fury for minutes, the heat between us rising. His smell and taste made my head spin, and I ravaged his mouth with mine, drowning in his flavor.

After what felt like an eternity of writhing moans, he stilled. Holding back the urge to push inside, his movements slowed. I rocked underneath him, desperate for his intensity to return. His length rubbed against my folds without entering, driving me wild with need. My whimpers grew louder, and I yanked my face away indignantly.

"What are you waiting for?" My voice sounded like a stranger. It came out frustrated and pleading. I needed him to ravage me. I needed to know he was real - that he would stay this time.

He lifted, looking down at me. "I haven't been with anyone for a long time," he answered. A look of uncertainty crossed his face. Our breaths were shallow and quick, matching the thudding heartbeats against our chests. What could I say to ease his mind? *I was with my husband weeks ago.*

A sudden urge of guilt pained my heart. I covered my eyes with my hand and turned my head away. The word *whore* came to my mind. "I'm sorry. I... I can't say the same."

"No, no," Killian whispered. "None of that." He took my palm from my face and held it down next to my head, entwining our fingers. He raised more, and the blanket dropped to his hips. His other arm reached underneath my lower back pulling my hips up. His eyes held mine and stilled my thoughts.

I couldn't look away.

Before I had time to react, he pushed inside me. In one motion, he filled and stretched me. A relieved cry escaped my lips. If this was being a whore, fine, then. I'll be Killian's whore. The glorious feeling of his body taking mine, of his cock thrusting mercilessly inside me, thwarted all negative thoughts. Nothing else mattered.

My legs shook while everything about Killian remained firm. His body moved with purpose, thrust after thrust. His breathing was even and thick. A sheen of sweat on his chest gave the slight indication of strain, but it only increased my need. Impossibly wet, more than I had ever been before, his movements quickened with ease. The tightening of my core rose, and I trembled underneath him.

His hovering body encased me. His jaw tightened, and the veins in his neck visibly pulsed. We were both close, and I clawed at his arms, almost near tears at the thought of our release.

"I love you," he confessed. "Do you know that? I fucking love you." A low growl came out after his admission. He brought himself lower to me, wrapping me in both arms, driving into me without pause. "I'm risking everyone for you." The weight of him against my chest, his skin rubbing against my hard nipples, made me cry out.

My mouth opened on his shoulder, and I bit down, screaming into his skin as the orgasm overtook my body. Shockwaves ripped through me, and I clenched against his hardness. "You feel so good," he gasped. "So fucking good. Worth every minute, every day, every year." I felt his heat pour deep inside, and the rumble of his chest against mine vibrated both our bodies in unison. "Fuck," he let out against my neck.

I'd known sex could surpass my experiences, but I didn't know it could be like... this. That moment with Killian consumed me completely. Everything else in the world faded to nothingness. Whatever he asked, I would allow. Anything he needed, I would provide. I granted him admission to every part of me, mind and body.

He owned me now.

I belonged to Killian.

After the tension subsided, he released me back to the comfort of the mattress. My limbs felt heavy and immobile. He hovered over me a moment, kissing my collarbones and neck. My body was still slick from sweat and bathwater, and his lips slid over my skin.

He lifted and sat on the side of the bed. I grabbed his arm with what little strength remained. He grinned back at me. "I've always loved you," I admitted.

His face remained unchanged. He brought a hand to my cheek and rubbed his thumb across. "I know," he said.

"Why did you leave?"

His face hardened, and he removed his warmth from the bed, heading to the shower. "That's a long conversation, and we'll have it, but not today."

He was leaving soon, and my heart sank. "Julie will be back after lunch," I whined.

"That won't be for a while," he hollered from the bathroom.

I curled into a ball on the bed, kicking off any covers. My body now felt overly warm. "What makes you say that?"

"I just know."

"Like you *knew* I was working at an art studio last week and a dark shuttle would take you away right before my eyes. Oh, but if you knew that, maybe you would have told me." My words came out with a snip, but I felt no anger towards Killian. My body felt too sated to be mad, but feelings of hurt and confusion remained. The sick feeling when they dragged him away into that transport returned. I never wanted to experience that again.

The water ran from the sink at full blast, and I heard a few cabinets shut. The shower turned on, and I took no response as all I would get.

Steam entered the doorway of the bathroom as Killian entered the shower. "Are you coming in?" His voice echoed from the room.

I rose from the bed we'd wrecked. Unable to refuse the invitation, I shuffled over and took a quick glimpse into the mirror. My tousled hair was everywhere, and slick skin and flushed cheeks looked back at me. But instead of cringing at my reflection, I smiled. A lucky woman looked back. A woman, content and satisfied, grinned in my mirror. A woman I had lost for so many years.

Killian's hand reached out and pulled me toward the shower, and I stepped inside. He wrapped his arms around my middle and held us together under the warm stream.

"Do you remember in school when we would sneak away? Do you remember how I would lay you down on that table in the storage room and worship every part of your body?" He moved his gaze over me with hooded eyes. "You feel the same. Your skin and your smell. Nothing has changed."

I nodded, closing my eyes at the happy memory. "You broke my heart when you left. You did it again last week. Why didn't you tell me?"

"Telling you wouldn't have changed it. It would have only caused you worry and stress. And things unfolded sooner than I thought they would. The only way I could let you know I would be gone for a while was to have it happen in front of your face. I came to find you the second I could. The second I was out of there."

I stiffened. "Wait, you knew they would take you."

"Yes. I needed some... time there."

My head spun. "Why? Do you know what happens when they find you disobedient too many times?"

Killian let out a soft chuckle. "That's well known."

"You can't just disappear again. You can't leave me again."

He held me tighter. "I'm here to take you with me. Please, trust me. I know what I'm doing. And... it's not just up to me anymore."

"Take me where?" I spit through gritted teeth. My fear intensified at the thought of Killian leaving me. The image of him walking toward the woods all those years ago flashed back into my mind. "Wait. To the woods?" I answered his question with one of my own. "You want to take me to the Blue Forest with all the criminals?"

He sighed. "You know so little. Please trust me."

"I know things," I shot back in defiance. But that felt like a lie the moment I said it. I hadn't even read the laws of coupling. I had never lived on my own until now. Each day, my environment surprised me. My entire life included my family, Julie, boarding school, and then Charlie. I knew Discovery Centers existed, but I never thought much of a place I would never visit, or so I thought.

How naïve am I? What do I know of the world?

"You know how to make beautiful art," Killian interrupted my thoughts. "Art that is suffocated by the City and their rules. You know how to love people despite their faults. You know how to make me come so hard I blackout." I blushed and put my cheek on his chest to hide my embarrassment. "But you don't know what's outside the City's borders. You don't know what the world, the entire world you live in, really is. You can't comprehend its size or that civilizations exist outside the environment they've brought you up in. This..." Killian made a circle around us with his hands. "Isn't all there is. It's such a small piece of the puzzle, you can't even imagine."

I gave no response. I didn't know what to ask. He was speaking in circles around me. I trusted Killian. Something had drawn me to him in school, and the connection only felt stronger now. I'd shared myself with him in every way, but he was only giving me pieces of himself in doses that I could handle. My spinning head couldn't grasp much more.

"I know you're trying to explain something bigger to me right now, but I just can't..." I trailed off.

"You don't know the questions to ask," he interrupted. "When you see it, you'll understand. Know that I'll take care of you. Do you want that? Do you want me and children? Children you don't have to leave on the doorstep of a boarding school. Do you want to be free?"

"I'm not free." I wasn't sure if that was a question or a statement, but Killian shook his head no.

"I don't think I know what you mean by free," I whispered into his skin. His woodsy smell still permeated my senses through the running water.

"No, Alaina." He rubbed his palms down my back and kissed the top of my head. "You don't."

Chapter 11

The Key

ALAINA

Killian and I remained in the shower until the water ran cold. His words may not have made sense, but our bodies understood each other perfectly. He pinned me against the shower wall, taking me once more. The sensation of control, and my lack thereof, thrilled me. I gave in to the feeling, letting it ease my mind and cloud my thoughts.

When he collected his things to leave, I didn't have the energy to ask all the questions that remained unanswered. Killian drugged my senses. Nothing seemed to matter after he sated me. My logical brain wanted to know the events from his week in the Separation Center. It troubled me to know he went through something unpleasant. *Was it because of me? Was Liam punishing him?*

His bracelet gleamed purple. The officials thought he tampered with it, but who did they think he was? If I saw him outside my apartment, should I pretend not to know him? And the most ridiculous thought that slammed into my chest filled me with shame.

Women would notice Killian.

They would throw themselves at his single status, and he would reciprocate to keep up appearances. Sure, the ratio of men to women eased my fears a bit, but few men carried themselves the way he did. He oozed confidence and sex.

All my jumbled thoughts entered my brain the moment Killian shut the door behind him. I reached out my hand when it slammed, but it was too late. "Fuck," I muttered under my breath. "What a time to be out of coffee." My rambling wouldn't make the caffeinated beverage appear, so I turned my focus to hide any evidence of our tryst from Julie.

I threw my bedding down into the laundry chute. Flashes from the afternoon entered my mind. I missed Killian with an intense ache. Closing my eyes, I pulled every moment back into my memory. His hands on my body and the feel of him inside me. The dirty things he said and the beautiful things he told me. And then... it came back to me.

I'm risking everyone for you.

That should have been the question I asked. In shock from his admission of love and mine, the statement became lost in the jumble of emotions and orgasms. The thought of Killian being taken away filled me with guilt already. Being responsible for endangering others seemed too much of a burden to carry.

With all of that hammering into my brain, I still blushed with elation.

Killian loves me.

Charlie said, "I love you," like a habit. An afterthought when he walked out a door or ended a call. I held no memory of a time he said it in passion. Not even one time. Maybe that's true for couples a few years in, but Killian pined for me. He carried his love for me during our time apart, and it had remained strong, burning between us.

I hadn't forgotten about our time together in school, but I pretended I did. I thought I was a fool after letting myself become so enamored with someone so different... so rebellious. Julie let me know her disdain for Killian more than once. She wanted to protect me. His ideas and feelings about the City were dangerous. She found Charlie a safe match, considering the alternative. Relieved with Killian's departure, she pushed me Charlie's way.

Sometimes, by myself, I would cry over the loss of Killian. Charlie never noticed, and I wasn't sure if Julie knew. We'd spent every waking moment together in school when I wasn't with Killian, but she'd never asked. After so many years, I wondered if I imagined our connection... our love. That's what it had been. Love.

I thought about my past, moving aimlessly through rooms, picking up knickknacks. Jupiter followed along at my side, happy to have my attention again. I mopped up the fallen water that created a path from the bathroom to my bed. The words played on repeat in my head.

I love you. I'm risking everyone for you.

After changing the sheets, I moved to the kitchen and waited for Julie. Maybe scrubbing the sink would make food appear, or at least coffee. As if I had manifested her out of thin air, a few soft knocks sounded down my hallway. I rushed over and opened the door, finding

Julie. Her hands were full of bags and the outstretched foot she knocked with dangled in the air.

Her appearance made me wonder if she pulled an all-nighter instead of going on a lunch date. Her hair fell undone on one side, and tendrils dropped around her face. She bit at her bottom lip, swollen and pink, with her red lipstick smeared on one side. She had skipped a tie on her dress, and strands hung frazzled on the side. *Or was her dress torn?*

"Are you okay?" I took the bags from her hands and ushered her inside. She reached down to the floor to lift a drink carrier filled with coffees and I whispered, "Oh thank you," hurling the bags to my hallway table.

"I'm better than most." She grinned and handed me a cup, but her expression left me questioning. Her face revealed a hollowness as if she had gotten sick or awoken from a nightmare. She made her way to the couch and inspected the dropped fabric on top. Pushing it around before taking a seat, she yawned and took a languid sip of her coffee. Jupiter curled up beside her, resting her head on her lap.

I moved closer with caution. "You look like you, I don't know. You look a little roughed up."

Julie smiled with her eyes closed and laid her head on the back of the couch. "I'm great," she insisted. "What are you going to do with all these pieces? Sell them at the market?" She spoke without lifting her head but motioned her free hand around my living room.

The idea hadn't occurred to me until now. The thought of the City having to approve the work annoyed me, but they would see them, eventually. Even if they only hung on my walls, someone would perform a maintenance check on the apartment. Part of the routine involved submitting independent artwork to the City. I might as well take my shot. It would come across better surrendered by me first, anyway.

I liked the idea of teaching. The few classes so far had gone smoothly, with limited rambling and a gracious audience. But the idea of becoming an artist again would be something to cherish.

Painting was a hobby, not a job, according to Charlie and anyone else I asked. Why had I listened to him in all things? Why did he make all the decisions, including the one to end us? In hindsight, that one was on target, but so many others were mindless.

Decisions like what we would buy at the store, what we ate for dinner, and even what I wore. He set them all out on a perfect platter, and I picked them up like the good little wife I was.

I read about people sewing their clothes once. They outlawed making garments independently, but secretly I yearned for the tools to try it myself. At the time, I understood. Or, I made myself comply and mistook that for understanding. Rules governed the residents for a reason, right? I followed along, complacent and happy enough. Not happy like the girl in the mirror hours before, though. That kind of happiness was new. *Is this what Killian meant by free?*

In school, my favorite teacher said the right subject would crack your mind open like an egg. You could try to undo the damage, but once the hit had occurred, it would force you to be open forever. No repair would piece you back together again. Killian had cracked my mind open like a volcano. It violently spurted emotions and ideas, destroying everything that lay dormant in its path.

I touched a canvas on its corner. "I just felt the desire, the strong desire, to paint. I never thought about what to do with everything later. Do you think they would sell?"

"I think lots of your art would be popular and sell. But the Blue Forest, it's a bit ominous. You would need the right buyer for something like that."

"You sound like Liam."

Julie blew air out of her cheeks with force. "Yes, well, I'm good at that most of the time. Not so much today, I suppose."

I took a large swallow of fiery liquid, unsure what she meant. It burned down my throat, warming my stomach. I sat at the bar chair across from Julie, ignoring the sting between my legs when I plopped down on the hard wooden seat. Killian entered my thoughts again, and I covered my smile with the coffee cup.

Julie continued. "You should share this with people, though. Fuck, give it away if you have to. It makes people feel something, you know. Your art makes a difference."

"Are you sure everything is alright? How was the... date?"

She crossed her legs, letting her top foot restlessly bob up and down. "I'm just too tired to fake it anymore today. It was great, Laney Bug. It was necessary."

Something about her tone had changed. Her words came out with a sharpness she never possessed before. And calling me Laney Bug hit me in the stomach. That marked the second time someone used the nickname. The prickling on my arms told me I missed something about today - something that mattered.

Will I ever lose this naïve nature?

My back shot straight, and I almost dropped my cup. "What was necessary? Fake what?"

She drew her lips into a tight line and raised an arm to her forehead, covering her eyes.

"We've kept each other's secrets before," I uttered. "You can tell me. What happened today? What..." Her laugh, sharp and jolting, stopped my sentence.

"No, we haven't," she interrupted. "Not really." She didn't move from her spot. A hole became visible on the side of her dress where the strings dropped on one side like they had gotten caught on something and ripped. Her knees were red and dry. She pulled a hair clip from her head and let the remaining strands fall behind the couch.

"I could," I whimpered from my seat. I should move to her and hold her. Something terrible happened to my best friend today, but I couldn't make myself move. "I can keep a secret for you," I insisted.

"And from me as well." She chuckled, a dry sound from the back of her throat.

My fingernails clawed at the cup, and I tilted my head. "What's happening here, Julie?"

Her leg continued to move up and down. It remained quiet between us for a moment. She took another sip. "Drink your coffee," she said. "You need it after your escapades today."

She knew something.

Maybe she knew everything.

"And do you need it? Do you need it for what was necessary?"

Julie rose from the couch. Her expression was lifeless and empty. "I got what I needed already." She chucked a small key in my direction. "Put that on your key ring."

I caught it in my right hand, a minor feat with my poor reflexes. It resembled the keys Carrie gave me last week. Small and heavy, with rusted teeth, I inspected the metal. I closed my fist, holding it in my hand so tight I almost drew blood.

"Julie, I don't understand..."

"And you won't. But keep those keys with you always, okay? Or it's all for nothing."

I nodded because I didn't know what else to do. My bottom lip quivered. I thought of Julie as the strong and beautiful woman I aspired to be. So sure of herself and this life they forced us to live, I hoped I could find the peace she did.

But she wasn't peaceful today. Today I worried something terrible had broken my beloved friend. And the sinking feeling in my stomach made me wonder if this, too, was my fault.

She made her way to the shower, giving me a quick hug when she walked past. I lost the sentiment in her curt embrace, and I felt like bawling when she pulled away. "Is this because of me?" I whimpered. For a moment, I thought she didn't hear me, but the door halted before it closed. It creaked back open and her soft expression dipped through the opening. She moved her eyes over me in the way a mother looks at a child, full of fear and endearment. Julie's face returned to her normal self for a moment. She placed her hand over her heart.

"It's *for* you Laney Bug. Not because of you. For you." The door shut with a soft close. My eyes remained transfixed on her until the last possible moment. When I heard the water turn on, I placed the key on my ring with shaking hands.

I marched into my bedroom and yanked open the top drawer, running my fingers over the cases until I felt the heavy crystal. I took my ladybug necklace from its case and clasped it around my neck.

Chapter 12

Trust

ALAINA

Julie stayed in my bathroom for over two hours. I checked on her occasionally, but her responses were only a grunt or groan from under the water. She took a shower and then ran a bath. I heard her leave the steam room she'd created for herself, and I waited for her to come and join me on the patio.

I scavenged her bags and found a few bottles of wine amongst the groceries she bought. Leaving a glass out for her on the side table, I settled in with a book, but mostly my thoughts. They were a dark mess of confusion.

She eventually sat next to me in a thin satin robe that clung to her damp red skin. There was a calmness in her demeanor, but a strangeness too. *Did it only take two hours to wash it all away, whatever it was?*

"I owe you an apology," she admitted.

"You don't owe me anything," I choked out. "I owe you. You have been there for me throughout these weeks from hell. You were always there for me, supporting me. You know, I realized sitting out here, that you cried when I told you I was going to paint only as a hobby all those years ago. You said working for the City would ruin me. And I was the idiot that took it like you weren't being supportive, but that wasn't it at all. You supported the real me. Charlie never did that. No one else ever did that." I swallowed the rest of my glass with long gulps. Julie lifted another bottle of wine from her side and bit her lip.

"I just stopped," I whined. "I never painted again after I told you that." I held out my empty cup. "I became someone else, and that was it."

"I did something I shouldn't have many years ago," she admitted. "Something that changed you. I... I regret it. I regret saying this to you now." Julie handed me a full glass and looked out over the patio. She opened her mouth a few times to speak but could only take in shuddered breaths.

"What did you do?"

"I chose a path for you. I thought it was the right one. I can't say anything more right now, okay. But I'm fixing it. I'll make it right."

I didn't know how to respond. She looked so broken. A different person sat beside me, and I couldn't push her to say more and risk losing Julie altogether.

"I've been thinking about a lot of things today," I went on. "I don't want to push you to talk about what happened. But I think it's only fair to tell you I really, really, really want to know what the fuck is going on."

Julie sipped and folded her legs underneath her. "I just need a moment to decompress," she murmured. I may not have understood what she meant, but I knew enough to drop the subject for the moment.

I nodded back and leaned toward her. "I love you a lot, you know? I would do anything for you."

"Oh, I know, Laney Bug," she assured, and gave my shoulder a weak tap. "And you can start by going out with Liam tomorrow night."

I pulled back in response and my jaw fell open. I fiddled with my necklace while Julie continued. "It's not what you want, but it is also what is necessary."

"He hasn't asked me out. He might have other plans."

"He doesn't," Julie deadpanned.

"Care to elaborate on this piece of the puzzle, at least? I'll do it. I'll do anything you ask. I don't know why you are asking, and I think you understand I have another interest right now..." I trailed off.

Julie twirled the wine in her glass in that way few people could pull off without looking ridiculous. Even in a wet robe on my overgrown patio, she appeared flawless. She flicked the flowering Madonna Lillies with her toes. "I didn't know it was Killian until I got here — until everything was in motion."

"You didn't know what was Killian? I don't think you can grasp my lack of understanding. I. Know. Nothing." I tried to keep the volume of my voice low, but Julie pushed her chair closer toward me and shot me a look.

"Well, I guess he wouldn't have much explaining to do," she whispered. "You trust him. You always have. In school, I thought you would disappear with him. There's just a lot, and I don't even know where to start."

"I would have," I huffed, exasperated. "I think I would have gone anywhere with him."

"I know. I... I knew that." She pinched the bridge of her nose and stood up. "Okay, well, if you ever move all the fabric off of your entertainment unit, you will see a message from Liam asking you out tomorrow night."

"Why do you know this?"

Julie raised her hand to shut me up. "Do you want explanations, or do you want to argue?" I fell back into my chair and tucked my necklace inside my shirt.

"Right now, I want both."

"I wish I could give you that," Julie admitted.

I had less frustrating conversations babysitting toddlers, but what could I do besides listen?

"He's taking you somewhere nice. We can get you a dress at the market tomorrow. At some point, Killian will take you. I don't know when or how, and I shouldn't even disclose that. You need to appear... calm with Liam... normal."

"Take me?" I muttered.

"Yes," Julie answered.

"But, why? Where?"

Julie poured more wine and moved to the edge of the patio. "I'll be an alcoholic by the time this one is done," she mumbled under her breath. She took a few deep breaths and sipped again. She plucked a lily from the pot and placed the flower behind her ear. "I need you to trust me the same way you trust Killian. I've kind of fucked up by not keeping it together. Again, I need to decompress a minute. I may just deflate right here in a sea of fermented grapes."

I brought my legs up and wrapped myself in a tight ball. I wouldn't get all the answers today. I may never get them.

"I'd like to lie down for an hour or so," she said. "Then I need to take a shuttle back home to my family. We have dinner with the boys tonight at their school. It's an orientation meal. Will you wake me up?"

"Of course." I stared outward at the metal gates that surrounded my home. I searched for Killian and maybe Liam, but only strangers passed.

"I'll get you tomorrow around noon. We can eat out somewhere and then shop a bit. But when I'm feeling more myself, I want to hear all the gory details about sex with Killian. I mean it. Paint a picture of his dick for the women that will never see it. That's something we would pay good money for!"

I blushed and bit the inside of my cheek. I didn't bother asking how she knew about our encounter. I didn't want secrets between us any longer, but she had nothing left to offer.

Her glass rang as she slammed it back on the table, empty. She dragged her feet with each step to my bed. She curled up into the clean sheets, her wet hair leaving a dark ring on my pillow. I went to my living room and took the coverings off my entertainment unit.

"System on," I said, and the screen flashed to life. Four new messages blinked. Three from my mother, and one from Liam. Both had marked each message with urgency, and I opened each one with dread.

A few hours later, Julie left without me berating her further. She seemed fragile somehow, like the wall between us came down and the girl behind it needed protection. I didn't know there was a wall until now, and I hated myself for that. I hugged her and told her I looked forward to seeing her the next day. She seemed half asleep getting into the shuttle, but for that moment, she was safe. That gave me peace.

The messages from my mother all begged for an update on my escapades while simultaneously talking nonstop about herself. The woman had an uncanny ability to be selfish and demeaning while appearing as if she cared at the same time. Each message left me confused and irritated. She berated me for fighting the way of things in one sentence and praised my beauty in the next. Like an older girl in boarding school, she intimidated me, even though I knew she saw me as competition.

As her daughter, I might have deserved her kindness, but she despised giving it to me. I pined for my fathers but they would take one look at my face, and press me for information. I wrote to them and that had to be enough for now.

Liam's message, I left for last. As expected, he wanted to take me to a City-sponsored event. He explained that although he had a few months left before he completed his marriage, we could date and that his wife already partook in the activity. *Well, isn't that sweet? Just sweep me off my feet.*

The end of his message, however, sent a chill down my spine. "Alaina, it's important you stay close to the right sort of people," he had said. "You may have some old friends that are looking for you. I understand the Discovery Center is new for you, and when we first met, I said I wanted to date you in a few months. I'm rushing our timeline together, but I want to keep you safe. It's no secret what else I want. But I understand you. I'm just like you. I hope you trust me."

I didn't.

Liam planted himself firmly in the danger category. His handsome nature drew you in, but for what purpose? Without Killian intervening, I might have found myself in his grasp. Something about him made me uneasy.

Music came down the hallway, signaling someone stood at my door. I flipped the screen to the camera at my entryway and saw a young man holding an enormous white box wrapped in gold ribbon. I powered down the unit and went to answer.

"I have a delivery for Alaina," the young man said. He fumbled with the oversized item and I took it, having trouble not dropping the box myself. I set my fingerprint on his screen and saw Liam's face next to mine in the top corner.

"Is that who sent this?" I asked.

"Oh, yes, miss."

I nodded, thanked him, and sent him on his way.

I stood in front of the package for a minute, trying to guess its contents. It felt like a trap to open. This whole place was a trap. I envisioned running through a maze, only to be caught at the end by a large metal snap. My life resembled an experiment more and more each day.

I untied the ribbon and opened the gift in a flurry of tissue that took over my kitchen table. I rolled my eyes at the packaging overkill but gasped when I saw the gown inside.

Lifting it, yards of deep red fabric unfurled. The bodice had a flexible cage inside, keeping the form of the dress perfect. Someone had folded the skirts so meticulously that not one wrinkle appeared. Julie meant it when she said we were going some place nice. This wasn't a dress. It was a ballgown.

A note fell from the gown. I held the fabric in my arms like a child and carried the dress to my closet and hung it. I rushed back to retrieve the note and ripped it open to find a white invitation written in gold letters.

THE CITY OFFICIALS TOGETHER WITH THE CITY COUNCIL

INVITE YOU TO CELEBRATE THE ERA OF PEACE

SATURDAY, THE TWENTY-SECOND OF JUNE
AT HALF-PAST SIX IN THE EVENING
THE COURTYARD BALLROOM
THE DISCOVERY CENTER 3

A twinge of excitement rushed through me, but it quickly replaced itself with fear. Killian would find me and take me. Julie said that much.

What would be his fate if he broke the law in front of the City Council? Liam knew people, important people, that would attend this event.

I'm risking everyone for you, rang through my mind. He was part of that everyone. He was at risk.

I'm not worth that. I can't lose Killian.

I shuddered, and trepidation coursed through my veins. What if his martyrdom was the last act of his life?

Chapter 13

Birthdays

JULIE

Alaina's gown would make any woman's heart flutter. When she showed it to me, I momentarily forgot Liam was behind the gift. Liam, misguided and self-assured, would stand next to her tonight. My skin burned at the thought. It wasn't jealousy, *was it?*

Officials had warned me Alaina would be under observation. Her records in school were enough to cause it, but her disastrous annual assessments sealed her fate. Liam was our best bet to manage her file, even though I hated to put him through this. I underestimated how much he would throw himself at her, but thinking back on his history, it made sense.

I tried to make him see reason, but I did it all wrong, and it cost me. The price was a bit of my sanity and self-respect. For a moment, standing in this closet holding a beautiful red ballgown, I forgot all that. Alaina would shine tonight on anyone's arm.

Alaina needed me here. She needed more of my presence than I could give. My tank never fully recharged anymore. After yesterday, I couldn't keep up my facade of the shiny, perfect City resident - not even for Alaina's sake. I hated myself for that. Her focus should be on her escape from the party and this City, not my well-being.

Last night went well enough, despite the exhaustion of the day. The boys toured the boarding school with awe and wonder. They couldn't wait to start the next chapter of their lives. They didn't know yet what it all meant, what they would have to give up. The City molded its residents to conform to *the way of things*.

The school confirmed both boys could enroll the following week, and I kept my smile planted on my face. Bile rose in my throat, but I choked it down, repeating to myself their time would come. Once children enrolled, school staff instructed parents to stay away for months to help with acclimation. It had felt like I dropped them into a pool of deep water. They would slowly disappear beneath the surface and fade from my view, where everything about them would drown.

My piece of shit husband nodded like an idiot droning on about how that would be best for our separation this year.

Once I thought of him as the strongest man I knew. Fuck, I hoped my boys would take after me more than him. They can keep his dark hair and height. Please let them have my will, my fortitude.

Alaina kept her questions to herself, but I could see the pitiful glances every few minutes. I hid my physical damage from her after examining myself this morning. Bruises on my hips and rib cage were the worst of my marks. Soon they would fade into nothing. No one the wiser except him and I... and anyone I showed the video stream to. A tightness filled my chest because I knew it may come to that. I always knew, but I did it anyway. I did what was necessary for Alaina.

"Will you be coming?" she asked.

I cocked my head to her. I trapped the fabric of the dress firmly in my fingers. I released it and let it fall back into the closet.

"To the celebration tonight. Are you coming?" Alaina repeated.

"No, I'm jealous. You are going to make men walk into walls in this gown. We still need to go to the market, get me some groceries, maybe find some jewelry."

"I'm going to wear this necklace," she said, holding the charm her father gave her in school. The ladybug meant more than just a nickname. Her father, Thomas, told her they embodied good luck, protection, and love. She needed all she could get. When he told us about what ladybugs represent, I remembered thinking he broke the law. They banned symbolism, except for the City crest. They forbid folklore and emblems, too. Anything that felt special was taken from us without explanation.

But that's what she loved about Thomas. He believed in bending the rules. Maybe not a full break, but enough to make you question things. Enough to give you something to hold on to. That's why she clung to Killian. I should have known it would be him to get her in this group. Of course, he would come back for her. I should have never forced him away.

"The chain is long, and I can tuck it into my dress," she continued.

"It's perfect," I said. After tonight, it wouldn't matter. Soon she could wear a shirt that read, *Fuck You*

Assholes, across her chest. I giggled to myself at the thought.

"I don't feel prepared for the market or tonight," she pleaded. "You won't be with me at the party, and I don't know when Killian is going to do this thing. I think I may have an idea. I think I know what makes sense, even though it makes no sense at all..." She rambled in half-broken sentences, and I held my hand up to stop her.

"I know very little about today. And to be honest, I told you too much. Do not look around the market or the dinner for Killian. Act as if Liam is the only person who holds your attention. Show genuine shock when you see Killian. Do you understand?"

She bit her lip and nodded slowly. She scanned my body once more, searching for the evidence of the day before.

I reached a hand to her. "Let's try to enjoy today. Carrie has a booth at the market. She asked us to stop by and visit. Is your painting in the living room ready? She would showcase it."

"A piece never seems ready."

"Okay, that sounds like it is. Let's do it. We have the time now that your outfit is all set."

Alaina wrapped the canvases in a thin cloth. I tried to help her as best I could, but I let her handle the pieces, scared I may ruin something so precious. Blue and purple trees stretched across the art. A low fog hung around them, with a beam of light peeking out from the center. The rays of yellow crawled through the fog and faded into the edge of the canvas. She painted a beautiful rendition, but when she felt the true heat of that sun on her skin and saw the blinding light from above, she would understand.

She placed them into a large tote and changed her clothes. Tucking her bracelet under another chain on her wrist, she let out a ragged breath.

She moved her head to mine and creased her brows. "Where is your bracelet?" she stammered. "You have to wear it to the market."

I took a deep breath and looked down at my bare wrist. My bag in the corner held a bracelet. Not the one issued by the City, but one that meant Alaina's freedom.

"I need you to switch bracelets with me today," I confessed. "And before you start, I'm not exactly sure why. Yes, it's illegal. And yes, Killian knows. And to make it even more fun, when we go to the market, I have to meet someone about some other illegal things."

"How can we switch? They match with our chips."

"It will work."

"That's not an answer."

I pinched the bridge of my nose and ran my hand slowly down my face. "I don't have all the answers. No one does. You have to trust me like I'm trusting others."

She moved the jewelry on her wrist and unclasped the band without further questions. Her fingers trembled slightly when she handed it to me. We waited a moment, and both bracelets flicked to life.

"I don't understand how that is possible," she said.

"I'm not the expert at the technology," I admitted. "But someone at the Rehabilitation and Separation Centers helped with programming. It's part..." I hesitated, careful not to reveal too much, but desperate to share more with my friend. "It's part of the reason Killian had to be taken and why I looked a little rough yesterday. I had a meeting, a lunch date, I don't know what to call it, with someone who is helping."

Helping may have been a stretch. I'd forced his hand and bent it to our will. I had known the transaction would have complications. I hadn't expected acceptance of our ultimatum without a fight. *What had I expected? Not what happened, that's for sure.*

I shivered at the memory. His hands were on me in anger and desire. We both hated ourselves a little for it, and maybe that's why violence permeated the act. His grip on my hips had been too tight when he'd slammed into me. His teeth on my neck had almost drawn blood. Tossing me around without regard, which had caused blue and purple marks to form hours later. Moments of sensuality mixed in with resentment. Flashes of loathing had crossed his face, replaced quickly by pure bliss. Our joint hostility moved from the City to each other and back again. And despite the pain, I orgasmed. I had come in such an intense wave I screamed his name and begged him to continue. I liked it, and I would have to live with that. He left with bruises himself. I'm not a saint, far from it.

"They are helping, but they hurt you somehow. Or did you get hurt together? I know I said I wouldn't pry. I'm just worried. I want to be a good friend to you."

"I really can't talk to you about it. I'm sorry," I admitted. My voice shook with uncertainty. "May I wear something of yours?"

"Besides my bracelet. Of course." She touched my arm and looked around the closet. After sifting through a few items, I chose a simple long sleeve black shirt and pants.

I tied my hair up in a loose bun. I wanted to feel unlike myself today. Maybe not like Alaina, but different.

"You look beautiful," she said from the doorway.

I tied the ribbon on the shirt around my waist too tight. The pressure reminded me to stand up straight and stay aware of my surroundings.

"Besides your necklace," I gestured to the open space, "Is there anything else you desperately want here? Any trinket or item that you couldn't live without?"

"I would say that's an odd question, but it's not, is it? I'm going somewhere. With Killian? Do you know when?"

"Anything else you would need in this apartment?" I insisted, avoiding any response to her questions.

Alaina placed her hands on her hips and sucked in her cheeks. She turned her head from side to side. Her shoulders stiffened while she dug her fingertips into her sides. "Jupiter and you, Julie. I need you."

"Jupiter will be well taken care of." The pup lifted her head from the corner of the room at her name, whined, and placed it down again.

I grabbed my bag and pulled out a leather satchel from the inside. Brushing past her, I kept my face stoic. She wanted a response from me, an answer to the unspoken question. *What would happen to me?*

I opened her front door and peered down each side of the hallway. Empty except for some potted plants and wind chimes. Residents had people to meet and fuck and hurt. An exciting life bustled outside these walls, exciting and empty. A life void of what mattered while citizens masked their pain with alcohol and orgasms.

"God, I hate it here," I muttered, unzipping the bag. I pulled out a small tool and wedged the flat piece of metal into the number six on her door.

Alaina scurried to my side.

I pulled the number slowly toward me, and the adhesive stretched underneath. "Tell me if you see anyone," I said, focused on the task.

"Okay, are you going to tell me what you are doing? And please don't say what is necessary. I'm getting as sick of hearing that as I am hearing *the way of things.* Yuck." Alaina shoved her finger to the back of her throat, mimicking a need to vomit. The number popped free, and I caught it before it clanged onto the floor. I removed a nine from my bag and painted fresh adhesive on the back.

I yanked a pack of cleaning wipes from the satchel and tossed it to Alaina. "Rub this on the door to clean it." She followed orders, moving her head back and forth, looking for anyone that might catch us.

I situated the new number in place and tossed the satchel back inside. "Ready to go?" I asked as if nothing just transpired.

Alaina paused, looking up at the door. She fixed her bag on her shoulder and pursed her lips. I walked down the hallway, assuming she would follow. Her scurried footsteps sounded behind me shortly after.

She met my side and brushed my hair behind my shoulder. "You know I love September. I love fall."

"Part of the girl handbook," I said. "Ciders and turning leaves. Pumpkin shit."

"Oh, yes, that's all good," she continued. "But I love it because every year we plan that apple picking trip. Do you remember last year? The ride back broke down. We had to carry heavy bags of apples almost a mile after we'd downed a bottle of wine in the fields."

I cackled out loud. "Right, and only when we got back did it dawn on us we could have just left the bags there and used another shuttle to get them."

"My arms were sore for a week!"

We laughed together entering the pedestrian walkway that led to the market.

"Your birthdays were always so much fun," Alaina reminisced. "I don't think I will pick apples on September twenty-eighth this year, will I?"

"Not with me," I admitted, and our laughter stopped.

Chapter 14

Yesterday

ALAINA

When Killian said others were in danger, I never imagined by others he meant Julie. I tried to picture a life without her. Julie filled all the empty spots in my heart, the spots Charlie had left barren.

It's easier to ignore the holes in your marriage when someone else fills them. She was always present and there for me, yet I knew so little about her. I had missed a vital part of her transformation somewhere in my haze. That's what my world had been before, a blurry haze of barely living. And I lost the Julie I thought I knew during that time.

Charlie's letter was proof of an empty marriage. He ended ten years of our lives in a few paragraphs. He didn't know me either. Anyone that knew me would understand I didn't belong here. Life, a decade at a time, would never work for me, the real me.

And in my stark denial, I neglected to see the changes in Julie. I missed the shift in her and ignored the person I was. The nagging voice that admitted the way of things was wrong. The me that wished things were different.

Our thoughts, as similar as they were, put her in danger and tore us apart.

That's where this all led, right? I would leave with Killian, and she would stay behind. I pictured her coming back to my apartment, leaving all the sheets on the walls even though she never paints. Would she take the sugar skull painting down or leave it?

I curled up on my bed and stared at the quote, "*She whispered back, I am the storm.*" Julie became the storm. She changed herself. I needed to do the same.

One hour to get ready was not enough time. I had to attempt an appearance of excitement. Faking it meant eyeliner and maybe a hairbrush. I moved into my bathroom with heavy feet. The mirror didn't reflect the sated woman anymore. A hollow being took her place.

Killian never appeared at the market. Bigger things needed his attention. Events where officials and maybe a council member glided through crowds of people they controlled. I could see them in my mind, toasting themselves to their greatness. Smug in their command over the crowd, over everything. That's where he planned to do something more than just take me. There was more to this than my ticket out. Hundreds of residents would attend, and the opportunity for... an attack perhaps presented itself.

But would he dare risk leaving me again? Everyone would call Killian a traitor, a criminal. Their reaction would be swift. No strike three after that.

Hours before, Julie and I had made our way through the market. We'd bought some food and earrings, then headed back. Our last stop was a stand that sold jewelry stamped by hand. Copper and silver pieces hung on the walls, chiming in the wind while people moved in and out. I scanned the charms, curious about how many designs the city vetoed for this artist. From what I could tell, they pushed the limits a bit.

"Are you done looking here?" Julie asked.

"I think I have all the jewelry I can handle," I chided, twirling the bracelets around my wrist.

She flicked her eyes to my wrist and clucked her tongue. "Yes, well, while I'm here..." she trailed off.

"Oh, I'll just step outside."

"I'll meet you at the apartment," she asserted.

"Okay, then." I took my queue to leave.

She disappeared behind a false wall. For a moment, I thought I saw Carrie when I craned my neck to look, but I couldn't be sure. I walked back alone, wondering in what state Julie would return to me. *What price will she pay this time?*

I heard my apartment door open and close with a thud. I jolted, smudging my eyeliner, and groaned at the mess on my face. Considering my poor makeup skills, I might have considered it an improvement.

"I know you aren't thrilled about this, but giving yourself a black eye won't get you out of it." Julie leaned against the door frame with a half-smile. She had every hair perfectly pulled back in place, and not a thread of her dress was out of line. I exhaled with relief.

"Worth a shot, right?"

Julie ushered me to turn and sifted through my makeup bag. "I'll fix it."

I relaxed my shoulders and popped myself on the counter, ready to let her take over and soak up every moment I had left with her.

"So, how did everything go?" I asked.

"It went fine. You need to take the keys with you tonight."

If she didn't have a grip on my eyelid, I would roll my eyes. That would be the extent of Julie's sharing on the subject.

"I take them with me everywhere." I lifted the ring from my bra, and she nodded in approval.

"Remember to keep your focus on Liam tonight. He's all you see, all you care about."

I remained still. Julie moved the cold liquid across my lid while I held my breath.

"He may be... unlike himself tonight. Did you see him on your way home? Have you talked to him since the message asking you to go to the dinner?"

"I haven't spoken to him. I replied to the message confirming I would go, and we had some back and forth about details. I thanked him for the dress."

"Just do your best to be relaxed. Distract him. Have his focus be on your night together."

"As opposed to what? Why would his focus not be on me? That seems to be all he cares about. Does he know Killian will show up? Is Killian in danger?"

"No, he doesn't. He shouldn't. He knows there will be a disruption." Julie paused, clicking the liner closed and choosing another one. "But Liam... Liam got thrown for a loop lately. He may try to sway your opinion. He may tell you some things that upset you."

"Like what? And why?"

Julie picked out more items I forgot I owned and placed them on the countertop. She worked in silence, sweeping brushes over my skin, standing back every few minutes to observe her work.

"Julie, what and why?"

Nothing left Julie's lips, but I noticed her fingers trembling. She shook her hand a few times before applying some powder. But despite her efforts to conceal it, I could tell nerves boiled below the surface.

"Julie!" I almost screamed.

"I'm working up to it."

"Well, I leave in twenty minutes."

She swallowed and took a comb to my hair.

"Okay, well, since you are mute," I huffed. "I'll take this time to tell you how sorry I am, Julie. I've failed you as a friend. How did I miss this?" I moved my hand wildly across her face. "How did I miss you not being... I don't know... you anymore? I'm so selfish, so stupid."

She shook her head and lifted her hand. "Please, stop. We don't have time for that. I purposely deceived you. There is no way you would have known I aligned with the refugees."

Even though I suspected that, hearing her say it ripped the air from my lungs. I bit my lip while tears pricked my eyes. Julie's entanglements meant the worst kind of danger. The harshest punishments await her future. Fear overtook me and the pools of water grew in my eyes.

"Do not fuck up this eye makeup," she snapped. I inhaled a shaky breath and tried to smile. She waved a tissue at my eyeballs, attempting to cease the impending tears.

"Julie, is there any way to stop this whole thing? This is so dangerous. I can live a life without Killian. I have this long. I cannot risk losing my best friend, my only real family."

"You're enduring a life without Killian because of me," she admitted. Her eyes darted around the room. She took a step backward. "I sent him away when we were in school. I told him he was too dangerous for you, and I threatened him. I didn't know then... I didn't know all the terrible things the City does. I didn't know a-anything," Julie stuttered. She brought the back of her hand to her mouth and let a few tears fall.

The shock hit me and sucked the air out of my lungs. I remembered Julie's mockery when I told her I wanted to partner with Killian, but I would have never expected her to do that. I put my head in my hands and breathed deeply, trying to absorb the betrayal. We were so young, and it was so long ago, but my anger was new. All the thoughts about what could have been poured into my mind, and I clenched my fingers into fists.

"Also, I fucked Liam," she spit out.

My head shot up. My brain misfired while the words tumbled around inside. My mouth dropped open, and I almost laughed. "What is happening, Julie?! What the fuck?"

Julie stared, eyes wide, and continued. "Yesterday. It happened yesterday."

"No," was all I could manage. I pulled myself from the bathroom counter, shoving her body out of the way, and paced the floor. Her betrayal about Killian subsided, and blood rushed through my veins, making my skin grow hot.

It was too much and too fast. I walked along the walls of my apartment, rage taking over my senses. "That vile piece of shit. I'll kill him tonight. What did he do? What happened?"

Julie held out her arms, palms down. "It's not what you think. Please sit down?"

"He's a rapist. He's an abuser."

"He's not," she yelled. Her voice echoed on the walls. I stopped and met her gaze.

"We have maybe ten minutes," she said. "Where are your shoes?"

"Where is your brain, Julie? Shit. We have to get out of here together. You can't stay here. What the hell happened?" My questions rambled out with choking sobs. I resumed my pacing, my dress flowing behind me and rustling on the dropcloth below my feet.

She moved to grab my heels. "Sit on the couch," she motioned.

I obliged, my movements robotic. "I'll kill him."

"You will not." Her fingers fiddled with the buckles, and she lifted my heel to her lap. "I'm going to talk fast, and I want you to listen. Can you grasp what I'm going to tell you? Are you able to calm down?"

I nodded, unsure if my weak response was a lie. The rushing sound in my ears slowed. Julie's smooth hands worked the clasp around my heel, and she gave my leg a gentle squeeze.

"I met Liam a very long time ago. That's a longer story than I have time for, but Killian will enlighten you one day. We remained acquaintances, and I remembered him because his story is told to our security detail in training. We omit names, but everyone knows. When his wife ended their relationship, he went insane at the Separation Center. His violence that day is the reason we have so much security there. He's not a terrible person. You can understand the pain he felt, what that did to him."

My heart broke a little for Liam. I remembered the feeling. I had wanted to hit someone or something that day, and I wasn't even in love with Charlie. Not truly in love. Someone Liam's size could do substantial damage. It sounded like he had.

"I don't think it's a surprise that my husband goes to the pleasure houses regularly." I bit my lip at Julie's words. We all heard rumblings, but I'd hoped she had ignored them. "In the beginning, when I gave a fuck, I would stalk him there. That's where I saw Liam with his wife, his first wife. He loved her, he still loves her. I know little about her, but she has Liam under her thumb. They met there in secret, but I don't think Rachel would be surprised. His first wife is a terrible person. She messed with Liam's head in a way I can't even describe. You think Charlie tricked you? You have no idea the depths of deception that are possible. I told him his secret was safe with me, and he's been more than happy to help me when I need a favor."

The pleasure houses were the only place where any illegal activity went unchecked. If you paid the right people, things slipped through. Even the City officials liked the place. Rumors of women and men taking credits for discreet appointments ran rampant. Liam paid to be with his first wife, someone he loved. My rage for him left me little by little as Julie went on.

"A lot has happened over the years, but about yesterday, I needed a big favor. And I needed it from someone working at the Separation Center. Guess who came to mind?" I nodded, eager for her to continue. Her grip on my ankle tightened, and I felt my pulse beneath her fingers.

"Liam became furious and insisted I couldn't hold his encounters with his wife over his head anymore. He said I didn't have proof, and he wouldn't help me. We argued, and I slapped him. I told him he was a fool and too scared to be himself."

She set my leg down. It felt heavy and immobile. She lifted my other foot and moved her gaze to it, avoiding my eyes. "He needed something against me. He needed the scales... even. Liam and I have always had some... tension between us. I thought it was physical for the longest time, but I've realized something about Liam he doesn't yet know about himself."

I reached my hand to her and intertwined our fingers. "He doesn't want love ten years at a time, either. He doesn't want to live this way. I think that's why he became so desperate to connect with you. Maybe he thought you would be a connection for longer than ten years. He could follow the rules and still be happy."

My mind ticked with the idea. She knew him better than I did, and everything hit me so fast. Now I was the silent one, with nothing to retort in this whirlwind of conversation. Julie looked at the time displayed in the kitchen.

"Five minutes," she said. She squeezcd my hand harder. "We had sex, and there is video evidence. We can extort each other if need be, but destroy each other at the same time. I've thought about it a lot. His request for the video confused me at first, but I was so desperate for his help - and a part of me wanted him. I'll admit that.

The sex was rough, and we both left with bruises, but I enjoyed myself."

She finished the other buckle and moved my foot from her lap. "Liam wants..." she trailed off. "Liam needs... someone to connect with forever. That act will bind us together forever. Neither of us could live with it exposed. Don't hate him, but understand he doesn't know who he is right now. Liam is lost."

She released my hand, and I stared at the red marks she'd left on my palm. "I think I understand," I whispered. "I trust you have a plan tonight, and I'll do what I need to. What will happen to him, to you?"

Julie turned on the entertainment unit, switching the monitor to my front door. No one had arrived yet.

"I don't know exactly. I'll stay here for long enough. My presence will confuse the officials so you can get away. They never make mistakes, you see. They won't accept that their programs have an error. And Liam, well, he needs to make some decisions, and quickly. He'll cooperate tonight, though. I don't know how he'll be or what he might say to you. I needed you to know this. I just wanted you to know I'm okay."

The screen lit up, and we both saw Liam walk toward my door. His suit jacket draped over one arm.

"I'll hide in your bedroom," Julie said and left the couch without a sound. I pulled her back, giving her one last hug. We held each other so tightly, that I couldn't catch my breath. "Don't mess up this makeup," she insisted, and I sputtered a laugh. "You'll see me again." Julie pulled away and left a kiss on my cheek. I watched her walk to my bedroom, stunned in silence.

Liam lifted his hand to my monitor, and the song chimed through the hallway. I stood up, looking at him through the camera. He shifted his gaze from left to right, fidgeting from side to side. I moved closer to the image, seeing him stretch his neck to one side, placing his hand inside his shirt to pull at the muscles in his shoulder. When he removed his grip, I saw the red scratches that moved from his chest to his neck. He straightened and re-buttoned his shirt, hiding the evidence of Julie's fingernails that had ripped through his skin just the day before.

Chapter 15

Options

ALAINA

People gawked from their windows as we walked along the pavement. The City was all but shut down for the event tonight, and those on the streets covered themselves with beautiful garments and jewels.

Liam gave all the polite nuances one does on a date. He remarked on how stunning I looked and gave me his arm. His smile came across with genuine ease. Maybe he had compartmentalized yesterday's events somewhere far away.

But then he flinched when I moved my arm into his. A solid jolt shot through him, and I knew the memory skimmed beneath the surface.

He recovered quickly, asking about my day and the art classes. I sauntered alongside him, feeling the stiffness of his body, and rambled about nothing. The music grew louder with each step. Soft violins played the City's anthem on repeat. We stopped within sight of the courtyard. Lights twinkled ahead, and I could make out laughter and the ramble of voices.

"Are you alright?" I regretted the question but felt inclined to ask. *Damn you, Julie, for making me care more about him.*

"I'm wonderful. I have a beautiful woman with me on a perfect night."

"Shall we... go in?"

Liam remained standing in place. He pulled me closer to him and moved his arm around my waist. The fabric felt thin under his fiery touch. "I... I don't want to go in just yet. Can we enjoy this moment, right now?"

I agreed and lifted my hand to his shoulder, brushing my fingertips on his jaw. He knew what lay ahead. He must, based on the forlorn look he gave the crowd.

He took my hand, clutching my fingers. "Let's walk a little. Around the courtyard here. No one will bother us. They are all on curfew or at the party." The City instituted a curfew on event nights. Security would mill about with scanners to see if anyone uninvited left their homes after dinner time - a veiled reminder that their reach was never far away.

"Of course," I said. It was the least I could do, and we walked in silence down the paths we routinely jogged together. Liam didn't speak. He looked at me as we walked, his eyes scanning my face for something. Unsure of what to say, I stared at the path ahead. I motioned for us to sit after only ten minutes, unable to stand the silence. Liam wiped the bench clear of leaves, and when I moved to sit, he pulled me into his lap.

"We can't ruin your beautiful dress on a filthy bench now, can we?" he teased. I curled up to him. The night had a bite of cold, and his body radiated heat. He cradled me, and I sank into his touch. It felt like goodbye, but neither of us could say it.

Everything Julie told me flashed back through my mind. Liam and I were similar creatures. He lacked the self-awareness I now possessed. An obligation to the City guided his day-to-day decisions, but underneath he was a man that thought like me.

Liam *was* lost.

The inner turmoil burned behind his eyes in the dim light. Not long ago our lives made sense. They folded into a steady routine, but chaos had seeped its way inside. My chance at happiness may have been close, but where was Liam's? It broke my heart, and I relaxed into his arms, stroking his cheek with my thumb.

His hands moved along my back with softness, and he curled his face into my neck. "It's going to be alright," I whispered. Julie must have told him I would leave. He acted as if these were our last moments together.

He let out a shuddered breath and caressed his lips on my neck. "Liam..." I muttered but didn't move. We sat alone in the gardens after weeks of flirting. I should have expected this.

His mouth continued the languid kisses while his hand slid up my dress. I tried again but remained in his grasp. "Liam. This isn't what you want." *But it feels good.*

His large palm slid up between my thighs. I froze, unsure of how to react, and confused about how I wanted to react. I needed his help tonight. Killian's face flashed in my mind. Guilt wretched at my stomach, and so did something else.

The flicker of desire flamed my insides as his mouth moved to mine. His soft lips pressed to mine, and he devoured my mouth, pulling me closer with every movement.

I kissed him back.

Our movements became an out-of-body experience. I left my sensible mind somewhere back at the party entrance. The naturalness of our embrace after so much time together, and the yearning to comfort him, had taken over. He wasn't who I thought he was, and he was in pain. His tongue pushed my lips apart, and I opened for him. He licked the inside of my mouth, releasing a moan. My body responded, opening my legs, and I whimpered back into his mouth.

I tilted my chin up, arching my back and catching my breath. He kissed my collarbone, causing my strap to fall to the side. It tickled my arm, sending goosebumps across my skin. All the while, he inched his hand further up my thigh.

"We have to stop this," I breathed. My voice escaped in a weak plea. I didn't mean it, not really. He pulled me tighter against him. His lips on my shoulder opened to a soft bite, and his thick fingers brushed the wetness between my legs. "Liam," I gasped.

"Don't you want to try with me?" he rasped. He looked up, desperation in his eyes. His mouth, wet and swollen, hung open in confusion. "We could have what we want and be safe, together." I couldn't speak. His hand remained still in my most sensitive areas.

Perhaps he had more self-awareness than I gave him credit for?

He slid his fingers further, but I pulled back, gripping his thick bicep in my hand and forcing him to stop. He groaned as I dug my fingernails into his arm. "Liam, this isn't..." But I couldn't finish the sentence. He removed his hand but kissed me again. *Tell him to stop, Alaina.*

The words stuck at the back of my throat. One arm wrapped around my back, holding me in place.

But he didn't have to.

I kissed him back again.

He separated our lips only to whisper promises to me, "I won't leave after ten years. We could be safe together. Stay." Then, he crashed his mouth back to mine.

In a moment of clarity, I yanked my head free, and Liam's teeth grated on my shoulder. "You wouldn't have to hide away with criminals," he growled. I felt the scratch of his bite, and I clawed my fingers into his skin. "We could be together... forever. I wouldn't leave you after ten years. We could have children and visit them as a couple forever in love, not with new partners. That's what we both want. No hiding and no danger."

My breathing became shallow, and he moved his lips to meet mine again. This time, I laid my hand over his mouth and shook my head. "Please stop," I whimpered.

His eyes filled with sadness, and he moved back, bringing more space between us. He tilted his head and bit at his bottom lip. "I-I'm sorry," he said and slid me off his lap. "I didn't mean to force you to..."

I shook my head. "You didn't," I said through soft tears. Guilt flooded my senses. Not only did I allow him to touch me when I proclaimed my love for Killian, but his idea planted itself in my mind. It rooted and created thoughts about a different ending to my story.

Liam wasn't the monster I made him out to be. What if I didn't have to commit a crime and found happiness? I could stay with Julie. She wouldn't be in danger.

With that thought, I remembered he had sex with Julie yesterday. The realization punched my stomach and bile rose in my throat. I gasped and placed my palms on his chest, pushing him away. I tumbled backward onto the bench, shuffling my feet underneath me as I stood. I faced Liam with wide eyes.

He buttoned the top of his shirt and ran a shaky hand through his hair. I stood immobile, shocked and ashamed. He moved to me and reached his arms out to hold me, but I turned away.

"No," I clipped.

"No, to what?" His expression was full of genuine confusion.

I bit my lip and craned my head toward the party. "No, I... I can't stay with you."

"You don't sound so sure."

"Because I'm not," I whimpered. Tears fell hot on my cheeks. He stepped forward, and I moved back.

"I'm the coward, Liam. I shouldn't have let that happen. What about Julie? I know... I know what happened."

He blinked, and his jaw fell open. "I'm not sure what happened with Julie. I can't figure it out. What I mean to say is... have you ever thought..." He moved closer to me and looked up at the darkness above. I saw him swallow, and a deep intake of breath pushed his chest outward. His muscles flexed against his crisp shirt, and I wished he would try to hold me again. *I wasn't sure.*

When he looked back at me, his eyes were steel. "Julie has her own agenda. It's not aligned with The City anymore. Did you know that?"

"She told me," I shot back.

"When? It's been years of this, you know."

I stiffened. *Years. She's hidden this for years.*

I shook my head in defiance. "Her agenda is to help me. She's my friend. She's risking everything for me."

"Is she?" he seethed. The muscles in his neck strained. He stepped closer, moving his arm around my waist, and pulled me against him. "You didn't know, did you? Not until they sucked you in, unable to escape the spider's web. Just like me."

I lifted my palm to stop his words. "Stop, please."

His hand cupped my jaw. The tears stopped, but my face remained wet underneath his grasp. He exhaled and his resolve left his body when he wiped my tear-stricken cheeks. I must have looked pathetic, crying and shivering. He left a tender kiss on my lips and released his hold.

"I can make you happy. Forever."

"I believe you think you can," I admitted. Neither accepting this as fact or fiction, but merely a truth he held in his heart.

"We n-need to get to the party," I stammered. "The City doesn't accept tardiness."

He nodded in agreement. I wiped my face with a tissue from my bag. After a few moments, he took it and fixed a few spots underneath my eyes.

"Okay, let's go," I sighed.

The soft wind and our footsteps made the only sounds until, once again, the twinkle lights and soft music appeared before us. I moved my arm back into Liam's and forced a smile. I needed the practice before we walked inside. Most attendees fit neatly into the narcissistic category. They focus entirely on themselves with no awareness of others. That meant no one would care about a puffy-eyed date, but I had to at least smile. I took a step, and my arm pulled on Liam's unyielding frame.

"We have to go," I pleaded.

"I think someone will drag you away."

"What?"

"When it happens, the distraction. I'm supposed to let you go. Let you go off and not report you missing for some time. But I could hold on to you. I could report it."

"And then your video..."

"She wouldn't do it if it's what you wanted."

I removed my arm and walked. I intended to appear resolute, but my mind spun. Liam caught up with me in a moment and brought his mouth to my ear.

"If you reach for me, I'll reach back. If you cry out for me, I'll find you."

He looked utterly sincere at that moment. He reminded me of Killian when things were new and full of promise. The way he would offer me something at lunch to eat or hold my bag for me. The pleading look on Liam's face was so sure that what he offered would lead to something bigger - something better.

I nodded, saying nothing, and kept walking.

Chapter 16

Champagne

ALAINA

My second glass of champagne went down in one long swallow. The bubbles burned my throat and warmed my belly. I studied the empty glass. An imprint of my lipstick graced the side. Foam crept up the inside of the decadent crystal. I considered smashing it on the pavement and making my escape, but Liam's arm gripped around my waist as he carried on with guests. Black suits cut in sharp lines littered the grounds. My stomach churned. If I could wiggle free from Liam, I could find a corner to sulk or vomit.

Out of the question. His body remained entwined with mine throughout the evening. He either interlaced our fingers in a tight hold or wrapped his arm around my middle. His firm grip on my hand or dress remained present, always.

He never let go.

How would anyone steal me away with his hold on me? But the sensation reminded me of our encounter moments before, and heat flushed my skin. His gaze was hopeful each time he looked in my direction. He expected an answer. He deserved one.

And when should I give it? How many glasses of champagne would render the verdict for the rest of my life? I flagged down a server, and he closed the gap between us. Another man intervened, bottle in hand.

"Rafael," I beamed. "Long time no see." I pitched my voice too high from the drinks. He studied Liam, who used his free hand to tell a rousing story about a small fire at the Separation Center to patrons around us. His eyes narrowed, and he refilled my glass.

"I think you should slow down, senorita," he muttered. "You will be on your feet for... a while yet."

I bit my lip and looked at the bubbly drink tempting me. "Yes, of course," I replied.

"I'll go see to Ms. Carrie." Rafael turned on his heel and left.

I cocked my head, confused. Carrie's attendance wasn't odd, but Rafael's mention of her struck me off guard. He walked in a straight line across the room and stopped in front of the willowy creature in a black dress. Carrie had her hair in a fanciful updo adorned with feathers and jewels. She looked the part of an artist tonight.

She had given me a key.

I had almost forgotten, but the piece of metal lay cold inside my dress. I touched my hand to my chest. They remained there, next to my ladybug, a hard outline just underneath the fabric.

Rafael and Carrie leaned into each other. Their conversation felt too intimate in the sea of people. They both turned back in my direction in unison. Solemn faces met mine, their stares intense and uncomfortably long. Then Rafael set his tray to the side, took Carrie's hand, and led her to the dance floor.

The interaction put me in a fog. I struggled to make sense of it.

"Alaina." Liam tugged at my middle.

"Uh-huh," I answered, with no force behind it. The champagne glass hung loose in my grasp, some of it spilling over the sides.

"What's wrong?" His voice came out panicked, and his grip tightened.

"Nothing," I shot back, alert this time. "Just the champagne, and you know, all the things. I need to use the ladies' room. I'll be right back."

"I'll take you."

I huffed, but I had guessed he wouldn't let me out of his sight for long. We made it to the restroom, where I found an enormous line. I let out another puff of air. "How are there so few women in the City and always a line?"

"This way." Liam tugged at my arm. "I'll let you into an office." A few brisk steps later, we entered an empty building. The sound of white noise filled the halls. I thanked him and headed for the restroom door, but he kept in step behind me.

I placed my hand on his chest. "You aren't coming in here," I pleaded. "Really, Liam, no?"

He shifted on his feet, looked up and down the hallway, then nodded his head. "I'll be right here, waiting."

"Okay, I just need a moment," I smiled. "And I want to freshen up."

I shut the door behind me and clicked the lock as softly as I could. I paused a moment, but Liam didn't object on the other side. I doubted he would barge in, but I needed a moment to myself. The party, and everything that came with it, suffocated me. My body felt clammy under the dress, and I never had a free hand to fan myself with Liam's constant hold and my ever-present champagne glass.

I moved to the mirror, and the cool night air touched my skin. I fixed a few stray hairs and grabbed a towel to dab at my face. Another breeze made me shiver and goosebumps covered my flesh.

Someone had left a large window open at the end of the room. The night air made its way through, and I walked towards it, my skin tingling. When I reached for the glass, a hand clamped across my mouth, quieting my yelp.

I knew his presence without seeing him. The scent of woods and the heat of his skin surrounded me. "Killian," I said from underneath his palm, reaching up to grab his arm. His hard chest pressed behind me, pushing against my back with every sharp breath. He released his hold and stepped back. I swirled around, smiling.

His furious gaze met mine, and my heart sank.

"Killian," I whispered, and lifted a thumb to my lips to shut them. I whimpered as he dragged his thumb down, pulling at my bottom lip, and flicking my chin down when he let go. He turned the faucet on full blast and stepped back, separating our bodies.

His eyes never left mine. His anger fumed off of him in waves that I could almost feel slashing my skin.

"Is there something you're upset about?" I tried again, my voice shaking.

"Where are the keys?"

I fumbled inside my dress, careful to unhook the pin that attached them. I reached out with a shaky hand to Killian. He took them and grabbed my wrist, hoisting me toward him. His force didn't hurt, but it startled me. A small yelp escaped my lips, and his eyes burned hotter. I felt the air from his mouth come out in harsh puffs against my skin. He acted as if he would lean forward and take a bite.

"I take it you saw what happened in the garden?" I blurted. I had to say it, to end this fury.

"No," he fumed. "If I had seen, I would have gouged my eyes out of their sockets. If I'd been there, I would have stormed over to that bastard and fucked him up. I would have gotten myself killed or exposed. So, I guess it's a good thing for both of us I wasn't there. I had to suffer through it by myself, hidden too far away to do a fucking thing about it."

I trembled. His anger seethed with every word.

"I'm sorry. I'm... so sorry. I don't know what to say."

"Well, everything you say I hear." He pointed to my bracelet and then his ear with sharp movements.

A silent moment passed between us. My skin flamed, and I choked on a silent sob. I stopped it all too late. "I'm so sorry."

His gaze softened.

"I won't leave you again. I meant what I said before. What happened earlier changes nothing for me. Nothing. I know this is confusing, and I know Liam got to you first. But he can't love you as I do. He's a man adrift."

I nodded. A soft knocking rapped at the door. "Are you okay in there?" I inhaled a sharp breath, and Killian grew impossibly still.

"Yes," I choked. I cleared my throat and continued. "I'm just fine. I need to fix my dress."

"Do you need my help?" He jostled the locked doorknob.

"No, I'll be right out." The movement stopped, and I heard the pace of his footsteps outside the door.

Killian's mouth took mine with a ferocity I had never experienced. His aggressive tongue invaded, and teeth clinked between us in his haste. His nails scratched into the sides of my arms, desperate and determined. He bit my lip, drawing blood as he drew back. "It changes nothing for me," he hissed into my lips. "Did it change things for you?"

I still ached for him. The memory of Killian inside me and the excitement of his nearness made me see reason. Killian meant freedom. True freedom. The notion had always been foreign until now. How many people had risked themselves to grant me this gift? There had to be a reason I didn't know. There had to be more dangers in this City than I could understand.

And Killian himself was gift enough. He could take me anywhere at this moment. He could whisk us into the forest, or fuck me over the counter while Liam tried to break in.

Liam's offer was enticing, but Killian's left me intoxicated with desire. He made me drunk with need not just for him, but for a life with him. He could give me everything. Julie made her choice years ago. I hated it, but I respected it. She would make it out too, someday. I had to leave her behind.

"I'm sorry," I pleaded. "I just got lost. I'm a coward. The idea of safety... I just... I'm so sorry."

His mouth shut me up, and I felt the dress loosen around my chest. He gripped the sides and yanked them down.

"We can't now."

"We aren't. You need to change into something less noticeable."

My skin burned bright red with embarrassment.

"Oh, right."

Killian handed me a thin long sleeve black shirt and pants. I changed while he looked over my bare body with hooded eyes. He adjusted himself and one side of his mouth lifted in a smile. "I'm still angry," he clipped. "Will you make it up to me later?"

I hesitated a moment before pulling the shirt over my bare breasts. He reached for me, running his hands up over my body, grazing my nipples, and then lowering the fabric to my waist.

"I'll need a lot of convincing," he quipped. He pulled the waist of my pants up and fastened the button. I went to kiss him again, and the door jostled once more.

Killian's face hardened. "We have to go. Now."

I nodded and looked at the dress left in a pile of fabric. So beautiful and set aside on a dirty bathroom floor.

"Will you miss it?" he asked and pulled me to the window. He reached down, cupping his hands. I placed my foot in the hold. He lifted while I grabbed the windowsill, hoisting my body up. I sat on my bottom at the ledge and curled my legs through.

"The dress?" I asked, before moving both legs to the outside wall.

"Your life."

The doorknob turned again. "Alaina!" Liam bellowed.

I jumped through, and Killian was on the grass beside me a moment later. He grabbed my hand, and we ran toward the tree line.

"You're my life now," I confessed. "It wasn't a life, so there's nothing to miss."

Our footsteps gained speed at the sound of Liam's voice growing louder behind us. Killian gripped my hand harder, but I didn't look back.

I left that life behind me.

Chapter 17

Reasons Why

ALAINA

The explosion rang out through the trees as we ran. They trembled from tip to stump, making branches and leaves scatter along our path. I screamed, and Killian pulled my hand harder. He ran deeper into the tree line that led to the Blue Forest.

"What was that?" I cried. A plume of smoke filled the sky overhead.

Killian didn't answer. He never looked back. "We are close to the first spot. Keep going."

My legs moved like lead beneath me. Every step away became more difficult than the one before it as we climbed over tree trunks, and I slipped on the slick rocks. All the while, Killian was unrelenting in the journey and yanked me behind him like a child. He offered to carry me, but I refused. He never let up the breakneck pace. My skin shivered from sweat and my lungs burned. Every inhale filled my lungs with cool air and smoke.

"Killian, please. What was that?"

"Julie is fine."

"And Liam."

He bristled, and his jaw rocked side to side. "It hurt no one. I promise. Just a distraction."

The sounds and smells grew further away as we pushed further into the darkness. A steady buzzing of the wall that caged in our City echoed with each step. Its closeness sent fear through me.

Rumors had spread about what happened if you touched the barrier. It electrocuted those that strayed too far, or you simply vanished into smoke. I believed they were fairy tales told to us as children to keep fear in our hearts about wandering too far. I wasn't so sure anymore.

The worst outcome if we reached the barrier would be detection and then imprisonment. That scared me more than death. The City tortured people, and I had information they wanted, names of those against them.

"Killian - stop!" I screeched, yanking back his arm. "P-people. Up there. Stop."

People's shadows lined the distance ahead. My mind raced. *How did anyone find us out here?*

"Keep going," Killian insisted. Sweat covered his brow, and his muscles strained against his shirt.

I shook my head in protest.

"There are others," he explained. "You aren't the only one leaving tonight. Let's go."

Of course. How selfish of me to think it would be just us.

"Julie? Is she coming?"

Killian gave a deflated look and shook his head. "Not this round, Bug. But soon."

My shoulders slumped, and I walked after him, running my thumb over my necklace. Another man, also dressed in black, spoke in whispers to Killian. He looked familiar, and I tried to place him in the hazy darkness. Killian handed him the keys from his pocket, and he returned to me and grabbed my hand.

There were maybe a dozen people grouped together. Everyone sat slumped over, hands on their knees, with heavy breaths. The escape had forced us all into a dead sprint.

The man took the set of keys and added them to a stack of his own. "Aiden," I whispered under my breath. Killian squeezed my hand, confirming my suspicion. I'd seen him with Killian the day the officials had taken him. He knew Julie as well.

Aiden set one key on a flat rock and crouched down. He grabbed a small device that looked something like a wire curved into a spiral and jammed one end into the metal. I widened my eyes and stepped closer. My mouth fell agape in curiosity. Killian's hand clamped onto mine, and I felt my blood pulse in between our joined fingers.

The key split in two, and a thin wire lifted from the crack, protruding from within. "What is that?" I asked, enthralled by what I saw.

"You won't like this, but you need to trust me."

"What's inside the key?" I stepped closer. The wires unfurled to a large C shape with a pointed edge. They flickered a faint blue in the moonlight, lit up by some invisible power source. *Had the device charged it?*

"It will hurt." Killian fiddled with my wrist, and my bracelet dropped to the floor. The purple glow disappeared into the loose dirt.

"What's in the key?"

"She's first. Aiden over here. She'll go."

Aiden came over with one wire. The blue light blinked and grew brighter as he drew near. "Hi, Alaina. It's good to see you again."

He drawled out each word in a soothing tone. But my nerves had taken hold. "What's in the fucking key, Killian? What is that?"

"It will hurt. You need to stay still. This will connect with your chip and upload our encryption data. We can then control it and get you out safely... undetected."

"It's just a chip in my arm. Why will it hurt? That wire is hair-thin. What does it do?"

Killian pulled me close against his body. He kissed me and then drew his mouth to my ear. "The others don't know me as you do. They don't know Aiden, either. They're scared, and we need this to move fast. I need you to be strong for them."

I moved my hand to the back of his head, ran my fingers through his hair, and kissed him again.

"Well, this makes us even then. I've made it up to you," I said, half demanding and half asking. My heart thudded in my chest, waiting for his agreement.

His grin meant I won, but his expression shifted when he lowered me to the forest floor. "They connected your chip to your median nerve. It's designed that way to induce a pain response if the City so chooses. Do you understand what I'm saying? The chip will cause nerve pain as a deterrent. So people won't remove it on their own."

I didn't know what the fuck he was saying scientifically, but I knew I would feel it soon enough. If I wasn't sure before about leaving with Killian, this sealed my fate. The City implanted us with devices that could cause crippling pain at the push of a button. The depravity made me sick.

I rested my head on the grass and closed my eyes. Killian's body moved over mine, holding my shoulders down and straddling my hips. Locked in place, I remembered the last time he wandered into the forest. Had he done this before? *He must have, and he knew the pain to come.*

Aiden's hand crept up my arm and felt for the right spot.

Blinding pain seared through my body. It radiated in every cell, every thought, and every molecule. It took every bit of strength left inside of me to remain silent.

But I did it for Killian.

I stayed quiet to make up for the betrayal of before. I showed him love by gritting through the worst agony of my life as if I felt nothing.

I passed out for a moment, and I awoke to find Killian in the same position, over another woman. His hand laid over her mouth to silence her screams.

A woman moved next to me, settling herself into the soft grass. She touched my forearm. "You are friends with Julie, right?"

"Yes." My voice cracked, thinking of my friend. The woman's arm had a large red mark with a handprint. They had deactivated her chip, and I wondered how long I was unconscious.

"I've been friends with her for a long time. She sponsored me, I guess you could say... for this. She talked about you and described you right before I left. Told me to look out for you."

"She's my best friend. I-I'm afraid I haven't been so great to her." We sat together in silence, watching people one by one go through the torture.

"They have to hide the cable in aluminum and silver to block detection. Antiques, like keys, get little attention from the City. It's distasteful to them but allowed. When you keep things in a tin box, someone looks twice to see what's inside."

"Make sense. Is that what all the keys are?"

She nodded. "It's a one-use deal from what I understand. Then it burns out once your chip gets updated. Takes years to collect the decoders without the City knowing. Julie was desperate to get yours. I'm glad she did. She was so worried about it."

My gut wrenched. Julie got the last key from Liam. I touched my arm with my fingertips. I knew a bruise would form where Aiden held me down.

Julie had sacrificed her body for me. She abandoned her self-respect and pride. Tears fell again, fast and hot, down my cheeks. It hurt to know she pushed Killian away all those years ago, but he'd chosen to leave. We were kids, and she'd wanted to protect me. Risking herself was too high a price to pay for that mistake.

"Hey, don't be sad. She wouldn't be. Your freedom is what she wanted more than anything. She never wanted what happened to her to happen to you or me."

I paused in thought, looking at this woman in bewilderment. "What's your name?"

"Erin."

Erin picked at some rocks beneath our feet while the men moved to another person. A few people sniffled, curled over on their sides from exhaustion.

"Erin, when I said I haven't been a great friend to Julie, it's because I never knew she was part of the, um, rebellion of sorts. It surprised me she turned against the City... against the way of things."

"She has to do that. She fakes who she is. It protects you and me and the next person who wants out."

I rubbed my forehead and moved closer to Erin. "What I mean is, I don't know what you are talking about. I don't know what happened to her. It's not my place to ask you... but please... what do you mean?"

Erin's eyes closed and her body tensed. I held my breath, afraid to push too far. But I would push her. I had to know.

"I guess I thought she told you. I'm sorry. I only knew because I was there. We worked together then, and she started bleeding at work. She went completely catatonic, and wouldn't get up from her desk. I didn't believe the lies they'd told us. She had a cyst or something, at least that's what the officials said. I knew I had to leave after that. I couldn't be in a place like this. I knew our City murdered people who didn't comply. But what they did to her, someone who'd complied to a fault, was murder, plain and simple. It was... horrible. It changed... everything."

Chapter 18

Left Behind

JULIE

I crouched outside the building and watched them leave. A part of me yearned to chase after her, not to pull her back, but to give one last hug, one last goodbye.

They disappeared into the wood line, running fast. Good. They needed to move fast. Liam's voice boomed from inside the office. I rounded the corner and climbed through the window as he busted through the door.

"Liam," I greeted him as he stepped inside the bathroom. Eyes wild, he opened each stall, slamming the doors one by one. I touched his shoulder, and he shook me off. "You know she's gone."

He raged through the room, finding nothing. A scream let out when he reached the window. Then he turned his anger toward me, spinning in my direction, raising his hands to my neck. He didn't touch me, but he made his frustration known.

I had a lot of shit to do, and his temper tantrum didn't frighten me. I undressed, tossing my outfit into the garbage.

"What the fuck are you doing?" he yelled.

"Changing into this beautiful gown," I snipped. I stepped into the dress and wiggled it over my hips. He raised his arm and, for a moment, I thought I had miscalculated and he might choke me or maybe even hit me. Instead, his fist met the wall. A large hole was left in its place.

"Dammit, Julie. You have ruined everything."

A lump formed in my throat with his words. I knew he wanted a partner forever, but maybe I lied to myself, thinking Alaina was an attraction of convenience. Maybe he wanted her and not just the idea of her.

"Call me Alaina, and help me with my dress," I choked out.

"What? Call you what?"

"You heard me. You had your fun. Now she made her choice. Don't make this harder than it is. Don't punish me or yourself. And button up this dress."

"What are you doing? You look nothing like Alaina."

"You really think they will notice? How long until they figure it out? I'm betting on a long time. Long enough for her to get away."

His eyes darted from side to side. I had a point, and he knew it. He ground his jaw, grabbed my biceps, and flipped me around. His looming presence sent a shiver down my spine. My hands slapped against the wall, bracing myself.

He yanked on the back of my dress. A few stitches ripped in the fabric, and he pulled on the hooks. My body rocked back and forth with each angry clasp.

"You're pinching my skin."

"You're fine. You like it rough."

I flushed with his honesty. A final zip up the back, and he whipped me back around. Our faces were a mere inch away. I could feel his hot breath on my lips. "Would you like me to escort you back out to the party? We can wait and see if anyone notices. You love to play games. Officials aren't that dense, despite what you think."

"They won't notice I'm not her from the back when we are running away."

His face contorted in confusion. He fumed each breath of air, still too close, but I refused to back away. He opened his mouth to speak, but the explosion took his words.

The walls shook, and the windowpane rang by my ear. I thought it would break, but the rattling subsided, and the screams from outside took its place.

I saw Liam mouth, "What the fuck?" but I couldn't hear the words with the ringing in my ears. I brought my hands to the side of my head and rubbed the ache there. He shook me a few times. His mouth formed words I didn't understand. I took his hand and started out the door, still deaf from the blast. He followed, his nails digging into the top of my palm.

We made it to the entryway of the party. Dresses and suits fled in every direction. The ringing stopped, and I could hear him screaming, "Julie, stop!"

But I couldn't stop. I had to keep going. *Follow the plan. The first day matters the most.* "We have to get out of here. We can't be around when they question us. And for fuck's sake, it's Alaina, got it?"

Liam moved his arm around my waist. "Where are we going?"

"Home," I yelled, probably too loud. My voice still sounded muffled in my ears.

The crowd thinned with every step, and the dull ache in my head increased. We made it to Alaina's apartment with the cloud of smoke behind us and without being stopped. I had moved some of my personal effects inside. Not much, but enough to fool someone at first. I put the furniture back in order but left some of the artwork out.

Tomorrow I would go to the studio and teach the children's class. Because of Carrie's careful planning, they never saw me and wouldn't know. Carrie and I would suffer a strike against us at some point. When the City found out what we did, they may skip rehabilitation and thrust us into the blue forest with our friends, no questions asked. People disappeared a few at a time, but this operation would make them look like fools.

The City doesn't kill women. There aren't enough of us to waste. *I hope.*

I wouldn't miss my piece of shit husband. My boys were another story, but it wasn't their time yet. *I'll come back to get the boys. They are safe for now.*

But tonight, those seeking freedom needed to get away. If Killian and Alaina had enough time to make it out with the others and to safety, then what I went through mattered. It made all the difference.

"What have you done, Julie?" Liam's voice sounded broken. He leaned against a wall, his large body hunched over. He rubbed his wrist, and I knew he hurt himself earlier.

"I told you, it's Alaina." I rifled through the cabinet and found a bottle of whiskey and two glasses.

"I won't call you by her name," he spat.

"Now, now. Calm down. Or are you planning on putting another hole in a wall? That helps our situation, don't you think?"

Sarcasm dripped from my pores with every word, but I was out of fucks to give. This was the part where it all went right, or it all went to shit. Either way, she would make it. I couldn't save my baby, but Alaina could survive. And she could have as many babies as Killian put in her.

Free.

"Why are you being such a complete bitch to me?" Liam moved to the couch and put his head in his hands. Red blood dripped from his knuckles onto the white fabric.

I handed him an ice pack from the freezer. "I'm in a shit mood. I watched my best friend run into the Blue Forest. And I'm scared for her."

"I lost a woman I care about today. I lost my chance."

"Your chance? What does that mean? You don't even know her. You just know what she could give you, what you could take. Just like everyone else in this place."

"It could have been different with her," he protested. "She is special, and you've probably killed her!"

"She's better off if she lives a week out there than an entire lifetime in here, and you fucking know it. And damn right, she's special. Can you even tell me why?"

I slammed a whiskey on the table in front of him. Jupiter came out of her hiding spot to sniff the gold liquid. He gave the dog a light smile and reached for the glass.

"She just is. It doesn't matter now, anyway."

"Give me that bleeding hand and tell me why you were drawn to her. Dammit - you're bleeding all over the couch."

"Why? She's your best friend. You don't think she's unique... special?"

He hissed when I brought a warm rag to his hand, wiping away the dust and debris. "She's amazing. Only a fool wouldn't try to be with her. Nevermind. It doesn't matter."

He looked up at me, giving himself a moment to take in a deep breath. He opened his mouth to speak but winced when I hit a sensitive spot on his hand.

It bled more with the wound opened, and needed stitches, which we couldn't accommodate. Butterly bandages and a nice scar were what I offered. "I heard what you said to her, you know. About choosing someone forever. I heard some other stuff too, but you know... been there, done that."

A huff left his lips. "It's safe to say what you and I shared was different. And, please, just let me die without knowing how you heard my conversation with Alaina. I don't want to know, ever."

The bleeding slowed, but the cut across his knuckles gaped open. I took a moment to get some medical gauze and tape from the closet. He remained mute for a long while when I returned. Only a groan escaped once or twice while I cleaned him up.

"I think I know why Alaina appealed to me so much," he finally spoke. "I'm not dense, but... I don't know. I don't know how to say it," he admitted. Something about his demeanor changed. His shoulders hung as he leaned forward, a pensive look crossing his face.

I wrapped the gauze underneath and around his hand and rested it on my lap. Red seeped through the white fabric, fading out to the edges. I brushed my thumb against his bare skin.

"No man wants to feel replaceable," he said, barely above a whisper.

"No real man," I echoed.

I had wrapped his hand from wrist to fingertips like a mummy. We could blame the injury on the explosion, although the blast occurred far from all the guests. The sound was deafening, but it hurt no one.

I examined my work. *Not bad for a novice nurse.*

"Is that what you think? That real men want the same woman? Because I wonder if it's a sign of weakness, loving someone like that." His voice quivered, and it broke my heart.

"It's what I believe. I haven't experienced it, but I want it to be true. My husband isn't... a good person. He hurt me in a way I can't begin to describe. But I think committing to one person, loving someone forever, takes strength."

He thought on that while our hands stayed entwined. I welcomed the moment of silence, looking down at them.

"What now, Alaina?"

I laughed out loud. My cackle echoed through the apartment. "Now that we are in private, you see things my way and call me Alaina?"

"I think, maybe, I've always seen things your way. I just didn't want to admit it."

I nodded and gave him back his injured hand.

"Thanks," he whispered.

"Will you help me out of this dress? I'm spent and need to go to bed."

He nodded and walked with me to the bedroom.

It took him longer to unfasten everything with the use of only one hand, but he managed. Once my dress lay open to him, he brushed his palm down the curve of my back. Goosebumps prickled at my flesh from the touch.

"I liked it," I admitted.

His hand froze. "What?"

His touch against my skin burned hot. I craved more of Liam. Memories of our afternoon together raced through my mind. It felt wrong, but I needed to feel something other than fear and anxiety. Liam would be a welcome distraction.

"I enjoyed fucking you. I came... more than once."

His hand flattened at the base of my spine. "I hurt you. I'm sorry for that."

"If you're beating yourself up thinking you forced me, I wasn't reluctant. I wanted it. I might even admit... I had a plan for it."

His hand moved underneath the dress, curling around my bare stomach. I leaned back into his chest.

"I won't take advantage of you again like that. I want to be... better than that."

I flipped the top of my dress down, exposing my breasts. I caught him staring in the mirror across the room. When I dropped the rest to the floor, his hand moved lower. His fingertips reached just inside the thin strap of lace, the only fabric left on my body.

His ragged breaths raced against my neck. "Don't," he hissed. "Don't tempt me like this. Don't tease me like this."

"I'm not teasing. I can be gentle too. It doesn't have to be like it was."

His hand trembled, and I reached for it, pushing him lower. I parted my legs and pleaded, "Please, Liam. Show me you're a real man."

Chapter 19

Missing

JULIE

Liam's chest rose and fell against my back. His large hand splayed against my stomach while his soft, sleepy breaths tickled the back of my neck. I wished I could bottle the fleeting moment. We were peaceful, almost... happy.

Dawn came quickly for us and ruined our cocoon of bliss. The sun shot blades of white across Alaina's blankets. I ran my fingers through the light and wondered how the heat of the actual sun would feel against my skin.

"Good morning." Liam's words brushed my ear and made me shiver. "What are you thinking about?"

"The heat of the sun," I admitted. He turned me over and creased his brow. I sighed at his expression. "You wouldn't understand. Maybe... maybe you will one day."

"I don't know what you mean, but I think I would like that."

Ice blonde hair fell in his eyes, and I brushed it aside. "I like you messy. Real."

"I like you naked, beneath me."

He pulled my body over his and spread my legs, drawing my center against his hardness. I rubbed him between my wet crease and rocked, desperate for more.

His hands trailed up over my body, cupping my breasts. I took his length in my hand and guided him to the right spot, and then music rang through the apartment. The chime signaled someone was at the door.

"Don't stop," he pleaded. His hands massaged my swollen breasts, pinching my nipples. I winced and pushed forward, but the music rang out again.

"I have to check it. You know I do."

He huffed a breath and released his hands. His arms flung overhead, displaying every muscle in his chest. I dismounted with disappointment, grabbed a silk robe from the hook, and tied it around my waist. Agitated at the interruption, I checked the screen for our visitors. Officials. No surprise.

But so soon?

I rushed back to the bedroom. Liam pulled his pants up over his bare ass. I bit my lip and shook my head free of dirty thoughts. "It's City officials."

"Okay, Ju... Alaina, is it?"

"Let's just stay away from names to be safe. I don't know what they know or why they are here. Follow my lead."

Liam yanked a shirt over his head and looked me over. "Are you going to put something on?"

"Fuck, no. Breasts are the best weapon I've got against these idiots."

Liam rolled his eyes, and we headed for the door with his hand on the small of my back.

Two men dressed in all black greeted us, one with a scanner in his hand. They had the City Crest pinned to their shirt. Both looked unfamiliar to me, and they didn't greet Liam by name either.

"Hello," I drawled with a wide smile across my face. I leaned into the doorframe and let my robe open a little. "How may I honor the City today?"

"The honor is ours to visit a City resident such as yourself," one man said.

Liam's forearms flexed as his fists closed and opened. I reached for his hand and noticed the gauze I had placed there yesterday was bloody and loose. He had torn the bandage in our night together.

"Nasty cut there," one official said.

"Yes," Liam agreed.

One-word answers. That's good.

I stepped forward and brought my hands to the tie at my waist. Their eyes drifted downward for a moment. "Gentlemen, how may I honor the City today?"

The other man scanned me, and a beep came from the machine. He did it again, and it made the same noise. He scanned Liam, and nothing happened.

"We need your identification," the man with the scanner said.

"Sure thing."

I stepped inside and grabbed my documentation. I handed it to them and brought my arm around Liam's waist to hide my shaking hands. His body was stiff and unyielding next to mine, even when my nails clawed into his back.

"We did not assign this apartment to you."

"Ridiculous. I live here. Come inside and see."

"Your name isn't Alaina."

"And who is this Alaina?"

The man pulled up her profile. My friend's beautiful face lit up the screen of his electronic device. She had been crying in the picture. The City updated everyone's files at the Separation Center. They would have snapped the photo after Charlie left her.

"It says here her birthday is June twenty-eighth." I tapped at the door on the 0928. "Looks like your files are... amiss."

"That's not possible," the man with the scanner said. He scanned me again. The red light flickered over my arm with rapid blinks.

"Will you stop that?" Liam seethed.

I placed my hand on Liam's chest and took another step forward into the hall. "It looks like they've mixed your files up. After the commotion last night, it's no surprise. If you are looking for an Alaina, you've come to the wrong place."

I noticed several officials wandering the corridor. They were everywhere. My heart beat wildly in my chest. *This is too soon.* Sweat prickled at my forehead, and I clasped my hands together to keep them still.

"Quite the manhunt here. What's going on?"

"At the moment, we cannot find this citizen." He lifted Alaina's picture once more, and I felt Liam tug at my middle, bringing me back inside.

"I think we've proven you have a clerical error. Perhaps try another building," Liam snapped. He slammed the door in their faces, and I dropped my head into my hands.

"How do they know she's missing so quickly, Liam?" My harsh whisper cut through the air between us. *Was I too quick to trust him?*

"I don't know."

"Is that so? You have no fucking idea?"

He backed away from me, a hurt expression crossing his face. "I don't. I did nothing to cause this."

I bit my lip and lifted my hands to him. He backed up further, raising his palm to push me off.

"I believe you, okay? I'm just startled. They have ten officials just in this hall. This is moving fast. We thought the bomb caused enough of a distraction. I thought they would take statements, not hunt down every guest like a dog."

Liam nodded and reached for me. I fell into his arms and let him hold me while my mind raced. "I wouldn't do that to you, to us. After that afternoon together, when I hurt you.... After last night. I promise I won't hurt you again."

"I told you before, you didn't..."

Liam left my response hanging and shot off to the patio. Once outside, he looked from left to right, his back muscles tensing with each passing second. "We have to go," he ordered, stepping back toward me. "We need to make a run for it. This will cause a City shut down in an hour. Don't you agree?"

He was right. All signs pointed to complete lockdown already, days before it should happen. The City would seal away everyone in their homes. Alaina may not have enough time.

He grabbed a leash and hooked Jupiter's collar.

"Go where?" I asked. "It's not easy to get out of this place undetected. We're on their radar now."

"Get out of this apartment or out of the City?"

"Both, but what are you saying? We can't leave the City right now."

Liam tilted his head and took another step toward me. "Was your plan to stay? They'll kill you! First, they'll torture you, and then you'll die!"

"They won't kill a woman."

"Yes, they fucking will. Are you insane? And if you think you can withstand the pain that they'll put you through, you're wrong. Can you guarantee you won't give up the names of people that helped Alaina? Are there people in this Center that will be safe when they're pulling your teeth out one at a time?"

My stomach churned, and I fought the urge to vomit. I felt the blood leave my face and my head spun. Liam dropped Jupiter's collar and pulled me against him. "I have decoders at my house. And my house is next to the forest. Do you know a way out?"

I nodded, and my heart sank again. I knew the location of several escape routes. The City had never hurt its women, but Liam was right. This was a bigger escape and attack. I had clearly underestimated their response. *And what if they threatened my boys?*

"You're right," I admitted. "I know a way out."

Liam's arms tightened around while Jupiter paced the floor. The noise of people scrambling outside grated at my nerves. I yanked my head back. "How many decoders? You made me angry fuck you for one?"

A mischievous smile crossed his face, and I returned the same grin. "When I got the one for Alaina, I grabbed a few others."

"Why?"

"I don't know, Julie. I honestly don't. Something inside me just said to do it."

Because he knew he wanted out.

I packed the most haphazard bag in our haste to leave. The front hallway was out of the question, and we couldn't scale the building.

We both stood staring at each other for minutes, me holding a bulging bag of snacks and panties and Liam holding the dog.

"Shit, what do we do? I don't know a way out of this building. Officials are still everywhere."

Liam rubbed his temple. He scanned the room and grabbed a ball from Jupiter's toys. He bounced it once, and the husky stood on its hind legs and begged.

"How far will she chase this?" Liam cocked an eyebrow.

"Really, really fucking far. How far can you throw it?"

"Really, really fucking far."

I bit my bottom lip. "Liam, you make me blush when you curse."

"And you make me blush when you come." Liam bounced the ball again. "Down, girl," he ordered. Jupiter heeled, and I adjusted the bag on my shoulder.

"We will only have one shot at a distraction," I said. "Can we get far enough away?"

Liam shrugged.

"That's not very reassuring," I whined.

"If they come, I'll try to cause a scene and let you get away. You are an approved guest in my apartment, so you can get right in."

I paced in circles with my hands on my head, as if another magical idea would come to me. Nothing did, and I knew we were out of time. "Okay, but one change to this stupid plan," I said. "We go together, whatever happens. I'm not abandoning you."

He took a deep breath and opened his mouth to protest, but decided against it. He gave one sharp nod, and we walked to the hallway.

Liam threw that ball so fucking far, I lost sight of it before it hit the ground. The husky barreled down the corridor, knocking over officials and citizens in her wake. "Bye, Jupiter," I whispered.

We raced the other direction to the fire escape and closed the door behind us with the softest click. And then I prayed again. I was still shit at it, but I prayed with every careful step while Liam clutched my hand.

Let Alaina make it.

Let us make it.

Let the damn dog make it.

The door at the bottom floor let out onto the side street. Liam cracked it open, and we peeked outside. Thankfully, only a few citizens stood around.

"Be calm and act normal," Liam said. "We can make it to my apartment in five minutes if we jog through the park."

Liam took the bag on my shoulder and wrapped the strap across his chest. "You ready?" He asked.

"Just one minute." I grabbed his face and pulled his lips to mine. I pushed my tongue inside and took what could be my last kiss from the man.

He lifted my body and pushed me against the cement wall. I bounced off it and knocked my head but didn't stop. I moved my legs around his waist and he thrust forward with gasps and moans breaking between us.

"We're going to make it," he hissed and ran his tongue across mine one last time.

I lowered myself down and cracked the door open again. Satisfied that no one of note was outside, we moved into the light.

Our first steps went unnoticed. Citizens in the distance barely looked our way, distracted by their conversations with each other and officials. We had made it to the edge of the gardens when I saw him. His dark eyes met mine and the look on his face told me some puzzle piece had just clicked inside his brain.

The soft gasp that left my lips made Liam's eyes grow wide. "What is it?" he pleaded, as we started our jog toward his apartment.

I gripped his hand tighter, tears threatening to escape. In all the planning, I hadn't expected things to move this quickly. I certainly hadn't expected to see him.

"It's Charlie," I sneered. "He knows."

Chapter 20

History

ALAINA

I listened while Erin exposed every painstaking detail. These horrible moments in Julie's life were laid out before me, and I never knew. Part of me wanted her to stop, but if Julie had survived it, I had to hear it. I needed to know.

The details of her tragedy made my stomach twist in knots, threatening to release its contents. The betrayal she went through - the pain. And she never told me any of it. She suffered silently. All the while, she used that anger to plot against the City.

I stayed silent while Erin told me about Julie's third child. An unfortunate fluke of science. Somehow, in the City's foolproof sterilization of their women, someone made a mistake. She kept her growing belly a secret for months. If caught, she would feign surprise at the news. If she told them she didn't know, they may believe her. She became pregnant by their error, and they *never* make mistakes.

In the end, Julie's husband reported it to the City. They had suspected something distracted her. She called into work, kept her office door closed the few times she went in and stopped visiting with friends.

A coworker filed a report referencing a mental health concern. Her husband was due for his annual interview, and they pulled him in for questioning.

He caved after officials presented him with the pictures. Detailed photos showed him walking into a pleasure house and then in the throes of ecstasy with a young woman, *not his wife*, on his lap. The selfish bastard never once asked what the baby's fate would be. Maybe he already knew. Either way, he spilled Julie's condition without hesitation or regret. The exchange took less than twenty minutes. He never fought for his wife or child.

They went to her home. They set her chip to a terrible ache that doubled her over in pain. Her husband allowed them inside shortly after.

She cried to him and begged him to take her away. He left her on the floor alone, in agony. They held her down and scanned the baby. She carried another boy, a child not worth keeping, not worth feeding.

After injecting her with an unknown substance, they saw themselves out. No one explained what would happen next. They simply left.

A message sent to her home devices provided dates for interrogation and debriefing. There would be rehabilitation, of course, but they didn't give her information on her unborn child's fate.

Four days later, the injection fulfilled its purpose, aborting the baby at twenty-eight weeks. She sat at her desk, refusing to move, and almost bled to death. Delivery started and contractions came back to back.

Medics sedated her and removed her from the office while Erin watched in horror.

She awoke in time to deliver a perfect, still-born baby boy. There was no funeral. Her husband stayed away from the medical center. A car took her home the next day, and she never said a word to anyone.

Erin was in a rage of her own about her missing brother. I didn't ask her more about that, but what she saw with Julie sent her over the edge. She confided to Julie that she hated the City and everything it stood for. Julie must have known she'd found a confidant.

Or maybe she was tired of carrying the burden and pain alone all that time. She told her story to her acquaintance that soon became a dear friend. No one else ever knew. No one else seemed to care, especially not her husband.

Together, they found the right people and planned a way out. They aren't hard to find if you're looking. The City scorned many people, more than we could imagine. More than we'll ever know.

"Thank you for telling me," I sniffled. "I'm sure that was difficult for you."

Erin crouched closer to me, her tone firm in my ear. "There are other people in the City like her. Others in positions of power that don't believe in the officials' agenda. We won't be the last to leave."

I thought of Carrie, Rafael, and my dear Julie. They remained behind. Were they stuck or waiting their turn? Had I taken someone's spot?

My mind drifted to Liam. Would he be angry or sad at my departure? Maybe both. Did he chase after us through the wood line?

Aiden and Killian lifted from the last person. Aiden heaved her limp body over his shoulder, and the group gave him their attention.

"We'll continue to the next checkpoint. It's a three-hour walk or two-hour jog. If you walk, stay with me. If you jog, go with Killian."

Killian made his way over to me, his expression terse at my tear-stained face. "What's wrong? Are you still in pain?"

"No - no. It's not that. I can... I can jog. I'll stay with you."

He looked at Erin, who had watery eyes and a shaky chin. "What did you do?"

"I told her about Julie... what happened to her."

He lowered his head, saying nothing. I threw myself into his arms and shook while he held me. His hands reached up under my shirt, making our contact closer, more intimate. "If you get tired, I'll carry you," he whispered into my ear.

He pulled away, grabbed my hand, and started running. I looked back for Erin while he tugged me along, but she was already gone. I saw her jogging ahead with the others, her ponytail bobbing back and forth.

Two hours of jogging in theory sounded impossible. In reality, adrenaline coursed through my veins and fueled my legs. My body responded to what my brain told it to do, but the pain tomorrow would be unbearable. The pace steadied, and our breaths began a uniform inhale and exhale.

No one spoke, and I counted steps in my head. I got to one hundred and then started again. Over and over to keep my mind occupied.

Killian looked back occasionally. My body ached and my lungs burned. But each time, I met his eyes, smiled, and kept going right behind him.

When he stopped, I slammed into his back, and he turned to grab me. "We're here," he said. "Last stop before we cross."

I wanted to ask what we crossed into, but my heaving lungs couldn't make words. When I tried to walk, my legs gave out, and I fell into his arms. For the last thirty minutes, my body had numbed, running on sheer will alone, and I crashed from the exertion.

"We rest now, Laney bug. It's almost over." I felt him lift my legs from the ground and I snuggled into his chest. The woodsy scent felt familiar, and I wondered if it came from this place. I heard Erin's voice when he laid me down, hovering over me. "I have a jacket to lie over her. Poor thing didn't get to train."

Killian's voice faded as they walked away. "I have something for us tonight. I'll lay with her. She's..." And then my eyes grew too heavy, and sleep took over.

I awoke in the dim light of dawn. The soft sounds of the woods surrounded me. Killian carried me in his powerful arms. I yawned and reached a hand to his face. His footsteps led us away from the group, deeper into the trees.

"What's going on? Where are we going?" My voice was barely audible after just waking up.

He kept his face forward, walking at a steady pace. "Not far." His hungry voice awoke my senses.

The group of sleeping strangers disappeared out of sight, and he lowered me to the ground. The grass below me wet my shirt with morning dew. I stretched my arms over my head, arching my back. Bones popped and my sore muscles stretched.

Killian stood above me, his eyes on my outstretched body. He lifted his shirt over his head in a fluid motion, tossing it to the side. His fingers moved to the buttons on his pants until he removed those, kicking out of them one leg at a time.

His intense stare never left mine. I undressed, desperate for him to take me again. I fumbled on the ground, removing my pants and shirt. I bared myself to him on the cool forest floor, and Killian lowered himself onto me. He stroked his length, which already leaked at the tip. His other hand wrapped around my back, and he brought his face to mine with a smirk. His lips had barely touched mine when he pushed inside me.

I wrapped my legs around him, meeting him thrust for thrust. The rough patch of ground under my back scratched my skin, but I didn't care. I enjoyed the sharp pains and wanted the evidence on my body that he'd taken me this way. His mouth moved from my lips to my neck, desperate to claim every inch of me, pulling at the skin with firm bites.

His hands cupped under my ass, lifting my hips to his, moving my center into the perfect position, rubbing my clit with every stroke.

Soft moans left my lips as the heat grew inside me. The intense tightening of my core got closer to its release. "I love you," I cried out. "I love you, Killian."

His movements became harder and faster. His hands held me in place while he fucked me with relentless force. "Don't forget it again. Don't forget you're mine."

"Never. Nev-" and my words cut off with a mind crippling orgasm. It ripped through me and took my breath. My body convulsed underneath him, pleasure rippling through my tired limbs while I dug my nails into his back.

When I grew limp, he hovered over me and withdrew himself. I whimpered at the loss of him. He had ripped away the physical connection to each other I so desperately needed to remain.

I bent my legs to my front, holding them against my chest. He pushed them to the side and flipped me onto my stomach. I gasped and scrambled to my knees. An arm wrapped around my waist, steering me toward his waiting cock. He entered me again, almost lifting my knees from the ground. He planted his other arm by my head, keeping his balance, and it shook from the strain.

Mostly quiet until now, he let out ragged grunts which grew louder with each movement. Tingling grew inside me once more, and I cried out every time he pushed deeper inside. "Don't... forget it... again," he demanded.

"I w-won't," I said with shaking breaths. He pushed and pulled my body against him, and I clawed at the grass beneath me to hold on. The sound of our bodies coming together rang out around us. He pulled up and grabbed my hips with both hands, quickening his pace as he bucked against me.

"Don't... hurt me... again. You're... mine." Liquid heat filled my insides, bursting out and dripping down my inner thighs. I screamed from another rush of pleasure, unable to control my trembling limbs. His hand came down on my right cheek, sharp and hard. It sent ripples of bliss like an aftershock, and he rubbed the sore spot with his palm until the sting subsided.

His hold loosened, setting me back down onto the soft grass. I turned to my side, and he cradled me from behind. His grip was tight but gentle. "I love you, too," he whispered.

I smiled in his arms, sated and exhausted. Minutes passed without words. Nothing needed to be said between us. I chose him, but he needed to claim me in this way. I wanted him to.

His fingertips brushed along the length of my arm. I giggled at the tickling sensation. "Say it again," I begged.

He smiled into my hair and pulled me closer to him, still naked and sticky and growing hard once more. "I love you."

"Tell me about the day you left."

Killian's hand stilled on my side, and he let out a long breath on my neck. "That's a long story, and we're short on time. I hated that day, but it's in the past."

"You said I couldn't go with you anyway, so I suppose it doesn't matter."

"It matters that I left you without saying goodbye. I shouldn't have done that."

I turned my head to the sky, squinting at the light that brightened overhead. "Julie told me what she did. She feels bad about it."

Killian pulled me tighter against him. "She shouldn't," he whispered into my neck. His words tickled my ear. "She was protecting you. Now it's my turn. I'll take care of you forever. You're mine... forever."

I wiggled my body into him, teasing him, loving him. He cleared his throat, running his fingers through my hair, down my neck. "Your chip controls your birth control, you know."

I moved my head to look at his face. "It does?" I knew so little about the City's control. When someone visited the medic, they didn't disclose how procedures worked.

His gaze, smug and sated, looked down to my stomach. "Well... not anymore."

Chapter 21

The Other Side

ALAINA

"Do you think that's something you should have told me, I don't know, twenty minutes ago?" Any tension in my voice faded quickly. I wasn't upset. Any sensible woman would have been, but I left sensible back in the Separation Center. Killian had brought up children the first time we spoke. His intentions were obvious from the beginning.

I wanted them. He wanted them, and we wanted each other.

"Maybe, but you distracted me. I've been thinking about being inside you again since... since I was last inside you," he chuckled. "I couldn't wait another second. It was hard enough to let you sleep at all."

"So you just turned my birth control off, assuming we would start making babies."

"We turned everything off for everyone. Your chip performs several functions. Several of which submit reports back to the City. So this was a happy coincidence."

"So my uterus wasn't singled out."

Killian let out a bellowing laugh. His firm body shook against mine, and I felt his hardness against my hip. I reached for him, but he took my hand and brought it to his lips, kissing it gently. "We have to get back. It's time to go."

"You say one thing with your words, but your body tells a different story."

He stood up with a remorseful grunt, adjusting himself. "Once we are settled, there will be plenty of time for what I want to do to you."

I reached for my clothes. I had flung my shirt over a bush, and my pants were nowhere to be found. Panic set in for a moment before I noticed Killian twirling them in one hand while fastening his buckle with the other.

"Settled, where?" I questioned, yanking the fabric from his hand.

"There is a spot in the barrier where we can cross. It's another hour's walk."

"And then how far?"

"A day's walk until people meet us with food and supplies. Then three more days' walk to town."

"Town?"

Killian held out his hand. "I can hear everyone getting up. I'm sure we woke a few of them. Let's go. It will all come together soon."

Killian had carried me only five minutes from the campsite, and my voice carries. Erin's face confirmed my suspicions back at camp. She folded her blanket and gave me a wink. I flushed with embarrassment and shrugged, causing her to giggle.

At some point last night, Aiden's group had made it to us. I had drifted off the night before as soon as we arrived, and I was glad to see everyone back together that morning. Killian and Aiden announced we would walk, but if they felt we needed to get to the checkpoint sooner, everyone would need to jog. No one complained, because what else could we do but agree?

Fifteen minutes in, Aiden announced it was time to pick up the pace. The jog wasn't a steady trot like yesterday. It was grueling and fast, like the initial escape from the party. It took everything in me to continue.

The forest thinned, and a buzzing noise intensified. It made my skin vibrate as if silent waves rushed against my body. The path under my feet became worn, walked upon by others before us. The woods seemed off somehow. I braced my hand on a tree to catch my breath and noticed it felt wrong. It felt... fake. I scratched its trunk with my fingernail and a brown film formed underneath. *Curious*.

Killian took my arm and yanked me away. I stumbled after him until we stood before a large grey building in the middle of the forest. Cement walls and a roof created an ominous barrier in front of us. The length of it had no apparent end from where I stood. No signs or windows were present. It appeared out of place, planted smack in the center of the outdoors, surrounded by strange looking foliage and trees.

Aiden looked at a device in his hand while everyone collapsed where they stood. "Four minutes," he deadpanned. He turned to the building, which had no visible door, and stared.

I tugged at Killian's sleeve. "What's this?"

"This is the crossover. The building here reaches several stories underground."

"Why is it so... so odd here? That tree felt... different. Look at the trees around the building."

"Nothing grows here. The currents from the power grid are too strong. Nothing here, the grass, the trees, is real. The rocks maybe, but it's a dead zone. It's too dangerous to be here for long. No one from the City comes out here, so it's the best place to cross."

I nodded, unsure of what he meant. I recalled the stories of people exploding if they touched the grid from my youth. I pushed the thoughts away. *They're just stories told to children to scare you.*

"One minute," Aiden announced. "We have ninety seconds to get through. If you hesitate, no one is coming after you. And it's a one-way, not a round trip."

I saw Erin give a comical salute out of the corner of my eye to Aiden. People advanced closer to the building, ready to sprint inside. I winced under Killian's grip on my hand, so tight it hurt. We would cross together or he would take my arm off.

Aiden counted backward from ten.

"Ten - nine -"

"*Alaina!*"

My name echoed in the woods behind us. It rang out in the distance, loud and unmistakable despite the hum of the City's barrier. Killian yanked us through the crowd, knocking others aside until we stood flush with the wall of the building. They moved their heads around at the sound of my name.

"What was that?" I shouted. "Someone just called out my name. Did you hear that?" Killian ignored me.

"Four - three -"

"*Alaina!*"

The cry sounded closer this time, and I whipped around, looking for the source. Branches moved in the distance, and my heart thumped wildly in my chest.

"Killian, what the fuck?" He pulled my arm towards his chest, wrapping our forearms together. Aiden looked right at him, stepped aside, and said, "One!"

The top of the building had split open with a thunderous groan. Rusted metal cracked under strain and sent shards of brown flakes into the air. The roof divided in two, separating in the middle, and straightened into the sky. We stared in awe at the large cement panels that lifted before us.

In a fluid motion, the front and back wall sank into the earth. They dug into the ground beneath with alarming speed, and dust exploded from all around us. Killian and I stood too close, and the muck in the air forced its way into my lungs, making it hard to breathe. I coughed and gagged, staring at a dark and blurred open void before me. Blinded by the debris, I felt the rush of people at my sides. Everyone shoved forward, and Killian moved me in front of him, plunging me into the smog. Elbows and backs bumped and collided, all moving through the haze.

I walked through the open hallway, unsure where we were headed. Bars in the center of the room rammed into my side and I cried out. Killian pulled me to the side. "That's the way down," he yelled. "We are going through."

Thankful for some explanation, I kept going.

A distant plea came from behind us. "Alaina, don't go. Alaina, please!"

The voice sounded familiar, but it drowned out in the noise of chaos and chatter around me. Dirt entered my lungs with every breath, so I didn't dare attempt to speak. I still couldn't see anything but a fog in the darkness. My dirty skin itched, and I felt others crowd against me.

Still in the hallway, I could feel a wall on one side. The dark and musty air cleared a little up ahead. The smell of rot filled my nostrils and coughing and footsteps echoed all around me.

"Will they get in?" Killian yelled forward. "Can you close it?"

"I don't know, and no." Aiden's voice rang from ahead of the crowd. "Eight seconds and it closes. Is everyone through?"

"Everyone that wants to be and maybe a few unwanted," Killian shot back.

My sight returned. My eyes had adjusted to the darkness, and the dust settled enough. I stopped walking and braced myself against the wall. There was a light maybe twenty feet ahead of us. Killian stroked my face, and my entire body trembled.

"Are you okay? We need to keep going."

Aiden rushed to our sides. Everyone else sprinted to the light up ahead. "You have to break off, Killian. I can't risk you with the group."

"I know. We'll meet you there."

Aiden handed him the backpack he carried. "If you aren't there two days after we arrive, I'll come back for you."

"The fuck you will. Stay with everyone. We get there when we get there. Don't worry."

They brought their foreheads together and put each other's hands on their necks. "I know what I'm doing," Killian affirmed. Aiden broke their embrace, jogged forward, and we carried on after him.

When we reached the light, it blinded me. It beamed down brighter and stronger than anything I had experienced before. I felt a searing heat on my skin. I shaded my eyes and crouched from it in shock. Killian handed me a pair of eye coverings. "These will help with the brightness," he said. "But the heat... you will have to acclimate. We have to go uphill. Do you need to be carried?"

I shook my head and put on the glasses with dark lenses. Immediate relief followed, and we started up at an intense angle while the group moved on an even path further away. I saw Erin as the last to go and caught her waving. I waved back, unsure when we would meet again.

"You'll see her in a few days," Killian promised. "But we can't put them in danger."

"In danger from what, or who?" He didn't answer, and we climbed.

Rocks tumbled around us at the uphill angle. My ass I so desperately tried to get in shape before burned and cramped with each footstep. Killian pulled at my waistband more than once to bring us further up what I now thought must be a mountain. I'd never hiked a mountain before. I'd only seen them from a distance.

When we reached a flat piece of land, he wrapped an arm around me, and we entered a dark cave hidden in the rock.

He worked quickly once inside, moving larger pieces of rock from the back of the cave to the slip of an entryway we just walked through. He stacked them with ease, building a stone door before my eyes. Each piece fits perfectly, like a pre-cut puzzle.

A large blanket was the last to come forward. He hooked it to the top of the entrance, pushing it flush against the rocks on every side. It blocked out every ray of light.

Then I heard them.

People.

Screaming my name.

And I recognized one voice.

"Alaina," Charlie bellowed.

Before I could react to the sound, Killian moved me against the cavern wall and pushed his palm over my open mouth.

Chapter 22

Prisoner

ALAINA

I scrambled under Killian's grasp. For a moment, the urge to reach Charlie overtook me. Our past had etched the instinct deep down into my bones to come when called. But he wasn't my husband anymore. The sound grew closer, and I froze.

He's the enemy.

"Alaina!" Charlie yelled. I patted Killian's arm and squirmed myself out of his grip. He brought a finger to my lips, reminding me to stay quiet. The cave was dim and cool, hidden from the sunlight. He took my arm, and we tip-toed toward the back. One hand skimmed against the wall and guided me further into darkness. I followed Killian, feeling my way until he sat cross-legged and pulled me into his lap.

"I'm sorry," I whispered into his ear. "I thought maybe... he was in some kind of trouble. What's he doing here?"

"Shh." Killian's fingers silenced me once more, and I pressed my lips against them. He brought my head to his shoulder, and I exhaled into his warm body. His heart thudded so loudly, that I wondered if they would hear it from the outside.

"Alaina, it's time to come home. We can't find Julie. We need your help."

I tensed but didn't make a sound.

"She's fine," Killian murmured in my ear. "It's part of the plan. She helped you escape. Don't make it all for nothing."

I nodded against his shoulder. My nails dug into his sides. I realized I was holding my breath and gasped in a rush of air. Killian rubbed my back, and the footsteps outside grew louder.

"He's kidnapped you." Charlie's voice felt closer than before. I had no reference of how far outside our makeshift door Charlie stood, but my heartbeat matched Killian's. Our chests thumped rapidly against each other. Quickened breaths warmed each other's skin. His grip around me hardened, pushing into my ribs.

"Too tight," I whispered, and he relaxed, but only a little.

"There's been a horrible mistake," Charlie continued. "He's a criminal. He threatened your life if I didn't end our marriage. I thought I was protecting you. Don't you see, baby? He's played you all along. He's got a vendetta against the City."

My entire body trembled in Killian's arms, but I remained silent.

He's a liar.

I raised my face to Killians in the dim light, and the look in his eyes terrified me. He shook his head *no* and brought his lips to mine. I hesitated to kiss him back, and he pushed harder, moving his mouth in a frenzy, desperate for me to match his lips.

"Laney, please," he begged in my ear. "Kiss me. It's me. Don't listen to him."

But I heard it, and I couldn't erase the thought.

"He's using you," Charlie pleaded. The sound faded this time. They were walking away. We escaped discovery, hidden together in the dark. "Come with me, and we can go back to our lives, our jobs, our apartment. Julie's husband is here. He's worried about you both."

"Alaina, it's Drew," Julie's husband yelled. "We need you to come home and help us find Julie. Her chip has malfunctioned, and we're all so worried."

That cleared my thoughts immediately. Julie's husband, the bastard who killed her son, didn't care about her. Drew was a liar. Charlie was still a liar. And I would kiss Killian in this dark cave until their skeletons rotted outside our rock door rather than go to them.

Maybe they could couple together and live out their days talking about which man was a bigger piece of shit. I chuckled to myself at the thought, and Killian's wild eyes met mine again. I put my hands on his face and kissed him, hard.

His shoulders relaxed, and he moaned against my lips. When I pulled back, I saw his eyes misted in the darkness.

I brushed my lips against his neck. "None of that."

"For a moment, I thought you would leave. You felt far away."

"Momentary shock is all. I'm with you. I'm here."

"We'll have to be here for a while. They will search the area from top to bottom. They won't go far inside the forest, but we need to wait. I have supplies. When it's time, we'll leave but only at night. Darkness is better."

"Whatever we need to do. I love you."

"Let's rest for a bit. You need to sleep. Lay down on me."

I yawned at the thought of sleep. Killian was right. The journey caught up to me and my eyes closed when he pulled me against his warm body. He rubbed my back, and I drifted away.

A few times in my slumber, the sound of voices shocked me awake. I forgot for a moment they loomed outside, yelling for me to surface. Promises of a normal life turned to threats throughout the night. *Baby, come back to me* soon became *you'll die for your treason.*

It firmed my resolve, and I remained by Killian's side. That didn't change the fact that it frightened me. Julie waited back at the Center, and I felt sure she was inside my apartment. She was alone and in danger.

If they had her, they would have brought her out here. At this moment, they didn't know where she was, but what would happen when they found her? She was an amazing actress, but this would be the show of her life.

With no idea what time it was, my eyes opened once more. Drips from inside our cave and the scurry of animals outside made the only noises. It must have been dawn or early morning. Killian awakened and wrapped his arm around me, rolling to his side.

"Did Julie force you to leave all those years ago?" It was a question that needed an answer. Alone together, waiting out our enemies gave him time to answer.

Killian's chest rose with a thick intake of breath. "I made a choice. The wrong choice."

"She said she threatened you. That's why she did this. It's why she risked herself to get me out."

Killian's head turned to the side, and he met my eyes in the darkness. I could make out the slow open and close of his eyelids while he thought about his response. "Julie loved you and so did I. I barely survived the crossing. She was right. Ten years apart was awful, but... not everyone made it across when I left. She'll be okay."

He couldn't know that, but I let myself believe the lie. I needed to believe it.

"Why are they so desperate to find me?" I asked. The thought ran rampant in my head all night. I wasn't special. They kicked criminals out of the Center. Why beg me to come back?

"They don't want you. They want me. They want the way."

"Like I'm supposed to know what that means, Killian. I know we have nothing but time, but if you could stop speaking in riddles, I'd appreciate it."

His face firmed, and he brought a hand to my cheek. "There's a world in these woods. More people than in the Centers. A whole world that was never taught in our history books, never spoken about in the City. It's heavily protected and for good reason. They want the way."

My jaw dropped. "That many people have been kicked out?"

He shook his head and laughed at me, at my ignorance. "No. They exile very few people from the City. Before the City became... the City, people broke off. The City, it's not the entire world. Shit, I'm explaining this all wrong."

"I don't understand. Why do they want to find the people that don't want to be found?"

"Some people they want to take. Some people they want dead. For a while, the division was peaceful, but more people have left the City. This isn't the only group. This isn't the first group or even the tenth. They are losing their stronghold. They can't produce girls. I don't know why, but it's becoming more of a problem. It's not a problem outside their territory."

"Territory?"

"I don't know how else to put it. I... let me show you. Do you need to pee? We can sneak just outside and you can see up here if you know what to look for."

"Is that safe?"

"It should be if we are fast. We'll leave tonight. We can't stay too long before Aiden sends reinforcements. He's a stubborn bastard."

He brought me to my feet, and we listened at the rock door for several minutes before making a space only large enough to crawl out.

"Any noise, you run, but I don't think they are in the area right now."

"What do you want to show me?"

"You're still my clever girl." He brushed his thumb down my cheek and kissed my lips. His hand cupped my ass, and he pushed me against him. I ran a hand underneath his shirt, feeling his muscles and the faint scars underneath. Flames rose in my belly. *Will I always melt at his touch?*

He looked me over, holding my body against his. "It will upset you. It's shocking, but I'm here. I'll never leave you again."

"Just show me."

We took a five-minute walk in which I found a spot behind a tree and peed in the most embarrassing moment of my whole damn life. I made Killian plug his ears so I could get anything to come out, even though I was bursting.

He motioned to a rock ledge that jutted out from the side of our path. He lowered his body and gestured for me to crawl alongside him. We moved to the edge, our bellies against the cool rocks and grass.

"Do you see it there? The curve. It gleams against the light."

I squinted, desperate to find what he meant. "I don't. I don't see it."

"Look over the trees. Look for the reflection."

I frowned. "What am I supposed to be looking..." And then I saw it and my stomach dropped out of my feet. Everything spun, and only Killian's firm hand on my back kept me in place. I laid on the earth beside him, but a part of me floated away. I almost screamed, but I caught myself and whimpered instead. I laid my head down on the rock underneath me and cried.

"What the fuck? What the fuck is that?"

"It's the City. It's an environment inside a dome." He gripped my chin and stared into my eyes. He felt my pain and confusion. He went through this once, too. "Controlled is... an understatement. It's a lot to explain, and we don't understand how it came to be. But this," he circled his hand above us, "is the real world. You lived in a sort of habitat, an old experiment. One that many years ago went... very much off the rails."

Chapter 23

Blood

ALAINA

Killian knew that inside the Discovery Center, he would look up to the sky and see nothing but a ceiling. He knew out here, he could raise his face to the sun, and it would pierce his retinas and burn. Nothing stood in the way of its rays.

I learned that fact mere hours ago, and I let the idea turn over in my thoughts. Officials and the council had fabricated everything. I questioned *the way of things*, but I didn't question the reality of my home.

Killian knew what a moon was. A white, round, cratered object that lit up the sky at night. It lit our way as we climbed over rocks and fallen trees, lighting our path to my new home.

This world outside the dome was messy and hot. Sweat poured down my back and matted my shirt to my skin. The temperature fluctuated between day and night, making the evening wind chill my sweat-soaked clothes. The thick woods had unknown noises that filled my ears.

But it was all real.

The City gave me a counterfeit. Scientists and politicians created it centuries ago.

"There was a time," Killian explained, "when people were so self-destructive they didn't know if humans could even make it. We killed ourselves and each other. There was war and fear and hate. They created the domes to save the children of this world... to protect them. But the power the leaders held... it became too much."

Habitats.

Countless habitats.

The world was enormous, bigger than I could ever imagine. When I looked at the sky at night, millions of twinkling lights filled the darkness instead of the pitch black of nighttime in the City. Bugs bit at my skin, causing red welts on my legs. I relished the sting.

This was the real world, and Killian's love was real. Ten years had always been a distraction, and one brought by the men that started our society so many decades ago.

"Why do it? Why force people into contracts of marriage?"

Killian looked up at the moon, hands on his hips. Strands of his hair whipped in the light breeze. I could make out his profile in the moonlight. "I don't know how it came about, but idle hands are dangerous. Emotions distract people, and if their focus is elsewhere..." He rubbed his jaw, scratching at his stubble. "No one at home, at your new home, can remember when that came about."

"Who all knows? The officials?"

"Everyone knows there is a wall, but a habitat... very few people know that. And fewer admit the City's isolation. They have talked themselves into the lie that the dome is everything. They convinced themselves only criminals are outside the City."

I grabbed a handful of dirt and rubbed it between my fingers. I let it go, watching the dark earth move in the wind.

All the City's bullshit about the way of things - lies. A scheme by adulterers and cowards to create a world that fits their desires. And I knew nothing different.

Killian held out his hand, and I took it, marching on in my hatred. It kept me going through my fear and exhaustion. Charlie and the officials still wandered these woods.

The path we took wound through trees and shallow rivers. Only once did we hear noises from other people, and Killian held me against a fallen tree in the darkness. We waited, and they left. I should have been nervous, but I felt nothing. I would leave Killian's side in death only. Knowing and believing that freed me from all fear. Together forever held true meaning in my fury. I would bring a knife to my neck and slice my skin to the bone if they took me from him. This forest, this life, this man, they were all I had to live for now.

They spread traps across the woods, and Killian knew the way. This was why officials from the City and their lackeys, like Charlie and Drew, wouldn't venture far outside their territory. Death was imminent just outside the border of their precious dome.

"Why do you think there are fewer and fewer girls born in the City?" I asked. We had walked in silence for hours. Killian had grown quiet, aware of my murderous mood. Rage seeped from my pores, and I could taste it in the surrounding air.

"I told you I don't know why."

"But what do you think? What's your gut tell you?"

He thought about that for a moment. Leaves crunched beneath our feet, and I waited.

"I think destiny is real. I think we all have a fate before us. There is a balance in things. The City is out of balance."

"And it's self-correcting?"

"It's self-fulfilling. They wanted men in control, men deciding. Now they will have it. And they will die out because of it. Only five percent of the births this year were female."

"They won't be safe," I whispered. "They'll get desperate."

"Clever girl. And they already are."

"Alaina!" A voice boomed in the distance, and we dropped to the ground. My face slapped on the dirt and stung my cheek. Killian's firm hand spread across my back, pinning me down.

"Killian," a male voice echoed.

Killian's eyes darted back and forth. The cry sounded familiar.

"Who is it?" I mouthed.

He lifted his head a notch with his hand pressing harder into my spine. My heart thudded against the dirt.

"Laney Bug!" Julie's cry rang out through the trees.

"Julie!" I tried to get up, but Killian yanked me back down to the earth. My breath left my lungs with a thud, and I fought him with all the anger that filled me.

"Let me up. It's Julie!"

"And she's with Liam. Stay down."

The familiar male voice was Liam. They were together.

I squirmed and spit in his arms. Julie was close. I could hear her voice, and Killian kept her from me.

"Liam helped us," I hissed in his face.

"Are you going to come to Liam's defense right now? Was it that good with him?"

Killian regretted the words the moment they left his lips. His face fell, and he withdrew his hold.

Heat surged through my veins, and I had the sudden urge to slap him across the face. I balled my hands into fists, collecting blades of grass and dirt in my palms.

"I'm sorry," he gulped. "I... I'm still upset."

"He's not a bad person. I told him, no, and I chose you."

He brushed his finger down my cheek. "Yes, yes, you did."

"Killian!" Liam's voice rang out, closer this time. Killian lifted onto his knees.

"Liam," he clipped. "Walk north."

I lifted to my elbows. "We can trust him. Julie would scream. She would tell us not to come out."

The sound of movement came closer, and I scurried out from beneath Killian. When I turned, Julie's face met mine. We sprinted the short distance between us and slammed together in a hug.

I cried. There was no stopping the tears. They fell onto her back, one after the other. Julie echoed my sobs until I felt the light pull of Killian's hand on my shoulder.

I released her and saw red streaks across my forearm. I gasped, confused, and wiped the stain with my hand. It was blood, but I didn't know I had hurt myself.

"It's my blood," Julie said. Her hollow face gave me a weak smile. Her skin was pale and when I looked her over, I saw the sticky dark liquid soaked into her sleeve. Her arm hung limp at her side and blood dripped onto the forest floor.

"What happened?" Killian growled from behind me. He stepped toward Liam, and they stood toe to toe.

"Now's not the time for a dick measuring contest, boys," Julie joked. But her voice was so light. She used all her energy in our sprint toward each other. She wavered and stumbled into Liam.

"We had trouble with the implant," Liam answered. He picked Julie up like a child. She went limp in his arms, but he didn't budge from her weight. "But we have bigger problems. They know Alaina is out here. Wherever the hell here is. Her first husband saw us making a run for it."

"Charlie, yeah we know," Killian clipped. "They've pulled him in to draw us out. They want the way."

"The way?" Liam's voice rose in question.

"He doesn't know shit," Julie mumbled into Liam's chest. "And I don't have the energy to explain it."

"Wherever you're going, Julie and I are along for the ride."

"Julie is welcome. What makes you think you are?" Killian reached to grab Julie, and Liam stepped back, clutching her against his body.

"Listen, Killian. I know I upset you about the... garden thing. But where Julie goes, I go."

"Fuck you, Liam. You're the City's lackey."

"He goes," Julie whispered. She turned her head to Killian. "He goes."

Killian grunted at her and then conceded, giving a curt nod and reaching for her. Liam gripped her tighter. "I have her," he said. "Let's walk. You lead."

Killian studied him. "Did anyone see you? You yelled out here like an animal. You said yourself, we aren't alone."

"We've been behind them for most of the time. We followed them through the barrier, and then through the woods. They've gone back."

"Not for long," Killian said. "They'll come back to find us."

"They have a plan of action for things like this," Julie added. "They aren't good at deviating. They can't be on this side of the barrier for over twenty-four hours. They'll have to get the council to approve what they do next. We have some time."

Killian ripped off the sleeve of his shirt, tearing the fabric at the seam. He took Julie's arm with care and wrapped the makeshift bandage around her wound. "They won't give up. This is different. We took too many this time."

I looked down, knowing I was one of the many.

"Then we need to hurry," Liam deadpanned. Killian pulled the bandage taught and Julie winced. He turned on his heel and we followed.

Killian jogged in front, and I huffed behind them, the last of my adrenaline coursing through my veins. His steps were like hammers into the ground, and the rhythm thrummed in my head. *How long have we been running?*

The night faded, and I couldn't find the moon. The stars disappeared from the sky. We had to be close. Daylight was coming. My foot slipped from the slickness of the forest floor, and I hit my knee. I heard the footsteps stop.

"I'm fine," I said, breathless, and rose to my feet. I wiped my hands along the front of my pants and, in the dim light, saw red smear down my thighs. "Julie! Is she bleeding again?"

Liam laid her lifeless body on the floor. Her stomach rose and fell with each breath. She had fallen unconscious. He felt along her arm, lifting it and inspecting the bandage. "It's not her," Liam scowled. "Are you sure it's blood?"

The light grew with every passing second. I stood in a puddle of red. The smell of copper hit my nostrils as I lifted my palms toward the men.

"It's blood. I'm sure of it." I scanned the ground. Trails of it led out in front of us. "Should we see where it leads?"

"We don't have a choice." Killian's words came out with frustration. He scuffed the ground with his foot and stomped along the trail. "The blood... it's the way to the checkpoint. Stay here."

"No!" Liam and I spoke in unison. Killian stopped in his tracks without looking back.

"We stay together," I said. I took Killian's hand and yanked him forward. The smell of blood grew stronger with each step. "How much blood can someone lose and live?"

"Hopefully a lot," Liam answered. He looked at Julie's limp body as he spoke, and my heart sank.

"There." Killian pointed and broke out into a sprint. A body rested on its side in a clearing up ahead. The buzzing returned, a sudden jolt to my eardrums. I covered my ears and groaned. "It's okay. There's a wall here. Our wall," Killian yelled.

"Could it be someone that left with us?" I asked.

"One way to find out," Killian answered, and he shot toward them.

He reached the end of the blood trail and cocked his head at the limp body. He crouched down and rolled them to their side. Their arm flopped in the dirt, then lifted for a moment, outstretched to Killian. Killian shot up, standing stiffly above the man. He backed up, almost tripping over his heels.

"Are they alive?" I asked through uneven breaths, running to them both. I came to a sudden stop in front of a familiar face. I think I screamed, but the buzzing was so loud around us that it vibrated the trees and muted my speech.

I registered Killian beside me, removing what remained of his shirt. He remained silent as well, lowering back down over the bloodied man.

What do we do with this?

He pulled the remnants of his shirt to shreds and began wrapping Charlie's wounds.

Chapter 24

Together

ALAINA

"The men in your life, Alaina," Killian snarled. "Like magnets, all of them."

Charlie grunted while Killian pulled the final bandage tight around his middle. Something had gutted him, and I fought the urge to vomit when Killian pushed entrails back inside Charlie's stomach.

"Why fix him up?" Liam growled. He paced with Julie in his arms, and I watched him. He looked at her like she was something precious and fragile. Julie was right about him. He wanted someone forever and someone to need him. He wasn't the type of man that could let go.

Killian continued tending to his wound. "I would do the same for you. This is no way to die."

"But will he die?" I asked. I didn't know if they heard me over the hum all around us, but both men looked up.

"Well, that depends." Killian turned back to Charlie's lifeless body.

I knew what he meant without further explanation. If we left him here, he would die. *But could we do that?*

"Did officials do this to him?" I asked. My stomach turned at the blood that permeated everything around us. The ground had a red tinge everywhere I looked. A headache formed at the back of my skull.

"That's a subjective question."

"Please, Killian. A straight answer, for once."

"These wounds are from our traps. I'm familiar with them myself." Killian pointed to the lines and circular scars on his bare chest. "But they wouldn't do this unless... unless someone held him against our barrier wall. Tried to push him through, maybe. It's only fatal if you keep going. Charlie doesn't seem the type to do that without being forced. And it's painful. I don't know if anyone that could withstand it."

I had wondered how he earned those pale lines that covered his body. Some scars appeared faded, others were fresh. *Had he tried to get through on his own? Did he set up the wall and receive some injuries in the process?* This wasn't the time to ask those questions.

The pool of blood under Charlie stopped growing. I sat in the dirt by his side. He was a stranger now, but then again, he always had been. We never knew each other, because we didn't know ourselves. *And where the fuck was Drew?* That bastard should have bled out right next to him.

"Liam, we need to talk." Killian jerked his head, signaling Liam to walk with him. "We won't be far, but it's hard to hear over the wall," he yelled in my direction.

I nodded as Liam placed Julie beside me. A soft huff left her body, and I ran my fingers through her hair. I lowered my lips to her ear. "They whispered, you cannot withstand the storm. She whispered back, I am the storm."

I thought she curved her lips into a smile, but with the noise and my exhaustion, I wasn't sure. I wanted to talk to her, to ask her what happened to her, and what she thought we should do. I needed her advice and her help. More than anything, I needed her strength.

The bloodied bodies of two people who had been with me my entire life lay at my feet. The blinding sun had risen completely now. I could see the puffs of breath that left their lips, Charlie's more of a struggle than Julie's. I saw the flicker of the wall a short walk away. I wondered about the world beyond it, and how life would be there. Julie's hand cupped mine in a gentle hold. I squeezed hers and took slow, deliberate breaths.

I closed my eyes and thought about the three of us years before in school. I imagined we were laid out on the lawn, staring at this forest, talking about who we wanted to become. All our plans felt so stupid and pointless. We were pets in a cage, but we allowed it. We never asked questions and focused only on ourselves. I had to match with someone. That's all I cared about back then.

So selfish.

I knew what we had to do.

Killian and Liam returned, looking worse than when they had left. Liam tousled his hair, now almost brown from dirt and muck. Killian's muscles in his chest were tight and clenched, a sign of his frustration. They hadn't reached a conclusion, but I had.

"We are... at an impasse of sorts," Liam said and crouched to reach Julie. He ran his thumb against her cheek and held two fingers against her throat, subtly checking her pulse.

"Liam's a fucking idiot," Killian snapped.

"We cross together," I said. My voice bellowed out over the hum. I said it without pause, without question. "All five of us. We have to be true to ourselves, to the reason we are leaving. I'm not a murderer."

"He won't make it," Liam sneered. "He'll slow us down and cause problems. He could lead officials to us."

I stood up and faced Liam. "You wanted to leave Charlie here? And Killian wanted to take him with us?" I had thought Killian would vote for Charlie's demise, but I misjudged him. He was a better man than that.

I felt Killian's warmth behind me. His hands moved to my shoulders. "We cross together," he said in my ear.

Liam clenched his jaw and grumbled. "I don't know where we're going. I guess I'm outvoted because my partner's unconscious."

"She would agree with me," I said. "Julie believes every life is worth saving, no matter what the City thinks. No matter what you or I might think."

Something in Liam's eyes softened. I remembered the first day I met him. His blue eyes might have flashed in anger then, but it didn't last long. His purpose was to have someone forever. He had decided that someone was Julie, and she would have sided with me if she could have. Which meant Liam now agreed that we cross together.

"I have other decoders," Liam said and set Julie back down on the same patch of dirt. "I grabbed what I saw when I got the one for Alaina. I don't know why, but today I'm glad I did."

"Good. That saves his arm. I don't think he would survive more blood loss." Killian reached a hand out to Liam. "No time to waste, man."

Liam handed the device over, and Killian got to work with Charlie's left arm. I moved to Charlie's right. "Should I hold him down?"

"He's barely with us. He shouldn't feel this." I saw Killian jab the wire into Charlie's upper arm, needling his way into the flesh. Charlie grunted and moaned. "Shit, maybe he's more conscious than I thought. This will hurt less than your gut, but stay still."

Charlie moaned again and rolled, pulling his other arm upward. It flopped back down, smacking the blood that pooled at his side.

"Hold him down," Killian hissed. I recalled the pain of the decoder, but Charlie's recent injuries looked much worse. I held his arm down and he pushed against me, grunting. His eyes opened from half-lidded to wide, staring at me. He swallowed hard a few times and moved his head down toward the arm I held.

"Something's not right," I pleaded.

"A lot isn't right," Killian retorted. "Look at him."

Charlie's eyes met mine again. They looked down at the arm I held, and then back at me. He opened his lips to speak. No words left. He tried again. "Chip..." he choked out.

I nodded. "Yes, we have to take it out. You'll die out here and we can't have you tracked where we are going."

He moaned again and coughed, a bubbled sound that brought red to his teeth. I winced. "It's almost over."

He pulled his arm up. I tried to hold him down, but he was strong. This entire endeavor was turning into a test of athleticism.

"Chip... more," he spits out between coughs.

"What?" I shook my head and cupped both hands around his bicep. He smiled, eyes growing wide. "Chip," he repeated and suddenly, I understood. He flopped his head back onto the ground and passed out. I moved my hands along his arm frantically until I felt it. "How many decoders do you have?"

Killian didn't respond. He removed the wire from Charlie's arm and said, "got it," to himself.

"Do you have another decoder?" I yelled to Liam.

"Why?" he shot back. "Are we going to troll the woods for the officials and take a fucking party back with us?"

"There's another chip. Right here!" I rubbed the hard nodule under his skin. "That's what he was trying to tell us. They gave him another tracker."

Killian reached over and the look on his face told me I was right. The City knew we couldn't leave him hurt and alone. He was my ex-husband who I cried and pined for in the Separation Center not too long ago. They thought they had us.

Bait.

Charlie was bait.

"This is the last one," Liam said. "I'm going to run the perimeter and make sure no one is around or watching us. But if there are more chips, we leave him. He dies, agreed?"

"Agreed," Killian said without pause. I said nothing, but I knew Liam was right. Killian went to work on the second chip, and I checked almost every part of his body for more. He flopped back and forth under my movements, completely unaware of what was happening and unable to tell us if there were more.

"I don't think there are any others," I said. "I've checked almost everywhere."

"Almost?" Killian asked as he pulled the decoder from Charlie's other arm.

I gave Killian an awkward look. "Almost."

"For fuck's sake, where is there to check?"

Liam walked up, out of breath, and red-faced. "I'm sure we're alone, so if you're done, let's go."

We both looked up at him with blank expressions. "What's wrong?" Liam asked.

"Well. Um."

"I can't hear you. Speak up."

"Well, I've checked almost everywhere on Charlie. For another chip."

"Finish then," Liam snapped.

I looked at Charlie's crotch. It was stupid, I knew, but I was on shaky ground with Killian and *my men*, as he liked to call them. I jutted my chin forward. "Almost everywhere."

"Fuck," Liam let out a frustrated grunt, throwing his hands in the air. He crouched down and unbuttoned Charlie's pants, careful with his bandages, and felt around. "All clear. Let's go."

I felt my face flame red. Killian shrugged his shoulders and stood awkwardly over Charlie. "Okay." I saw his mouth move, but he said it to Charlie, not us. He pulled him up, cradling him like a child, and walked toward the bolts of light in the distance.

"Single file line," Killian yelled. The noise grew louder. Killian's voice sounded like he was far away, not right in front of me. Liam carried Julie behind me, and we walked forward like schoolchildren.

After a few minutes, Killian stopped in front of a wall with flashing beams of light. It vibrated and shook directly in front of him. A thick pulse of noise loomed over everything and it blocked my view beyond. I was in awe of its ominous presence. It looked scarier than the City's but the refugees didn't put forth the effort to conceal its danger.

"What are you doing?" Liam screamed from behind me. Killian didn't respond, and I wondered if he had heard.

"What are you..." I started.

Killian yelled back, "Deciding!"

I didn't know how to respond to that. He turned and set Charlie down. "I have to set off the barrier," he said. "To let them know we are here. It will flicker while they observe who is trying to cross. They will bring it down when they see us."

Killian's hand reached out toward the beams of light. He hesitated a moment and then jutted it forward. A bolt shot out, blasting Killian in the chest. The smell of burned skin came next, and I flew over him.

"Are you okay? What the fuck, Killian?"

He moaned and bent his chin down toward the wound. A perfect circle of blood pooled and then dripped over the side. That's where the scars were from. Every time he crossed, he suffered. Every scar was from helping others across.

He caught his breath and lifted to his feet. "I don't know how many more times I can get electrocuted," he joked. My eyes grew wide and my jaw dropped. "Don't worry. I'm not going back now that I've got you." The wall flickered to an unobstructed view of trees. It disappeared once, twice, and then, on the third time, the forest continued before us with nothing in our way.

Killian stumbled once, lifting Charlie into his arms, but he rose on the second time with him in tow. "Move," he yelled, but the buzzing had stopped and his words rang clear in my ears.

I ran behind him and turned to make sure Liam and Julie were at my heels.

I froze in place for a moment. The air left my lungs as I brought my palm over my mouth to scream. Liam caught up to me and bent down to my face. "Alaina, keep going," he ordered. I walked backward after him, unable to turn around.

I bumped into Killian moments later. "This is far enough," he said. "Let's wait and make sure it closes. Don't look at it."

I said nothing, and Killian's hand grabbed my shoulders, whipping me around. My head was the last to turn, stuck on the spot until it whipped back in his direction.

"The... the bodies," I stuttered.

I saw dozens of them. They tumbled over each other in piles of limbs. Decay and blood mashed together on the forest floor.

And one of them was Julie's husband, Drew.

Chapter 25

Martyred

JULIE

When I came to again, we were still walking. The walking never stopped. Well, Liam walked. I rocked in his arms, a natural sway with each step, wandering through this fucking forest.

I wanted to be grateful, to appreciate the miracle of being here, but all I felt was pain. Every movement brought sharp needles of agony burning through my arm, taking what little energy I had left.

The makeshift stitches only held my wound together at the surface. A gaping hole of melted flesh lay beneath.

What Liam and I didn't know, what we couldn't possibly have known, is what the City does when you attempt to deactivate your chip and they find out. Maybe we were close enough to the City center or Charlie tipped them off.

Either way, they knew.

Liam had to go first. I didn't know if I was strong enough to disable his chip with one hurt arm. I described the decoding process while working on him, and I'd only seen it completed once. We thought we were lucky when everything went smoothly, albeit painfully. He grunted and let out some cursing, but then it ended.

I knew when Liam began the process on me, he might fumble around, and I would feel pain. It had to be done, and I expected discomfort. The unending torture that followed - that was a surprise. My City electrocuted me from the inside out while Liam watched, desperate to help me.

He had moved the decoding wire into my arm, and I bit onto a wooden spoon, ready to start. A few moments later, blood poured from my arm in buckets, and we knew we were in trouble.

I screamed and writhed in agony. Liam pulled the wire out, thinking the searing pain and destruction to my body would cease if he removed the decoder. But he was wrong. The pain continued, worsened even. When I passed out, he reinserted the device and deactivated my chip. We smelled the burning flesh for hours afterward.

"It took too long for me to deactivate the chip." That's what Liam told me in the woods. He was unfamiliar with the process and so much of my muscle had been... destroyed. It was hard to see what he was doing in the mess.

That's not what happened.

The City did this to me.

When I heard Drew's voice in the woods, I thought I had hallucinated from blood loss. *Had we led them to us, or were they here first?* With my mind looped in an out of conscious thought, I couldn't know. We made it this far with sheer luck and no other choice.

And Liam.

The plan we once had was now a mess of blood and reckless decisions, but we had to keep going.

I later discovered Drew *had* been here with Charlie, threatening my best friend, pretending to care about me, and doing the City's bidding. Then he got himself killed like the fucking dumbass he always had been.

And I must have entered an alternate reality because Killian was hauling a half-dead Charlie in his arms like his first-born child.

Fuck you, Charlie. You belong in the dirt along with Drew.

The moment the thought hit me, I wondered if my sadness would follow. I loathed Drew, but he was the father of my boys. He should be in the City looking after them. *Someone needed to look after them.*

I wasn't a crier. Alaina brought it out of me more than anyone else. Despite the ache in my chest when I was fully conscious and able to process the news of Drew's death, I had no tears for him.

I would save those for worthier causes.

My boys, Carrie, and Rafael, all remained out of my reach. Others had their part against the City, but their involvement was untraceable. I saved my tears for my friends — for people that I loved.

"What were you deciding?" Alaina asked. Her words came out slowly. She was tired. We were all so tired.

"What?" Killian asked.

"When we crossed the refugee barrier. You stood there and said you were deciding. What about?"

Killian laughed. A loud and guttural sound that echoed all around us. I smiled to myself. My eyes remained closed in hopes I could sleep again, but it seemed I was awake for good this time.

"I was thinking about making Liam break the barrier and get his chest seared. Maybe even Charlie, if he wasn't half-dead already."

"And you wanted all the glory?" Liam barked from behind us. "Or are you a masochist?"

"They would have seen you and killed you on the spot, Liam," Killian shot back. "And I think I've proven to be more of a sadist lately."

I chuckled against Liam's chest. "Julie?" he whispered to me.

"Is she up? Her timing is good," Killian interjected.

I turned my head towards him and saw them in the distance. Transports moved in our direction, and this, I thought, was a reason for tears.

Killian cursed while they settled Charlie and me on the floor of a vehicle. He wrapped a rope around Charlie to secure him in place and wedged a seat cushion against my side. The ride would be bumpy, and I grimaced at the thought.

Alaina fell asleep once we were on the move. We had been traveling for hours on foot. The others had made it to our new home the day before, and Aiden didn't wait. *That glorious, stubborn bastard.*

"We are too close to the wall with transports," Killian hissed. "They shouldn't have risked it. They should have met us on foot, as planned, with supplies."

"We wouldn't make it," I choked. "I... I wouldn't make it."

His face grew solemn. I felt his eyes scan my broken body. He nodded once and lifted himself to a seat by Alaina, resting his arm around my sleeping friend.

"Are you comfortable?" Liam asked, making his way inside.

"Fuck, no," I said. "But I'll make it."

That might be a lie.

I knew I was close to death. My heart had a slow rhythm and with each pulse, I felt a small trickle of blood leave my body. Breathing had been difficult. I had to think about each intake of air and focus on filling my lungs, feeding my body the precious resource. I refused the water offered to me. I couldn't imagine how to swallow it or keep it down. I needed intravenous fluids and a shit ton of painkillers.

Aiden was in the transport ahead of us. He thought I couldn't hear him when he ordered our driver to go at maximum speed for the rest of the journey. No one with medical training came with them, and he knew I had little time.

What should I do with my last moments, if these are my last moments?

I thought seriously about killing Charlie. I even thought up how I would succeed at the task. It wouldn't take much effort. I could remove his bandages and his guts would fall out from what I heard.

Alaina had insisted I wouldn't leave him to die. Old Julie would have felt that way. The bitter woman I was today might kill him out of spite for being a liar, for being Drew's friend. I would never tell her. She didn't need to know me like that, so full of hate.

He won't make it, anyway.

It was a three-day walk to town, but how fast could the transports get us there? I did the math in my head. We were slower than expected moving on foot thanks to injuries. These transports had huge tires and, thankfully, good shocks.

We would be there in a few hours.

I had a lot to think about, given that time. Liam looked at me like he owned me during our journey. I made Liam promises. I'm not a saint, I'm a survivor. Could we trust each other? Were we in a relationship of convenience? I doubted Liam's infatuation with Alaina would fade overnight? Now he was with her, at least in proximity.

I heard Liam snore in the seat at my back. Killian drifted to sleep minutes later. None of them had anything left, and they might awaken to find me dead.

The last thing I would see was Charlie. *Fuck, that's awful.* He was still a problem. I looked over at him, examining the lifeless man who took shuddered breaths while the transport weaved through the woods.

His body moved slightly with each turn and bump, but no blood formed underneath him.

Shit, maybe he'll make it. Or maybe he's already dead.

"Hey," I whispered. We lay close to each other on the floor of the vehicle. My body wedged up on my good arm, and my lips pointed to his ear. "Charlie," I said again.

No response.

I grunted. We hit a hard turn, and he swayed to one side and dropped back, flat on his back. His face contorted, but it could have been a reflex.

"Dickhead," I spat, louder this time.

His eyes blinked open slowly. He looked drugged and slurred something back to me.

"He lives," I hissed and rested my head back down on the floor.

"I'm s... sor...," he slurred.

"Don't waste your breath."

"Sorry," he got out.

"Yes, you are." I closed my eyes, wishing I could turn away from him. This was the worst pillow talk I'd ever had, and I'd left Liam with bruises not too long ago.

"Drew," he continued.

"Oh, Drew's dead," I snapped. "You probably should be, but here you are." Everyone remained asleep. A hollow sound of wind rushed against the walls. Another bump and we both groaned.

"I kn... know," he stuttered. "Sorry. I h-had to."

I opened my eyes, and Charlie looked right at me. His eyes were no longer empty and lifeless.

"Had to what?"

His lip quivered, trying to speak.

"Had to what?" I asked again.

"To kill..." he trailed off. "Us."

We stared at each other, letting minutes tick between our silent bodies. I didn't trust him, but he had my attention now.

"Kill us?" I asked. "You had a murder-suicide with my husband or something?"

"They... they would have come."

I never thought of Charlie as a coward, as Liam had described him. He was safe, easy, and maybe even a little boring. He abided by the rules and didn't like confrontation.

But a martyr?

Would he die for Alaina, for others?

I didn't know anymore.

"They... are," he said. A trickle of blood left his lips. He left Alaina after ten years. That didn't make him a monster. I hated him, but he never visited the pleasure houses with Drew. I couldn't see Charlie killing his unborn child, but then again, Drew caught me off guard with that one.

"They are what?" I echoed. My neck craned toward him. The slow pump of my heart sped up. Blood rushed from my arm and dripped down the front of my chest.

Charlie's eyes grew wide. "Coming. They are coming."

Chapter 26

Sanctum

JULIE

"He hasn't woken up yet?" Alaina's voice cracked with the question. She paced in the small white room. Light beamed in through the windows, warming my skin.

We had made it. Every damn one of us.

I was told familiar faces lined the streets when we arrived, cheering and crying happy tears. Friends I helped last year ran to the town center when they learned of my unexpected arrival. But after my conversation with Charlie in the transport, my memory went blank. Our arrival was a black void in my memory. I woke up with tubes running out of my arms and throat and Liam resting on a cot at my side.

In the last hour of our journey, a fever had taken over. My conversation with Charlie had manifested into some kind of panicked episode. I'd started hallucinating and convinced myself the City had followed us.

Killian later told me what had happened. My body burned from the inside out, overtaken by infection, making me sound crazy. No one believed the threats were real, but I feared the City coming here. I believed what Charlie had said in the transport. He had said they were coming, *didn't he?*

They put me under for two days, treating the fever and my wound. Charlie remained in a coma one room over. Liam slept like a puppy by my side. My head pounded and my body ached. They may have removed most of the tubes, but I still felt the burn in my throat and soreness in my hands and arms.

"Fuck," I hissed. The nurse pulled the string on my stitches taut, and a bolt of pain hit me. She had numbed the area, but I still had some feeling.

"Almost done, dear," she mumbled, and I fidgeted in my bed, eager to escape.

I continued my conversation with Alaina. "I didn't imagine what Charlie said. I know I sounded out of my mind on the way here..."

"You were crazed," Alaina interrupted. "A complete maniac."

"Yes, well, I was out of my fucking mind with fever, but... I remember what Charlie said. Clear as a bell. I remember the way his face looked and the way he said it. He told me they were coming. I would bet my life on it. The fever dreams came later."

"It's not that I don't believe you."

"Then you don't believe Charlie."

Alaina stopped pacing. She went up on her tiptoes to see outside the window. "I just want to talk to him when he wakes up... if he wakes up."

"I do too. I know what he said, but I have more questions. He knows something."

Alaina tapped on the window. "They're still out there."

"My receiving line?"

"Yep. Sitting on blankets in the sun, reading books I've never heard of before. Wearing clothes I couldn't even dream of. No bracelets. No fear."

My body tensed. *They should be afraid.*

The nurse finished and cleaned her area. She pulled Liam aside and gave him instructions about caring for my wound. I would never regain full use of this arm, but I could live with that. I'd cut it off myself if it meant freedom. This wasn't how I wanted it to happen, but I was here. I was grateful. And Liam was the obedient partner, collecting gauze and making notes on a tablet.

I rolled my eyes and grunted, edging off the bed. Liam met my side a moment later, helping me to my feet. His fingers brushed the inside of my gown, making my skin tingle. Fuck him for being so attractive *and good with those hands.*

Alaina looked back at us with a smile. "Remember when we would do that at school?" I asked. "We would set blankets out on the lawn and study together. I remember Killian would be around, staring at the woods."

"Yes - I... Yes, I remember that," Alaina said, biting her bottom lip. "It feels like another life. Another..."

"World," I finished her sentence. "It very much was. So, I heard you got kicked out of the communal housing."

Alaina's skin turned bright red. She clapped her hand over her mouth and groaned. "Oh, shit. I bet I'm a laughingstock already. What did you hear?"

"Just that Killian fucked you senseless in the cots and the others said it was fine in the woods, but enough was enough. They volunteered to help finish your house if they didn't have to hear your moaning and squeals anymore."

Alaina slapped my good arm. "That's not true!"

"It's an exaggeration, but it kind of is."

"Well, I'm the first... um... citizen this round with a finished house, so jokes on them I guess."

"You're the first refugee, you mean?"

She moved away from the window and sat in the corner chair. Liam wrapped his arms around my waist from behind.

"Refugee," she said, letting the words slowly fall from her lips. "That's what we are."

I nodded, and Liam pulled me against his chest. "Our house is ready," he whispered into my ear. I froze. *Our house? What other promises had I made to this man in my fever-induced insanity?*

"Liam... I appreciate everything you have done. And — and, I like you," I stuttered.

"You have to stay with someone," Alaina stopped me. "You will be on strong antibiotics for a long time, along with pain killers. You need rehabilitation for your arm. I volunteered you for a family home. Liam will help you."

My mouth formed a straight line. Alaina's intentions may have been good, but a part of her wanted Liam coupled off. He was still a significant problem in her and Killian's perfect world, and it was easier to keep him preoccupied with another woman.

I clucked to myself and looked back out the window. Someone had to keep an eye on him, anyway. He didn't choose to leave the City, and this town will want him watched. I might as well get some orgasms out of the deal.

I moved closer to the window. My nose went flat against the pane of glass. "Erin's out there."

Alaina shot up. "She is? Can we go say hi?"

"Sure. I take it she found you?"

Alaina gave an eager nod. She already had a hand on the door handle. Liam reached behind me to lift me, and I pushed him off. "Okay, that's enough. I can walk. It's not that serious."

"No," he said and lifted me in one motion. I hated how the act turned me on, sending a rush of heat through my body.

Alaina stopped by Charlie's room again on our way out, but she couldn't gain entry inside. "I don't have access," she huffed. Last I heard, he was unconscious but stable. I needed him to wake up. He had things left to say.

Dozens of people stood when we exited the medical unit, me in Liam's arms and Alaina hovering just behind us. Killian jogged up to us and clapped. Then the encore of cheers ensued and the cynical side of me took a back seat. At that moment, the emptiness inside me subsided. The damage to my soul healed a bit more when I saw their faces.

Good people.

People like me and Alaina.

Maybe Liam too.

Alaina shot around us to hug Killian, which turned into a kiss full of open mouths and teeth, and I felt Liam's chest rise in a chuckle. They couldn't keep their hands off each other.

Alaina broke free and greeted Erin. Liam walked us over and sat me down on a blanket with the women. I exhaled. A slow release of breath I had been holding for what felt like years.

"Liam," I cooed. My acting skills took over once more. "I need some girl time."

"Sure thing," he agreed.

He went back into the medical unit with Killian, and Erin took my hand. "I can't believe you're here." She reached her other hand out to Alaina. "Both of you. And healthy." She looked me over once more. "Healthy-ish?"

The sun beat down on my skin, making it blush. I would sunburn, and I reminded myself to explain that to Alaina if Killian hadn't already.

"How about not dead?" I smirked. "That's all I've been shooting for the past few days. Not fucking dead is just fucking great."

Erin shifted her gaze from side to side, and Alaina stiffened. No one sat around us within hearing distance. I lifted to my good elbow. "Spit it out," I snapped.

Erin's demeanor changed as she tilted her head and rubbed the back of her neck. She smacked her lips and edged closer to me. "People are upset about the extras. Not you, of course. But... Charlie and Liam are causing some problems."

"I'm fucking upset about the extras," I added.

"Stop," Alaina whined. "We did the right thing. And Liam saved your life."

"It got all fucked up is all I mean," I countered. "We weren't supposed to be here. My boys are back in the City with no parents."

Ever since I let my guard down with Alaina, I was messing up everywhere. I had put her in danger when I went to Liam for the decoder. That's when I started comingling our alliances. Business or pleasure became a mixed bag. I had lost my focus.

Our careful plan went to shit the day after her escape. How did that happen? I didn't account for something *or someone*. Liam swore he had nothing to do with it, but I kept replaying the night over and over again in my mind. It was a blur of blood and anger and sex. I couldn't figure it out.

And now, with the threat of the City at our heels, it felt like everything was falling apart. And Charlie needed to wake the fuck up.

"Finding Charlie may have been a blessing in disguise," Alaina interjected. "Did you hear about the wall? Sanctum's wall? All the dead bodies there?"

We were in Sanctum, then. I knew Alaina would be safe, but I never knew the location Killian would take her or the name of the town. That was by design. If the City tortured me, I could never give her up.

"The City has been trying to get people through for some time," Alaina continued. "They even put extra chips in Charlie when he couldn't pass through. We removed it, but Julie swears..." Alaina drifted off and looked at me.

"I swear Charlie told me the City is coming. Then he passed out, and I got so sick I lost my damn mind, and here we all are, together," I huffed. "The refugee camps control the wall. They know people are trying to get through. They killed them, Alaina, to protect us."

Alaina huffed out a breath and wiped her palms on her thighs. "I'm just saying, we know the City is responsible for their deaths. We know they're getting desperate, and Charlie may know something useful."

Erin looked around once more and took a deep breath. "Are you sure you aren't trying to make a reason for your ex-husband to be here? It would be normal to still have... feelings for him. I'm not saying he'll get banished as sick as he is, but... I don't know. I'm just saying people aren't happy."

"And here comes Killian again, so let's talk about something else," I hissed to both women.

Killian jogged over, and Liam walked at a steady pace behind him. The moment I saw their faces, I knew something wasn't right. Alaina's smile dropped, too, and I struggled to stand. Alaina made it halfway to them by the time I got to my feet.

"What's wrong?" I yelled across the grass. The surrounding voices hushed at my words, ready to eavesdrop on our conversation. I felt the stares settle on me, and I braced myself against Erin. She hooked her arm into mine, and I yelled again, "What's going on?"

Alaina let out a scream and covered her mouth with her hand. Killian's face was stern, but he reached out to her and held her. Whatever he said to her, he kept himself void of emotion.

Liam kept walking toward me. Hushed whispers began around Killian and Alaina. Liam reached to put his hands on my arms and pulled them back, remembering my injury. He took a cautious step forward and reached for my good hand, and held it in his.

"Liam," I growled. "What is going on?"

"It's Charlie." Liam squeezed my hand harder as if I would run. "He's gone."

"Define gone. Missing?"

Liam shook his head and stepped closer. "He's dead."

I held my breath, knowing I would never get my answers. I wondered if Liam held my hand so tight because he thought I might hit him out of frustration.

My instincts had been off lately, but I knew at that moment, deep in my soul, someone had killed Charlie.

Chapter 27

Tomorrow

ALAINA

"Stop watching the footage. You're driving yourself crazy." Killian pulled at my shoulders, but I shrugged him off. The monitor consumed my thoughts. I watched it over and over, looking for clues, examining every footstep, every person, every moment.

Video feeds ran along the borders of the refugee towns. Our new home, Sanctum, recorded the surroundings of their barrier wall. They recorded the entire town, but unlike the City, the footage was free to everyone.

Once I discovered this and considered what Charlie had said on the transport here, I became obsessed.

"Please, baby," Killian pleaded. "Come back to bed."

I had to stop at some point, but something was there. Charlie was dead, and this was all we had to go on.

I couldn't understand why I cared so much. His injuries had been severe. It surprised no one when he passed. But something wasn't right.

He died after making it all the way here. He had round-the-clock medical care, and no one tried to revive him?

Julie seemed off about it as well, but she hated Charlie. I assumed she blamed herself for wishing him dead time and time again. But something nagged at the back of my mind. His death meant something. I had to dig further. I had to know.

I restarted the footage again. "Just one more time," I said over my shoulder, and Killian retreated with a groan.

The screen flicked to life again. I saw officials with Charlie and Drew. The group paced around the wall for a half hour. Then they disappeared from the camera's view. When they returned, Charlie rubbed his arm and looked down at it a few times. *That's when they put in the second chip.*

They all talked for a few more minutes. Charlie was looking down and Drew wasn't facing the camera, so I couldn't read their lips. I'm not especially skilled in that talent, but I could have tried.

Then an argument broke out. It was a violent disagreement that started with yelling and ended with shoving and an angry right hook from Charlie. Blood sprayed from Drew's mouth and flickered into the frequency wall at their side.

Drew grabbed something from his pocket and tried to speak into it. Charlie knocked the object from Drew's hands. It tumbled to the ground at their feet. They continued to fight, and Charlie knocked Drew to the ground.

Charlie scrambled after the device and stomped on it, crushing it under his boot. Drew got up, and Charlie pushed him into the frequency wall. He held him there while Drew thrashed and fought. They spun and switched places. Now Charlie fought and clawed at Drew's face. Spurts of blood covered the ground, and I saw Charlie's feet step backward, further into the wall.

Then the footage was filled with flashes of light. Bolts of bright white shot out, making the playback nothing but a blinking white screen. The picture in front of me hid what happened in those precious moments.

I froze the spots between the flashes again and again, but I couldn't make out the picture. When the blinking light stopped, Drew was gone and Charlie stumbled forward and hit his knees. He fell to the ground, holding his stomach. I scrolled the footage forward. No one else came, and Charlie didn't move. An hour later, the video showed Killian at his side.

The same loop over and over. Nothing new. No clues to show what Drew had in his hand that Charlie destroyed. Did Charlie kill Drew to protect us, or was that storyline already written in my head? Maybe I saw what I wanted.

Killian's hands ran through my hair when the screen turned black. He brought his lips to my neck and grazed them across a sensitive spot. My skin prickled, and I closed my eyes. They burned from constant hours in front of the screen. Killian's warm chest pressed against my back, and I knew I'd completed my research for the night.

He reached around me and shut off the monitor. "That's enough," he whispered.

"I know," I breathed. "I need to step away from it. There's something in this footage, but I'm too close. I need to sleep on it."

"I know what you need," Killian hissed into my skin. He pulled me back into his lap and moved his hand around my waist. His fingers fiddled for a moment with the tie on my shorts and then found their way inside.

I arched my back against him. "We have to be quieter," I moaned. "There have been complaints."

Two fingers entered me at once, and I groaned, already louder than I had intended. The sensation overwhelmed me and pulled my thoughts from the recording. Charlie and Drew's last days felt far away. Their moment by the wall was a mystery I couldn't unlock, and it made me crazy. But Killian's touch made me completely insane.

"More," I begged. He moved his fingers in and out of me at a steady pace. The heel of his palm rubbed my clit, and I matched his rhythm with my body and my breath. His other hand moved underneath my shirt. "Please," I repeated.

"Unbutton your shirt," Killian whispered.

My shaking hands moved to my nightshirt, freeing the silken fabric and dropping it to my elbows. Killian growled and slid eager hands over my breasts, pinching and pulling at my nipples. I bucked against him from the sensation.

He pushed inside me a few more times and then removed his touch. I cried out in protest. "Turn around," he commanded.

My legs already wobbled underneath me as I moved to face him. He unbuckled his pants, pulling his cock free. I salivated at the sight of him stroking the length. The way his mouth fell open and his large hand wrapped around himself made me desperate to have him inside me.

I moved forward, but his open palm pressed against my bare stomach, holding me back. "Watch," he said.

And I obeyed.

I kept my eyes on the show, the way he pumped his length in front of me, teasing me, torturing me. He moved faster, and a sheen of sweat formed on his chest. His eyes remained locked on mine. I reached down, seeking my release, and touched myself in return.

"Clever girl," Killian hissed. His stroking was now fevered and his breaths came out heavy and thick. "Take... your panties off. Show me."

And I obeyed once more.

I couldn't say no to Killian. I didn't want to, either. Every sexual encounter with him brought me pleasure. He wouldn't rest until he knew he'd left me sated and lifeless.

He kicked his pants further down and spread his legs wide, continuing to pump himself.

"Please, Killian," I breathed. I continued to stroke my clit and inched closer to him. He didn't stop me this time.

His low voice rumbled, "Show me more. Just get yourself close. I'll do the rest."

I nodded and sat spread apart on his thighs, leaving a space between us. Every part of me was open to him, my body, and my heart.

He loved me, and I loved him. We said it all the time now. We said it every time we left each other, if only for a minute. I swore I repeated it in my sleep.

"I love you," I panted. "I need you. Please."

He cocked a smile. "Take it."

And once again, I obeyed.

I placed my hands on his shoulders and pressed myself against his chest, his cock at my entrance. I cried out when I slid down, taking him completely. *Fuck the noise complaints.*

"Fuck, I'll never tire of this," Killian groaned. His hands grabbed my ass and thrust me up and down at a ferocious pace.

Every time my skin slapped against his thighs, the air knocked from my lungs. "So... close," I breathed.

"Me too, Laney. Me too."

I held myself against him with his cock buried to the hilt. I rocked my hips, gasping and moaning. His fingernails dug into my ass, and I returned the gesture, scratching along his wide muscled back.

"Fuck!" he roared. He exploded inside me as I came with him. The rushes of pleasure coursed from my core and poured throughout my body.

I rocked more until he halted my movements, holding my hips still. "Stop. I... I can't. Oh, fuck." And I felt his pulse inside my walls slow.

I disconnected our bodies with a moan, and I walked to the restroom on unsteady legs. Killian gave a soft chuckle behind me. "I love you," he shouted after me.

"And I love fucking you, too." I laughed and flicked on the bathroom light.

We cleaned up, and I took a hot shower. I let the water rush over me until my skin pruned. When I opened the door to our bedroom, puffs of steam billowed inside. Killian rested on his side with his tablet in hand, reading.

"There's a town meeting tomorrow," he remarked. "There will be an important discussion and vote. They mandated everyone to attend." His eyebrows creased together, and he sat up.

I let my towel drop, but his focus remained on what he read. "What's that mean?" I attempted a playful walk to the bed and stretched myself in front of him.

"Sanctum is not like the City. Rulers don't decide everything. We vote."

"We who?"

"All of us. The refugees. We all vote to decide on important matters."

"Like what?"

Killian let out a puff of air and looked up. "Fuck, you look good naked," I smirked in response. "Put on some clothes if you want to just talk." I wiggled under the covers and pulled the blanket to my neck. "Overkill, but that works," he mocked.

"Am I allowed a vote?" I asked.

"Yes. You are a citizen, a refugee."

I thought about the concept, still confused by the notion. Never in my life did my opinion matter to decision makers. There were laws, and you followed them. The City said it was, and so it was. I never questioned *the way of things*, and they didn't ask for my input. "Okay, so what are we voting on?"

"It doesn't say, but I have a guess."

Moments ticked by. I rolled my eyes. "Do you want me to guess? Is this a game?"

"No, I just... I'm not sure, but they haven't decided what to do with Liam. There is still the unknown about Charlie's warning. They didn't call this meeting over what meat we store for winter or if we can resume visits to the other civilizations. It feels bigger than that."

I didn't bother to ask what he meant by storing meat for winter. In the past few weeks, I had learned I didn't know what seasons truly were in the outside world.

"Whatever it is," I said and ran a finger down his cheek, "we'll figure it out together."

Killian nodded. "It's at two o'clock tomorrow." He pulled my blanket down, exposing my bare stomach. He placed a wide palm over my reddened skin. "We will have enough time for the appointment."

"Are you coming to the clinic with me?" I asked.

Killian kissed my forehead. "I wouldn't miss it. I think tomorrow may bring lots of surprising news."

Chapter 28

Risks

JULIE

The room felt hot and overcrowded. I tried to protect my tender arm from the horde of people, but they collided with me, wandering throughout the space. The town meetings never started on time, but I didn't know that. I waited and watched, ready for something to happen. I brushed my thumb over a coin given to me upon entry. I was told it was for a vote.

Everyone came over to my shadowed corner to say hello. My attempts to hide failed now that I was out in the open. I had retreated to my home with Liam after Charlie's death, and today's sudden influx of strangers made my skin crawl.

They talked about everything but Charlie, and everything but what brought us all here. No one seemed certain of the agenda, but rumors spread like a wildfire throughout the town. Liam pretended it didn't bother him, but he stayed home, complaining of a headache. Worry filled his thoughts. I caught him pacing in the night, mumbling to himself.

I wasn't much help to him, consumed with my plans. I'd spent the last few weeks focused on getting better.

Hours of painful rehabilitation and exercise filled my days. I ran long distances with my arm strapped to my body in a sling, ignoring the throbbing pain from my wound. Liam trailed behind me, cursing and agitated with my resolve.

He supported me despite his objections. Sex had a way of making a man agreeable. And all we did was argue and fuck - in that order. The disagreements seemed less important after the fucking.

Lately, our encounters had held a twinge of violence. Our time together teetered near the edge of safety. We had always maintained a subtle undertone of loathing when we were together. I found part of Liam irresistible, but I blamed him inwardly for the unspoken things. He represented the City and everything I hated. He'd loved Alaina first or at least lusted for her. And I wasn't sure I could trust him.

Did he have a part in Alaina's botched escape or Charlie's death? Did he still think of Alaina? Did he think of her when he was inside me?

All those questions rushed to the surface when we were together. He wanted to be gentle with me because of my injury, but every time I pushed him to his limits.

Last night, with the stress of the impending town meeting, something in us broke. I slapped him hard across his chest, leaving a red handprint. He groaned and gripped my hips tighter, grinding me against his body.

Then I went too far. I hit him in the face once, then twice. My hands made their own decisions, and I struck him until he grabbed my wrists. I screamed from the pain in my bad arm. A panicked look crossed his face, and we both came to our senses, frozen in time and shocked at my actions.

"I can't do this anymore. I can't be like... t-this with you," he stammered. "I need to find you again. Find us." He scrambled out from beneath me, and I said nothing. My mouth opened and closed as I sat on our bed naked, with no explanation for my actions.

He crept back into our room in the middle of the night and held me gently. I felt his warm breath on my hair, and I caressed his arm that wrapped around my middle. We didn't speak about it in the morning either. He complained of his headache and murmured about not being considered a refugee anyway, and I left.

Alaina arrived with Killian and was all smiles. Her worries were behind her and that gave me relief. All I wanted was for her safety and happiness. She appeared to be both when she sauntered over to me.

"You're late," I deadpanned.

"These things never start on time," she said and waved her hand around the room, then placed it on her stomach.

"You couldn't tell me that this morning?"

"Sorry. It's been a wild day." She beamed at me and gave me a side hug.

"What was that for?"

"Just because I love you," she shrugged.

A voice came over the room and asked everyone to quiet down and take a seat. Alaina sat next to me and waved over at Killian. He couldn't make it to us, caught up in a group of people. He gave a shrug of defeat and sat with other refugees a few rows over.

"Do you want me to trade places with him?" I asked her.

"No need," she said and held my hand. She was affectionate today, but her touch helped me relax. I hadn't realized how wound up I'd become in anticipation of this meeting.

An elderly woman came into view at a podium. White hair fell just below her shoulders. She wore a maroon suit with a long bronze necklace that hung down to her stomach. Her smile was wide and kind.

"Thank you for coming today, citizens of Sanctum," she said. Her smooth voice echoed throughout the room. The crowd nodded and raised their hands to their chest, palms pressed together. Their fingers curled around each other, making a fist in the center of their chest and holding it there while standing. Alaina and I looked around, confused. Killian looked back at us and repeated the motion. I tried it and felt ridiculous, but I followed along. When everyone released their hands, I did the same.

"We have an important matter to discuss. I understand there are several concerns that anguish our inhabitants of Sanctum. I wish to remedy that today with your help. We will vote on these matters and extinguish the concerns."

She moved her chin to her chest and brought her hands together in the same motion. The crowd mimicked her again. Alaina and I repeated the action a few seconds after everyone else, still feeling out of place.

"Liam of Discovery Center 3, please come forward."

My entire body tensed and I gripped Alaina's hand, my arm throbbing with the pressure. Alaina's jaw clenched and her eyes grew wide. She had to expect this. I know I did, but the words leaving this woman's mouth still made us coil up with nerves.

Everyone grew quiet, with only a few creaks from the turning of bodies in chairs. I saw Killian out of the corner of my eye, darting his head around the room. He met my gaze, and I shook my head, "no", in his direction. Killian stood and walked toward the woman. Each footstep sent a trepidatious ripple throughout my body.

"Your Honor," Killian addressed the woman. "Liam is not present today. I will stand in for him."

"As you wish," she answered. "The subject at hand is regarding his citizenship. Are you willing to speak on his behalf?"

"Yes," Killian said and stood by the woman. His size towered over her frame, but her presence commanded the room. He curled his shoulders downward and tilted his chin toward the floor. She had power here, and Killian knew that.

"Liam of Discovery Center 3 has breached Sanctum's borders without the vote of its citizens honoring a request. If Sanctum allows his residency, a separate vote will take place regarding penance for these actions. But first, Killian, would you like to say a few words in request of his citizenship?"

Killian nodded and took a step forward. I heard Alaina let out a shuttered breath, and I realized I was holding mine. I exhaled and felt my eyes burn with impending tears. *Fuck, I'm falling in love with Liam.*

"Liam risked his life to protect others on our journey to Sanctum. His encroachment on Sanctum was unintended but necessary to save the lives of my... partner, Alaina, and our friend Julie." He pointed back to us and a few heads turned. Killian motioned his palm upward with a flick, and I assumed he wanted us to stand. We rose to our feet a moment, scanning the room with befuddled expressions, and then sat back down.

"Yes, and we will discuss Julie's citizenship status after Liam's," the woman said.

"What?" Alaina and I both clipped in unison. I stood back up, and Alaina shot to her feet as well. The woman raised a finger to speak, but Killian interjected, "Please take a seat." His hard gaze shot to us, almost pleading with us to oblige without question.

"Yes," the woman said. "We have a just system. We appreciate everything you do for our safe havens, Julie, but we must vote for your residency as well. It's only fair, but it's only a formality."

I hesitated for a moment and sat back down. Alaina followed with a huff, clearly displeased by the circumstances. She brought her palms to her stomach, moving one hand back and forth. I noted her actions and refocused on Killian.

"Regarding Liam," Killian continued. "he showed courage, persistence, and honor, helping others escape the City and bringing them to safety. These are qualities that would benefit Sanctum. We would be lucky to have him as a citizen."

The crowd grumbled, and my pulse quickened. These bastards had already made up their minds.

"Can you align your citizenship status with his, Killian?" the woman asked.

"W-what?" he stuttered in response. They looked at each other and the crowd shifted in their seats.

"If Liam were to break our laws, we would banish him from Sanctum. If we align your citizenship status with him, you would then have to leave as well. If he possesses the quality of character you describe, it should be no issue. So I ask again, can you align your citizenship status with his?"

Killian paused and looked outward at me and Alaina. She lowered her head. A minute passed, and the woman cleared her throat.

"No," Killian clipped.

"I see," she acknowledged, placing her hands on the edge of the podium. "Do you have anything else to add before we vote?"

"Just that... I think he would be a good citizen, but I can't risk abandoning Alaina and my..." he stopped short. He swallowed and raised his shoulders. "I must reiterate the bravery he displayed on our journey. I owe him a debt of gratitude."

"But not everything," the woman added.

Killian's eyes bore into hers. He said nothing and stepped down.

"Would anyone else like to speak on behalf of Liam before we vote?"

I sat frozen in my seat. Alaina kept her gaze downward, rubbing her hand across her stomach. I felt a tear fall. *Dammit, stop crying.*

"Then we vote," she said before I could rise to my feet. I felt the room spin around me. Everything moved too fast. "Please bring your tokens to the front in an orderly line. Where Killian stood would be a vote for Liam of Discovery Center 3 to become a citizen of Sanctum. The basket to my left would be a vote for banishment."

"We're leaving!" I shouted over her words. I didn't recognize the sound of my voice. It came out with a low rumble, threatening anyone to question my resolve.

"Julie," the woman said. "Is that you?"

I stood. The room turned to me. Faces filled with confusion looked back, but my focus remained on the leader up front. "Liam and I are leaving. I know how this vote will turn out."

"Then you must be mistaken about your citizenship vote. I can all but guarantee Sanctum wants to have you here."

"But I don't want to be here... without Liam."

When I said the words, I knew they were true. Liam and I were two special brands of fucked up. We didn't belong in the City, but we didn't belong in Sanctum.

We belonged together. Both of us were broken, both of us forgiving each other for all the mistakes we had made.

Alaina tugged at my arm. "Why are you doing this?" she pleaded.

I took her face in my hands. Her tear-filled eyes looked desperately back up at me. "I'm sorry. I won't see your belly grow or hold your baby in my arms. But I'll be back. I'll meet her."

Alaina's tears came out in buckets. A throaty sob escaped her, and she begged again, "Please don't leave me. I just got you back. Why are you doing this?"

Killian walked over to us and held Alaina in his arms. I looked around the room, thinking about the faces I saw. I knew some of their stories, but they didn't know mine.

"I request permission to go back to the City with Liam," I said, attempting to sound more respectful.

People gasped and stood in outrage.

"So he can tell them where we are and the City can come to kill us all?" a man yelled in my direction.

I realized at that moment, that banishment may be a word for death. They didn't trust Liam to keep Sanctum's location safe.

"They are already trying to get here. You know that," I shot back.

Alaina's sobs quieted, and Killian moved to my side. "She's right," he added. "It's a matter of time before we have a breach."

"We already have a breach with Liam!" another woman yelled.

"Silence!" the woman at the podium bellowed, and the room quieted. "Julie, explain your request. We will vote. No other outcry will be necessary. Do I make myself clear?"

The room of refugees lowered their chins down and placed their palms together, seating themselves.

I walked to where Killian had stood and cleared my throat. "I wish someone had given my son a chance," I began. The words made my heart pang with hurt, but I continued. "The City took his chance away, his chance at life. He was my third child, and they killed him because he was a risk to their perfect system. Liam is a risk to Sanctum. That's frightening. I'm scared too, but I will take a chance on him. I ask you all to do the same."

A few people shuffled in their seats, looking at each other. "The City's birth rate was under five percent female this year. I'm not sure if you all knew that. You're isolated here, and thoughts of the City feel far away. It's easy to pretend all that's behind you. You made it, right? You're safe and free. But the City is still there, right outside our borders. I look around this room of men and women, in equal quantities, and I realize you don't see how rare that is in the City. I walked here and saw more young girls playing in the parks and visiting shops than I have in years in the City. You're at risk, even if Liam dies right here and now. The City isn't going away. I ask for permission to go back with him and not for another rescue. I want to take down the officials and council. All of them. I want to burn it to the ground."

A few nervous laughs escaped the deafening silence. I heard the wind outside rustle leaves and a man in the front row coughed.

"I'm not saying I'll be successful," I continued. "But I'll die trying. My son deserved a chance. So does Liam. So do I."

"I'm going with you," a woman's voice shot out from the back. She climbed on top of her chair and shouted again. "I'm going with you!" It was Erin. Her chin jutted forward, and she rested her hands on her hips.

I nodded to her, and she smiled. She jumped down and walked to the podium. "Where do we put the coin to vote yes?" she asked.

"The podium," I answered. She flung a bronzed flat piece of metal on the wooden shelf and stood by my side.

Killian and Alaina stood and made their way toward me. They placed their coins in front of me. Alaina put something in my hands before they stepped away, and I clasped it inside my fist.

Refugees stood, forming a line in front of me. They pulled out their coins and tossed them one by one to vote. Then the sounds of clanging metal echoed throughout the room until the pieces spilled over the sides of the podium. They placed only a few coins on my side. I knew the vote before they were done.

I stepped down from the platform and out the doors with Erin at my heels. I looked into my fist and saw Alaina's ladybug necklace in the palm of my hand. I fastened it around my neck and kept going.

Time to tell Liam.

Time to take a risk.

Time to save them all.

The Center's End

THE CENTER DUET, BOOK 2

The conclusion of the Center Duet, The Center's End, is available in the Kindle store in both EBook and Paperback format.

Buy now or read on Kindle Unlimited.
Below is chapter one.

Julie

"I don't recall inviting him."

Erin frowns at me. She's shaking out our bedding, now dirty from spending over a week outside. When you look at the Blue Forest from the city, the view of the Jacaranda trees is beautiful. Shades of blue stretch out over rolling hills that peak into mountains. While you're in it, however, everything is brown. It's dirt and muck. Shades of earth cover our clothes and tools. It's as dark and nasty as my mood.

I'm tired of looking at the ugliness.

I'm tired of bathing in a stream.

I'm tired of walking our border scanning for City officials.

I'm tired of Aiden never shutting the fuck up.

"He's in his element," Erin says. She's exhausted too, and I'm adding problems when we have enough already. "And it's just easier with four. Everyone has a partner when we split off. You can handle some small talk."

"We never split off!" I argue. "This conversation is the longest I've gone without hearing Aiden's voice."

"That's not true. Everyone is on edge right now. I understand you're agitated..."

"Agitated? At this rate, we'll have our first casualty before we cross the border."

"Julie, come on. This isn't your best morning. I hear you, but Aiden's here, and I'm glad about it."

I groan and pull at my ponytail, yanking the band out to put it up again tighter. I'll take my aggression out on my scalp. I feel the dirt in my hair and mumble obscenities to myself.

Liam and I didn't take long packing up after the town meeting. I know how to make a dramatic exit. We spent a few days gathering supplies and meeting with the rulers of Sanctum. When we said our goodbyes at the town center, we found Aiden ready to go. Erin didn't look me in the eye for an entire day. She'd known he wanted to join us and chose not to ask me. This means all my complaints go straight to her, and I have plenty of them this morning. His presence makes a rough start on top of an already difficult trip.

"He never stops talking," I hiss. "I don't even know what he's talking about. It's not about our mission, that's for damn sure. It's not about his scans or anything that could help us. He went on for hours yesterday about the demise of organized sports. What the fuck is that? Why the fuck do I care about that?"

I made the mistake of asking Aiden why he kept complaining about the world's lack of outdoor games. That sent him into a lecture about my ignorance on the subject. Much like a child, if you tell Aiden not to do something, that's all he thinks about... and talks about. He's obsessed with sports that have different sized balls in them. It's senseless and confusing.

Football... Soccer... Tennis.

Why are there so many balls?

He drones on about the generations before the dome, convinced things were better in the shadow times. I don't know, and I don't care. I want a new way of things. People go from one dark story to another. We need a fresh start, and that begins with freedom from the City's rules.

Erin packs the last of her things in her backpack. "This is the only place where he feels he can speak freely about his thoughts and ideas. Liam urges him on, you know. Your man isn't talking as much, but he's part of the conversation."

"He's not my man," I deadpan. Even though I can only make out her profile, I notice the exaggerated eye-roll she gives me.

"Didn't sound like it last night. Sounded to me like he owned you in your corner of the woods. And if the complaint department is open about this little foursome, might I remind you how incredibly awkward that is? I'm sleeping next to a man I hardly know listening to you have angry sex with your... whatever the hell he is. And damn, Julie, you sure are angry."

I kick up some dirt when I stand. "If we split into two groups, we solve the problem." I'm acting like an angry toddler. My exhaustion isn't helping this conversation. I can act my ass off when needed. Shit, I spent years in the city playing the part of the perfect employee and resident, but my guard is down.

I feel like I'm breaking into a million pieces. I felt so certain the day we left Sanctum — so sure I could infiltrate the City as soon as we reached the border. Now we can hardly find a spot to cross that doesn't have a recent patrol on the other side of our barrier. I huff, picking up the gear, refusing to continue the pointless conversation with Erin. She won't split off, and she's right. There's only one scanner, and we are stronger together if we encounter a surprise guest.

I grab the bag with our heaviest tools and my grip fails. Sharp pains take my breath, reminding me I'm not as strong as I once was. A whimper leaves my lips, and I pull my arm back to my chest, rubbing the sore spot.

"I've got it." I hear Liam say from my side. He takes a few swift steps in our direction and heaves the bag over his shoulder. His muscles pull and flex through his shirt. He's not trying to show off, but I almost drool looking at him. "You need to be careful of your injury."

I nod, letting my hand fall to my side. The sting runs up and down my limb and I ignore it, pretending I'm fine. He reaches his hand out, running his fingertips down the scar. Erin walks toward Aiden. He's five minutes ahead of us, and I hope we can keep some distance today.

"It's not your fault," I say. I'm not sure if that's what he wants me to say or if I want to remind myself. Liam and I have a constant push and pull with our feelings. So much hate fills us both, and it's often misplaced. I don't want him to hate himself for what happened when he removed my chip, and I can't hold it against him. We need to save our loathing for the City.

"I've been thinking," Liam whispers. He moves his hands to the straps of his backpack and turns to start after Erin. I follow but keep the pace slow. I can't handle Aiden's ramblings about goal lines and bouncing spheres for another second. "We should split up after we descend from the hills. Two of us go to Carrie's art studio and the other two go to Rafael's restaurant."

My body stiffens. It's not the time to deviate from the plan. We have one, maybe two officials that can get us into the dome during their patrol. We can't risk asking them to take us further.

"Wherever we cross, we need to go to the closest location. It's too risky to have someone sprinting to the other side of The Discovery Center." I wonder if we will make it there or end up in another part of the City with the distance we are traveling.

Liam holds out his hand, and I take it. I lie to myself, thinking it helps me keep my balance over the rocky terrain.

The truth is, I like his touch. I crave it. I refuse it sometimes because I don't fully know Liam. Alaina has faith in him, but she's too trusting... too hopeful in his case. I wish I could talk to her about these thoughts, but I don't know when I'll ever see her again. I listen as he continues. I want to believe he doesn't have an agenda — that I can depend on him. In our most intimate moments, I do.

No matter what, I need his help. I'm stuck, wavering between the sure and unsure parts of my mind.

"I have a connection with a shuttle driver. He can get us across. I know he turns off the tracking devices to deliver officials to the pleasure houses. The City looks the other way about it. He'll do it for me."

I don't ask Liam how he knows about this driver or the commutes to the pleasure houses.

I know.

I've known his secrets for some time now. My heart breaks for a moment, remembering how hurt he was back then, refused by the woman he thought he would spend the rest of his life with. She teased him along, meeting him in secret to keep his affections burning. He would do anything for her, and she used him.

"How would you get a hold of him?"

"Rafael has the contact. It's all done outside the City's reach. We need to split up in case..."

"I know why," I cut him off. "But we have to cross the border first, and so far, that's not going so well."

Our scanners reach to the other side of our border wall, looking for any sign of people or equipment that could stop us or record our crossing. The City's reach has grown worse, and it's been a struggle. They are positioning a stronghold, and there are signs of attempted crossings in two spots. They want into Sanctum and the other civilizations. They want the refugees, especially the female ones.

It's awful to be right sometimes. I'm sure of my purpose more than ever now, but it weighs on me. I feel the pressure of keeping so many people safe, and I can't even cross the damn border.

"We will find our way. We received a message from Sanctum earlier. Their video feeds show less activity further west. We just have to keep going. I wish we would have taken a shuttle, though."

"We can't afford to take that from the refugees. What if they need to run?"

Liam nods in agreement. "I know. You just seem so..."

"Tired. I know. It's Aiden. He never stops talking."

"Give the man a break. There's a chance that your injury and being on foot for a week is why you're tired and being short with him."

"I'm not being short. He's annoying."

Liam smiles, sputtering a laugh, and it lifts my spirits. He's filthy, like the rest of us. His ice blonde hair is a tawny brown, and his face has days of sweat and dirt, but his bright smile is contagious.

"He enjoys pestering you," Liam admits. We pick up the pace, drawing closer to Aiden and Erin. Aiden's scanning a section of the wall, his face undiscernible as he reviews the screen in his hand. I groan and mumble curse words under my breath. Erin looks over his shoulder, standing on her tiptoes.

"He's not a fan of you either," Liam whispers in my ear. "You two are getting under each other's skin right now. It'll pass."

"What the fuck am I doing to him?" I snap. My voice carries while the distance between us closes in.

Aiden keeps his face on the scanner, but he heard me. "To start, you fuck like a hyena. No one can sleep until you're done riding Liam every night."

Erin sputters a laugh, and I stop in my tracks. She covers her mouth with her hand and leans against Aiden, falling apart into giggles.

"Mind your business. Don't be a creep."

"It's not like I have a choice in neighbors. Shall I pick another chalet in the lush accommodations of this fucking forest?"

"You had a choice to come. I didn't have a choice but to let you tail along."

"For your information, Erin asked me to come. She didn't want to be a third wheel."

I give Erin a sharp look. *I knew it.*

"All we hear every night is your nonstop moaning in these woods," Aiden continues. "So what if I talk too much? I'm trying to drown out the ringing in my ears from your squeals. You can't stand a history lesson in sports, but I have to listen to the Julie and Liam freak show. He's quiet. We don't hear a thing from him. You can't cover her mouth or something, man?"

"Okay, okay," Erin stops him. "That's enough. Once we cross and get a shower and maybe some privacy... right, Julie?"

I cluck my tongue and Liam squeezes my hand, a chuckle leaving his throat.

Fuck, Aiden's right, but he's still an asshole.

"We are truly sorry about all the loud sex," Liam concedes. "What's the scan say?"

"You aren't sorry. I guess I wouldn't be, either, but don't throw stones in your glass house."

I suck in my cheeks, taking a deep breath. I don't respond, but I bob my head a few times, acknowledging that he has a point.

"The scan is clear," Aiden says. "We can pass here."
Aiden hands the device to Liam. My heart thuds in my chest, and I drop my jaw, staring at the readout. He's right, and we need to move before it's too late.
For the first time in a week, no one speaks, and I'm surrounded by silence.

The Center's End is available on Kindle Unlimited, EBook, and Paperback.

About the Author

Liz Hambleton writes imperfectly beautiful romance. Her heroines are always strong-willed, and her heroes are resilient. Her characters live in alternate worlds and futuristic times, and putting yourself in their stories lets you escape reality while still feeling the power of true love.

If she's not reading, she's writing, and her deep adoration for the written word shines in everything she creates. Liz is married with two children, two large dogs, and a fish that refuses to die.

Connect with Liz for other works and important updates:

Sign up for my newsletter on my website for Affluence's extended epilogue, extended scenes, giveaways, and more: https://lizhambletonbooks.com/

Home - Liz Hambleton Books

Other works on Amazon are under my author page: https://www.amazon.com/~/e/B08N9XXBK8

Visit Amazon's Liz Hambleton Page

Like Liz's Facebook Page: https://www.facebook.com/LizHambletonBooks/

Liz Hambleton Books (facebook.com)
TikTok: @lizhambletonauthor
Instagram: https://www.instagram.com/lizhambletonauthor/

@lizhambletonauthor • Instagram photos and videos

Made in the USA
Monee, IL
09 April 2024

56174784R00166